ANIMAL DESIRE

THE DESIRE SERIES BOOK 3

BARBARA DONLON BRADLEY

ONE

Heather sat in her rooms, feeling very trapped. There had already been a few little complications with her pregnancy and now she was under house arrest.

She looked around but didn't see anyone in sight. Storm had been talking to Kuarto via the screens and must have moved into another room so they could discuss her condition without her hearing it. It didn't matter. She finally had a few moments away from those two overprotective men, who swore they were just looking out for her. How? By restricting just about everything she normally did? Well, she planned on taking advantage of their absence. Bracing her arms against the rests of her chair, she pushed herself to her feet.

"Sit." Storm's voice was right at her ear.

"Where did you come from?" She turned to look at him in surprise. Heather was positive he would be gone longer than a few seconds. Did he have radar? Then she realized he probably knew her intentions because of their mindlink. It grew stronger every day.

"Sit." He crossed his arms over his chest. "Mate's orders."

She parked herself back in her chair. Not happy with the

turn of events. She couldn't stop the pout she felt take over her features. "I need to move around a little. Sitting still is driving me crazy."

"Your doctor said you needed to relax and you haven't done that."

"I can't help it." She shifted in her seat. "It's boring, just sitting."

"Heather."

"Fine." She mimicked his pose by crossing her arms over her chest too. Being trapped in her rooms wasn't how she wanted to spend the first weekend she had to herself. So what if her readings were a little off.

Kuarto didn't like the heightened levels of her heart rate, blood pressure and pulse and had recommended she not do anything strenuous. Storm took that as she wasn't allowed to do anything and he wasn't allowing her any leeway.

"If I rest can we go for a walk later?" Heather looked up at him, giving him her best smile.

"It depends on how well you behave." He watched her with a raised eyebrow. He knew she was up to something.

"I promise." She stood.

"What part of sit do you not understand?" He gave her an exasperated look.

"I'm going to lie down. Rest as demanded." She gestured toward their bedroom.

"About time you came to your senses." He scooped her up in his arms.

"Storm." She loved the close physical contact, but she could walk a few feet without any trouble.

"How far along are you?" He didn't show any signs of putting her down as he carried her into the room.

"Six months." She rested her head against his chest. There was no way Storm was going to let her feet touch the ground, so she might as well enjoy listening to his strong heartbeat. Let it calm her the way it always did.

"And how much further do you have to go?"

"About twelve more." She sighed. "I get it. I need to take care. Don't want to make this worse as I get further into the pregnancy because I didn't behave now."

"I see you were listening." He set her down on the bed.

"My heart, I haven't done anything crazy. You've been with me, you know." Heather looked up at him. "The elevated readings are probably from something I ate."

"Until we're sure, you will do exactly what is expected of you. I don't want you to take any chances." He placed a soft kiss on her lips.

"Aren't you going to keep me company?" She patted the bed beside her, giving him her most seductive smile.

"You know, if I join you, you won't get any rest." He captured her lips once more with his. This one was deep, heated and left them both a little breathless.

"I was kind of hoping for that." She knelt on the bed. Placing her hands between her legs, she leaned forward. Heather had learned this little pose. If she leaned the right way, it allowed him to see all the way down the front of her dress. She got her way a lot when she did it right.

She watched as his eyes started to glow. Over the last few months, he had developed the glowing eyes when he was aroused. A smile spread across her face.

"They're glowing, aren't they?"

"Oh, yeah."

He dropped to his knees on the bed and her smile got brighter.

"You know, I'm not sure I like this smug look you get whenever you're about to get your way."

"What look?" She tried to appear innocent, but couldn't pull it off any better than he could.

"You know what I'm talking about." He placed his hands on her shoulders and eased her backwards. Once he had her

7

prone, he lowered himself and started to nibble on his favorite spot on her throat.

"But we're both getting our way." She tilted her head so he could have better access. Arousal flowed through her.

He released the seams of her dress. "You still need to rest."

"And I will." She worked on his shirt seams as well. "This will help relax me so I can rest."

"You are incorrigible." He opened the gown and allowed his hands to roam her body. He pressed kisses along her collar bone and down the center between her breasts. "I have noticed these have been very sensitive lately."

"I know. Highly annoying for me." She closed her eyes as he gently caressed them. "Sometimes the material of my gowns aggravates them and sometimes it is very arousing. That's not supposed to happen. You would think it would be one way or the other, not both."

He pressed a chaste kiss on the side of one breast, then the other. "And now?"

"They want to feel your hot mouth on them."

He gently lathed one, waiting for her to react. A quick intake of breath was her answer. He turned his attention to the other one, making sure he didn't cross that fine line between pain and pleasure. Storm used the mindlink they shared to know what gave her pleasure and what hurt so he could be as gentle to her breasts as possible. They pebbled quickly and he could feel much more attention would be painful, so he moved to her abdomen.

Every morning, he spoke to his children. A ritual they both enjoyed because it always led to something more. Placing little kisses across her belly, he spoke to them again. Now that she was showing, it made her pregnancy very real. He paid homage to the life growing in her, drawing a few giggles as he did so.

"That tickles."

"You laugh while I'm trying to arouse you?" He climbed back up her body, placing soft kisses wherever he wanted. He loved the computer system in the underground compound. It only took a thought to remove their clothes.

"Sorry." She touched his face softly. "But you know I've become more ticklish since I've started to show. Can't help it if the slide of your tongue makes me laugh instead of moan. I think it's the children causing it. They feel a lot of joy when you talk to them and it manifests as laughter."

"So you are going to blame the innocent lives growing inside you?" He looked into her eyes, laughter and desire glowing in them.

"I'll try to react better next time." She touched his face with her fingers again. "If you wish, I'll moan for you right now."

"Woman, you are talking too much and there is only one way I know to quiet you." He slid in deep and watched in satisfaction as her eyes closed and a smile spread across her face. The next stroke had her looking at him, need swirling in her eyes. Her muscles constricted, making her sheath tighten against him. He loved the way her body hugged him, the way they could share each other's response when he pulled out and drove back in. Heather tilted her hips so he could penetrate deeper. Each time he filled her, he went as deep as he could. Her body accepted every thrust. He picked up the tempo as the friction between them increased.

Her breathing became labored. He could feel little spasms wracking her body. She was close. Very close. Storm shifted his weight a little and filled her once more. He felt her reach for her orgasm.

So close.

He felt the evasive release start with the heat in her belly, then it moved outward, toward her extremities. Her whole being shattered as it overtook her. She whimpered as it overpowered her.

Storm pressed soft kisses against her hairline. His heart.

He continued to move in and out of her. His turn. Everything started to build inside her once again. He could feel both his delicious arousal as well as hers. Her muscles held him in another tight grip, increasing the sensations. He ground his hips against hers and their worlds exploded. They floated in each other's arms, not wanting to come back to reality.

"Wow, I never get tired of that." She touched his face.

"You are phenomenal, my heart." He pressed his lips to one cheek, then the other before he worked his way to her throat.

Someone banged against the door loudly.

"Did I mention your brother was coming to give us the results? Clothes for the two of us." He mumbled it against her neck. He lifted his head, knowing the moment was gone. "Enter."

More loud noises came from their main room.

"Don't think so." She closed her eyes, hiding the disappointment he felt flow from her mind.

"We'll have to continue this after he leaves." He pressed another kiss against her throat.

"Is it safe?" asked Kuarto. He stepped into the room once he was sure they were covered. "I've had my share of your sexual exploits." He tapped the side of his head. Heather knew he still hadn't quite forgiven either of them for mentally connecting with him just as they hit their orgasms.

Storm sat up and pulled Heather into his embrace. "So what is going on with her, doctor?"

"Well, I have good news and bad news." He crossed his arms and watched the two of them.

"Is there something wrong?" Heather looked down for a moment as she rested her hand against the slight swell in her stomach.

"Nothing is wrong, but the diet I put you on isn't working. Keeping you from exercising didn't help matters either."

"Really? Does that mean I can resume my normal duties?" She was excited to hear about that.

"Yes." Kuarto didn't look happy. She could tell he didn't like not knowing what was causing the weird readings.

"So what is the problem?" asked Storm.

"I can't figure out why she's having these issues. We get rid of one ailment and another one crops up. Nothing life-threatening, but enough to drive us all crazy. Heather, you must be tired of all the restrictions."

"I'd love for them to stop." She was glad Kuarto stopped talking about her like she wasn't there.

"And they are. This time I want you to eat whatever you feel driven to. Whenever you wish to eat. My only request is that you allow me to keep a log of it. Same thing with activities. We've kept you from doing things that maybe we shouldn't have." He pulled out a small medallion on a chain. "Wear this so it can record everything I need to know about."

"Yippee, another medical scanner." She took it from him. "You know I have a tendency to break these things."

"So I have heard. I made sure this one is a little more durable than the other one and it's subcutaneous. Once you put it on, it will sink into your skin and stay there until I remove it. Harder to damage if it's inside you." He slipped it over her head then turned to Storm. "I have one for you as well."

"No."

"Your body is going through changes we don't understand. This will help me figure out what is going on."

"Find another way, doctor."

"Don't be stubborn. I will go to the council and make them aware of what is going on with you if you refuse, and they will force you to wear it." Kuarto held it out to him. "Is that what you want?"

Heather grinned. Kuarto might be taller than Storm, but Storm's muscular physique overshadowed Kuarto's slimmer frame. Storm's build intimidated others, but it didn't seem to bother her brother. He just proved it.

Storm glared at him, but took the necklace and put it on. "Thank you."

"Heather?" the voice of the computer interrupted. "You have a communiqué coming in from Earth. Shall I route it to the main screen?"

"Earth? What could they want?" She looked at Storm. She slid off bed and stood in front of the main screen. "Yes, computer. Make sure they don't see any more than my head. I'm still not sure how to explain how I got pregnant, so the less they see the better."

The face of her old commander filled the screen. "How are you doing, Heather?"

"Sir?" Her brow creased. "I wasn't expecting to hear from you. Is everything alright?"

"Yes, it is." He gave her a smile. A fake one the military taught them all to use. He wanted something. "The president wishes to extend the hand of friendship and invite you and your family to come to Earth for a visit."

"That's very kind of you, sir, but I'm pretty sure we're going to have to decline." She smiled back. Storm would never go along with it, anyway.

"As an officer of Earth, you are commanded to come home for a few days." The smile had disappeared. He was serious.

"Why?" She realized she said the wrong thing. "Sorry, sir. I meant no disrespect, but I thought it was understood that once the treaty was done I wouldn't be back."

"Consider it a strong recommendation. Somehow, information on you has leaked to the press that has most of Earth up in arms. You need to come here and show them everything is alright. I'll send you the files the media has been broadcasting. I don't care how you do it, but you need to come home and fix this. Now."

"Yes, sir." She cut communications and sank back into the bed. "Crap."

"My heart?" Storm had moved to her side.

"Nothing." She slapped a bright smile on her face. No need to worry him over something that was probably minor. He and Kuarto had been talking to each other while she spoke to her old commander, so she wasn't sure what he had heard. "Computer, can you show me the files sent from Earth?"

Several files loaded at the same time. The print ones were easy. All she had to see were the headlines. They all had the same theme. They knew about her being wounded while doing the exercise several months back. The news now had something they considered concrete to paint the Vespians in a bad light. They made it look like she was being held against her will and being treated badly.

Now she knew why she needed to go home. She looked at Storm. How was she going to get him to go along?

"They feel we are mistreating you?" Anger laced his voice. It wasn't good to upset her mate.

"Maybe a little?" She touched his heart. "They just don't know how it is between us."

"And you want to show them they're wrong." He returned the gesture.

"Yes." She scooted closer to him. "I won't be gone too long."

"No."

"Storm." She was given a command and had to go home.

"You are not going anywhere without *me*." He shook his head. "Especially back to Earth."

"You want to go with me?" She knew he wasn't a big fan of Earth. The last time he was there he was forced to do something he didn't want to do, so she hadn't thought to ask him.

"Of course." He frowned at her. "Why would you ask that?"

"You didn't seem to like being there the last time."

"I found you there." Slipping his arms around her, he pressed another kiss against her mark.

"And I'll take that as my cue to leave," Kuarto commented. He headed for the doors.

"Doctor, you will accompany us." Storm continued to nibble on Heather's throat as he gave the command.

"No 'please'?" Kuarto turned to look at them before grabbing his heart in mock pain. "I'm wounded."

"It's a good thing he's your brother," Storm murmured against her skin. "When do you want to leave?"

"I don't know. Um, how many people will we bring with us?" Heather always had trouble thinking when her mate distracted her. She hadn't planned on bringing a huge contingent. She understood why Storm wanted to bring Kuarto. With all the weird little things she had been through since she became pregnant, she agreed, but they didn't need a lot of people. Then it dawned on her.

"Crap!" her body tensed at the realization.

"What?" Storm sensed her unease and lifted his head to look at her.

"I can't go to Earth now." She touched her stomach. "How would I explain this?"

"Your pregnancy? You won't be there that long and you are barely showing. They probably won't even notice." He smiled, trying to reassure her.

Heather knew he didn't understand why she was so upset about this, but she knew she wouldn't be able to waltz in, say her piece, and waltz back out again. There would be questions and interviews. Their life would be dissected into tiny little pieces.

"There shouldn't be an issue with you traveling as you're not due for a while." He looked to Kuarto, who hadn't quite made it out the door yet, for reassurance.

"It's not that. How do I explain my pregnancy since I have been sterile all of my life?" She hated this. Frustration filled her. "Especially since Vespia has asked Earth to donate DNA to help eliminate the same problem in their population?"

"We'll hide it." Storm tilted his head as he studied her.

Although she knew her mate well, and knew he would never treat her like she was some sort of specimen, she felt like she was back on Earth being poked and prodded by the Earth doctors.

"Kuarto, do you see what I see?" Storm touched her cheek.

"I do." He ran his scanner over her, which Heather tried to slap away. She was really tired of the constant impromptu check-ups.

"Behave." Storm stopped her by grabbing her hands.

"What?" She wasn't happy with either of them.

"Look at your hands."

She looked down and found them glowing. So it wasn't a food reaction after all. Heather looked up at him, under-standing the odd look he gave her a few moments ago. "You saying I glow when I get upset?"

"It looks that way." Her brother looked at his scanner. "So you need to relax. Not let everything get to you."

"Fine." She took a deep breath, trying to calm herself. "So, how do you plan on hiding my pregnancy?"

"The material used for the uniforms hides everything on the body. We'll utilize it." Storm placed his hand on her cheek again. "We'll work it out."

"There is a cloth used by the ancients that can hide your pregnancy and is more flexible than the material in the Vespian uniform," commented the computer. "I can create one outfit you can wear under any of your garments, Heather."

"That will be fine, computer," said Storm.

"I don't see how this is going to work." Heather flopped back against the mattress. "Knowing Earth as I do, I will have to be very diligent."

"Well, I'm going to inform my mate of our trip." Kuarto turned and left.

"You really think that was why your brother was anxious to get out of here?" He leaned down to nibble on her throat once again. "You know everything will be fine, right?"

"I know. It's just not the right time with all the little things happening with me. This stupid glow, for example." She looked at her hands. "As far as my brother, I think he noticed your glowing eyes hadn't dimmed through any of what just transpired."

"You saying I have a one track mind?" He used his fingers to release the seals on her dress he had thought back into place only a few minutes ago.

She laughed as she worked on the seals of his clothes as well. "When it comes to me you do."

Storm grinned. "You know me so well."

———

Storm watched his mate on the screen from the main deck of their ship. She hadn't been getting enough sleep, so he ordered her to their room to rest while they were heading to Earth. By the way she was tossing and turning, she wasn't doing what he demanded.

"You really need to get another hobby." Kuarto stepped up to his side. "Spying on your mate isn't a good one."

"I'm worried about her." Storm turned to look at him. "She's not getting enough rest, and it shows. How are these humans going to perceive the darkened circles under her eyes?"

"We can mask that, and you know it. Her readings are good, so are the twins. What she needs is you." Kuarto placed a hand on his shoulder.

"What do you mean?"

"I have found she sleeps best when you are at her side." He held up a small pad with the readings from her monitor. "You can send her to your room and demand she rest all you want, but she doesn't seem to relax as well. I'd recommend you rest when she does."

"So you're saying if I were to lie down with her she'd get the rest she needs?" Storm gave him a questioning look. "You do know who you're talking to, right?"

"Libido aside, it sure wouldn't hurt. Perhaps the sex is part of the equation. I'm sure it relaxes her."

"Whatever you think is best, doctor, but I'm not responsible if she doesn't get any rest since this is your idea." Storm walked into their small room to find his mate feigning sleep. Her eyes were closed, but he could tell by the way she lay there that she was wide awake. "I know you're awake."

"I'm sorry. Just can't sleep." She sat up and looked at him. "Did you come to rescue me?"

"Sorry." He sat on the bed. "Your brother suggested I come and join you. He believes you rest better when I'm with you."

She scooted over so he could stretch out beside her. "True, but we don't always rest when you're this close to me."

"Well, right now, we have to be good." He pulled her into his embrace and rested his head against the pillows.

"We're always good. I think it's one of the reasons why we can't seem to keep our hands off each other." She snuggled against him.

He chuckled as he tightened his hold on her. "We have a

few hours before we arrive on Earth, so we have plenty of time. You need to rest first."

"And are you going to keep your hands to yourself?" Her voice came out soft. He could feel her body relaxing against him. Sleep was already setting in.

"I can't promise anything." He pressed a kiss against her forehead as she slipped deeper into slumber.

"I can help you break that promise." She practically sighed her answer. Even in sleep, she wanted him.

"My heart."

———

The ship landed in the designated area and powered down. Heather stood beside her mate, nervous about the next few minutes. She hoped to have a private landing, but was informed that the media and the military were already there, waiting for them. She had lamented about what she should wear, her uniform or civilian clothes, and decided on the civilian. She was the ambassador's wife and that was the role she felt she needed to live, but now she wasn't sure if that was the best choice.

The first group of people off the ship were the Vespian guards brought along as protection. Next went the staff and servants needed to run the embassy while they were there. Then the council, which had come along. Heather wasn't real sure why. Her brother and his mate were next. Then her and Storm stepped off the ship.

To her dismay she was treated to a military welcome.

"Sir." She saluted her commander. "I apologize for not dressing appropriately. I thought we would receive a private landing like most dignitaries get."

"I do apologize, Heather. Your dress is fine, in fact, it is probably the best thing you could wear but the media got wind of you coming home and there was no stopping them."

She smiled. Heather knew better. "Sure there is, sir. Don't forget, I used to work in security."

He didn't respond to her, just gestured to a podium.

"What?" She looked at it in shock. "Sir, you do not want me talking to them. It won't be pretty. Why can't I just release a statement?"

"They won't believe it. Be yourself, Heather. I think it's what is needed."

She looked at Storm for a moment before she shrugged and walked to the mics. People started asking her all kinds of questions. She had to raise her hands in order for them to quiet down. "I'm not here to field any questions you might have. If you have questions, submit them in writing to me and I'll decide which ones I want to answer." She looked out at all the people there to pull her life apart and anger filled her. "I have thought about what I would say to you when I finally got my chance to speak and the only thing that keeps popping into my head is how dare you! These people rescued our planet. Gave us a mineral we desperately needed and you pay them back by perpetuating these awful lies? I am happily married to a man who adores me. End of discussion."

Heather stepped away from the podium and walked to her mate. Slipping her arm around his waist, she leaned into him, as she led her entourage off toward the waiting vehicle.

She had looked at her hands while she was speaking, and her wonderful glow had started again. It wouldn't be good for one of the cameras to pick it up. Heather didn't want to end her tirade so abruptly, but she couldn't take a chance the glow would get worse.

"I don't think your commander was very happy with your statement." Storm pulled her close.

"Don't care." She rested her head on his chest. "They wanted a spectacle and that was what they got. Minus the glow." She held out her hands to show it had started again.

———

Once they were in the embassy, she found herself relaxing a little. This was where it all started. It was hard for her to believe less than a year had transpired. It seemed like a long time ago.

They were given the same room, but this time Heather was the one in charge of decorating the rooms, so the stark white décor was gone, replaced with nice neutral tones to set a calmer mood. She dropped to the couch once she was sure she'd have a few minutes and rested her head against the back of the cushions.

"My heart, are you okay?" Storm sat beside her and touched her face.

She lifted her head and smiled. "You worry too much."

"And you push yourself too hard. You didn't have to make sure everyone's room was to their liking before resting. I could have assigned that to someone else."

"And I would have been following them around to make sure they did it right and you know it." She touched his face with gentle fingers.

The doors to their rooms opened as her brother walked in, hands over his eyes just in case. "Thought I'd remind you about a particular box you wanted to be delivered."

"Oh, right." Heather sat up. "Is it here?"

"Yes. The staff wasn't sure where to put it. I rescued it before it was stuffed in a closet."

"Have them bring it in," said Storm. He stood to make sure it was done to his satisfaction.

It took four men to carry the box into the room. At Storm's direction, they placed it on the floor next to the room's mainframe and left. Once the room was clear, Storm stepped up and pressed the buttons to release the seals. As it opened, he went to the couch and sat next to Heather.

Once the box opened, small metal wires extended out and

attached to the main computer. It didn't take long for the system to be integrated.

"I see we have arrived." The computer was quiet for a moment. "So this is Earth. I do have information about it in my database."

"Sorry to keep you in the box the whole time, but no one knows about you, so we couldn't see how we would explain the need to bring our own computer." Storm looked at Kuarto. "As it is, you need to be very careful when you speak to us. The security grid might think you're an intruder."

"I can place my information into the system so it will recognize me." It was quiet for a second or two. "Done."

"Good. Do diagnostics on this embassy to make sure our security is at one hundred percent. I'll be waiting for your report."

"There is a call for Heather from the Earth government. Shall I rout it through?"

"I guess." She sighed. Sitting up, she plastered a smile on her face. Her old commander appeared on the screen. "Hello, sir."

"Have you been watching the newsfeeds?"

"Sorry, sir." Heather shook her head. "We haven't had time to see what my little bombshell caused."

"Your speech has the whole planet buzzing about you. The honesty of your feelings seems to be what they're all talking about. They find it refreshing and heartfelt."

"Only because I called them on the carpet, sir." She was happy they were taking her words at face value.

"Yes, well, your itinerary has been altered because of it."

"Altered? How?" She had just gotten the huge missive on where they wanted her to go and who they wanted her to see. How much of that had changed?

"We're getting lots of requests for you and your husband to be interviewed. They wish to give you a chance to tell your side of the story." He looked away from the screen for a moment. "I'm sending you what the government wishes. You'll see a lot of them are very simple and it won't take much to make the necessary changes to cover everything. But there are four things that are not negotiable. They wish to have a dignitary function, an awards function, your interview and a military presentation."

The data streamed across the screen. Storm took her handheld and downloaded the information into it so she could sit comfortably and go through everything.

"I'll take a look at it, sir." She took the small device from her mate. "I'll need to clear this through the Vespian ambassador."

"I'll be waiting to hear from you."

"Yes, sir." The moment the screen went dark she dropped her head back against the back of the couch again and moaned. "I can't believe this. They just expect me to make all this happen."

"My heart, why do you let this bother you?" He pulled her into his embrace. "We have people who can do all of this for you."

"Would you give this to someone to do if our roles were reversed?" He didn't answer her. "Didn't think so."

"You need to calm down."

She looked at her hands. They had a feint glow. Sitting the pad down, she looked at Storm. "If this keeps up, it's going to cause a problem."

Kuarto knelt in front of her, scanner in hand. "You need to stop getting upset over every little thing."

"Oh please. You're the same way." She watched as he used his scanner. "If you're going to break out that scanner of yours every time you see me, and you see me all the time now, why am I wearing this stupid monitor?" She tapped the spot where it sat beneath her skin.

"Because they do two different things. This." He held up

the scanner. "It is going to do the quick scans where your monitor is doing the deep scans. If you remember to remain relaxed so your protective protocol won't take over and skew the readings."

"I'll try."

"You ready?" Kuarto asked Storm.

"Yes." He looked at Heather. "You going to be okay?"

"Yes. I have plenty to keep me busy." She held up her pad. "Can I ask what you two are up to?"

"We'll see you later." He gave her a wonderfully heated kiss before getting up and leaving with Kuarto.

"Of course not," she said to herself.

She sent a message to Anseri and asked if she could speak to her. Thankfully, her mate's mother was available. "How may I help you, Heather?"

She explained what her old government wanted.

"What is the awards ceremony?" asked Anseri.

"Normally, they are pinning officers with their new rank. They also use this time to award new medals and special commendations. I'm assuming they're going to give me a commendation for the treaty."

"And the military presentation?"

"They wish to see a demonstration of the Vespian military. They will also do a demonstration of their military. It's normally the best of the best. I've seen so many things done. It's pretty wide open as to what you can do." Heather tapped her pad against her leg. "I can see if they will tell me what the Earth military is doing, so we know what will complement their program."

"Whatever we present will have to go through the head of security."

"I expected that and will be speaking to him later." She hoped Storm would agree with what she thought would wow the audience and not give any secrets away. She sure would like to show what she had learned from working with

Vespian security but wasn't sure if he would allow her to participate because of her condition. He could be very over-protective at times.

"Then let's leave that for last. This schedule will work best for us if your government will go along with it."

"Thank you. I'll speak to them. Hopefully, they will agree and make all of our lives easier." She got up and headed back out into the hall. Now all she had to do was schedule the interview.

TWO

Why did she have to do this anyway? She hadn't ever been approached to talk to the press before and didn't want to talk to them now. But Heather wasn't given a choice or she would have turned it down. Just standing there thinking about it upset her. One quick glance and she knew she was starting to glow a little brighter. Hoping no one noticed yet, she headed back towards their rooms before it got out of hand.

She had questioned her old commander about the interview when she gave him the suggested schedule approved with Anseri. She wanted to know how they found out about the exercise where she had been wounded.

What she found out was the government had already set her interview up with the most outrageous newscaster on the planet. All she had to do was give them a time. How was this going to work?

She passed Toki, deep in thought.

"Are you alright?" She touched Heather on the shoulder.

"Of course." She tried to smile, but knew the glow hadn't disappeared. Anyone who knew why she glowed would know she was lying.

"Right." They heard a noise behind them which made Toki wrap an arm around Heather and guide her into the first available room. Storm and Kuarto were sitting at a table, probably discussing her.

Storm stood at the intrusion. "What happened?"

"Something has upset her," commented her brother.

"Where did you get the clue, Kuarto?" she snapped. Her attitude wasn't going to help. "Sorry. My government has already set the interview with a newscaster who's known for taking your words and twisting them. I hate this."

Storm stepped up to his mate. "And I hate seeing you like this."

"I'll be fine." Once she got past the interview, she would feel a whole lot better.

"Sure, if you like glowing like this. At least I'll be able to see you in the dark."

"That's not funny." But laughter at what he said did escape her.

"I see your sense of humor hasn't left you. That's always a good thing." He took her into his arms.

Heather looked up at him, grateful he didn't seem to be phased by what she was going through. He lowered his head to hers, drawing her into a kiss that had her forgetting everything but the two of them. She felt his tongue rub against hers, sending little shivers of desire down her spine. He made her feel precious and cared for. When he broke the kiss, she didn't feel any of the anger that had filled her earlier. Her only thoughts circled around her mate and the way he made her feel. "Wow."

He opened his eyes and smiled down at her. "I'm going to have to remember that."

"What?"

"That kisses to melt your toes stops you from glowing."

"Really?" She looked down at her hands. "Hey! It did work." She looked back up at him with a bright smile. "You have my permission to do that anytime. As long as they're all like that last one."

"Promise." He gave her another kiss, just as deep and long.

———

"At least they went along with the first schedule we gave them." Heather sat on the couch, pad in hand. "The dignitary banquet is in three days, so we'll have time to get everything ready."

Storm handed her a cup of coffee. "I'm still not sure you should be drinking that."

"My doctor cleared me and I've been good about how many cups I ingest in a day." She set the pad down and took the cup. Sipping the hot brew, she closed her eyes and smiled. "Please don't take this away from me. I'm being forced to stay away from so many foods right now I could just cry."

"It's only for your protection." He sat down beside her. "Kuarto has loosened his restriction on your diet since we figured out what has caused the glow. Once he figures out how to stop it all together, I'm sure they will all lift."

"Well, I have a request." She set the cup down and turned to face him. "There is something I'm craving and you can only get it in one place."

"And what is that, my heart?" He pulled her into his embrace.

"I want one, no two of Henry's tacos. They are very bad for you, but I don't care. They're delicious and something I'm craving."

"What is a Henry's taco?" He rubbed his hand up and down her back.

"Henry is a proprietor of this little restaurant that I used to go to all the time." She shifted so she could look at him. "And it's not very far from here."

"So you wish to see this Henry as well as eat his food?"

"Please?" She pressed herself up against him, giving him her best smile. "I promise not to ask for anything else while we're here."

"Right. You will forget, and I will want to make you happy once again." He touched her face. "Let me do a little investigating first, and I'll let you know."

"In other words, you want to make sure my doctor agrees with it and you plan on checking out the restaurant before you let me within ten feet. And if you approve, you will shut the whole place down so I won't be in danger."

"You know me too well." He lowered his lips to hers and gave a quick but heated kiss. "I will try my hardest to make this work."

———

"You really did shut down the restaurant, didn't you?" They stood outside the small place, Heather surrounded by guards. She frowned at the thought of these men with them all the time. "And this is going to get very old. Are they going to go everywhere with me?"

"They are here to protect us and yes they will accompany us whenever we leave the embassy." He ushered her into the restaurant. Three guards were in front of them.

Heather noticed the use of the word us. Storm wasn't going to let her out of the embassy by herself. Ever.

"Sorry. We're closed." Henry looked up at the guards when they walked in. "Are you them Vespians? The ones who decided I shouldn't be open to the public so some dignitary could try my food?"

"They're just trying to protect me, Henry. They mean no

harm." The men parted so he could see Heather. She gave her friend a hug.

"I'll be damned, Heather Drexel. Heard tell you ran off with one of them Vespians." He returned the hug, then released her and stepped back. He smiled as he watched Storm put a possessive arm around her. "You don't seem to be mistreated. Knew you were too bullheaded to let anyone get the best of you."

"He knows you well, my heart," Storm said, his face close to hers.

"Henry, I want you to meet my husband, Storm. Storm, this is Henry. He was like a father to me while I was learning at the academy."

"She didn't have anyone to watch over her. Other than Bear and he was always working." He walked back behind the counter after he shook Storm's hand. "You want the usual?"

"Yes, please." She sat at the counter, watching as he created her favorite.

"So, hear you people are having a big party tomorrow night." At Heather's nod, he continued. "Heard you're going to have a surprise guest, knowing how the two of you have behaved before, I think it would be wise to make you aware Bear is in town for your gathering."

"Bear? Thought he was assigned at some little Podunk outpost."

"Only giving you a warning." He set a plate in front of her and then one in front of Storm. Henry hooked a thumb at Storm. "Has he ever had a taco?"

"Not that I know of." She looked at her mate. "Have you?"

"No." He looked at the food dubiously. "What is in it?"

"Beef, cheese, onions, sour cream and his special sauce." Heather picked her up and took a bite. Her eyes closed as the flavors she had been craving exploded in her mouth. She always thought these were better than an orgasm until she met Storm. But they still were her favorites. A little moan escaped her.

"I see." Storm picked up his taco and held it the way she had. "Food makes you moan where an orgasm doesn't?"

Heather felt the heat of a blush fill her cheeks as Henry laughed.

"Girl, don't tell me you still have the title of ice princess even after marrying this one."

"I believe I have melted that image a long time ago," Storm said, and winked at Henry. "It's just she is very quiet and to hear her moan over a taco caught me by surprise."

"Storm." She put her taco down.

"Sorry, my heart. Didn't mean to upset you. I just wonder if I need to speak to Henry about that moan. I never know when I will get one, but he might know the secret, since all he has to do is cook for you to get that wonderful sound."

"Good Lord." She hid her face as the blush deepened.

"She once told me they were better than orgasms," commented Henry.

"Really?" Storm turned his full attention on Heather. "Do you still feel that way?"

She wanted to kill Henry. That wasn't something she had planned on telling her mate. But she pulled her dignity around her and looked Storm in the eye. "You have the picture that answers that question."

"I do, don't I." He took his first bite of the taco and grinned. "This is very good."

"The two of you are evil." She popped the last bite into her mouth. As much as she would love another one, she needed to make sure her system would accept it. She had been eating Vespian food for a while and had adjusted to it, so switching back might cause trouble. Especially with the pregnancy. "May I have two to go?"

"You can have as many as you wish." Storm had finished his plate as well.

"Henry, I hate to eat and run, but I know we're keeping your normal patrons from enjoying the cuisine and I can't be responsible for that." She stood and gave him another hug. "Thank you."

"Good to see you again, my dear."

Heather turned to Storm. "Thank you."

"For a taco? I should be thanking you for teaching me about orgasmic food." He wrapped his arms around her and pulled her in for a kiss. She melted against him as his tongue swirled against hers. The kiss held so much promise.

"Heather?" At the sound of his voice, she turned to look at Henry. "There is magic between the two of you. I could see it in the short time you were here. You need to let the rest of the world see it too. Show them that Al guy was wrong."

She felt cold at the name. It couldn't be the same man. Heather grabbed Storm's hand for support. "Fair complexion, blond hair, about my height?"

"That sounds about right. There's a picture of him in the news archives. He's the one who started the rumor about you in the first place."

"Thank you, Henry." She went to him and gave him another hug. "You are a true friend."

As they passed a guard, Heather commented, "Invite him to the banquet. And find that archive."

Their transport waited for them. She entered first, then Storm followed. As soon as the door closed, he pulled her into his lap. "I don't know what it is about that picture, but all I have to do is think about it and it makes me want you." He lowered his mouth to hers, drawing her tongue to his, making her forget about what they had just learned for a moment. "Too bad this thing travels so quickly or I could have my way with you right now."

"You know they will leave the door closed until you say to open it." She rested her head against his chest.

"I see you have been paying attention. Now that your glow is gone again, we need to see what Al is up to."

"You realize he drew us here." She lifted her face so she could look at him. "This whole visit is a ruse to get us away from the safety of Vespia."

"You're starting to glow again."

"I just wish he would leave us alone."

"And now you're brighter." He touched her cheek. "If you don't calm down, we'll never get out of this transport."

"I know." She sighed. Heather closed her eyes for a moment, trying to calm herself down. The one thing that always worked for Storm was making her forget about everything but the two of them. He had a way about him to take her focus off of what was bothering her. Could she do the same? She focused her thoughts on the way he made her feel for a few moments and opened one eye. "Any better?"

"Not really, my heart." He smiled at her. "Your emotions are what cause this, not your thoughts and I know what it takes." He nibbled on her neck. "If I can get you into the embassy, I can take my time peeling your dress off you. It would give me all the time I want to pay homage to your body the way I like to. Show you just how precious you are to me."

She sighed, and relaxed against him.

He opened the door and urged her out.

"I'm guessing the glow is gone?"

"No, but has faded enough for you to step out into the light and I'm hoping as long as I keep telling you what I want to do to you once I have you naked and in our bed, we can get indoors without a problem."

She felt that to her toes. "Why does something so simple affect me so profoundly?"

"Because you know what happens when I get you naked,

bed or not." He pulled her close so she could see the glow in his eyes. "I start a fire deep inside you only I can put out."

The door was right in front of them. Stepping into the cool interior allowed Heather to relax a little. As much as they wanted to run to their rooms, Storm's mother was in the main hall which stopped them.

"I wish to speak to the four of you." She had already captured Toki and Kuarto and forced all of them to follow her.

Heather wasn't in the mood to hear some sort of speech about what she wanted from them during the dinner the next evening and her persistent glow showed it.

"Oh, my." She looked from Storm to Heather. "Perhaps we could talk about this later, after you two rest a little."

"That would be wonderful, Anseri. I do need a few moments to get my glow under control."

"Of course, my child."

Storm took Heather's hand and led her back into the hall so they could head to their rooms.

"So, how long have Storm's eyes glowed like that?" asked Anseri.

"Um, a couple months now." Kuarto knew he had better answer her, but also knew Storm had worked hard to keep this from her. "Why?"

"Oh, no reason. Just find it interesting that Heather glows when she is frustrated and now her mate's eyes glow when he becomes sexually frustrated." She touched his hand. "We'll try to have this conversation again later."

He and his mate nodded. Kuarto looked at Toki when her mother had left the room. "How come I never made that connection? I should have spotted the correlation long before this."

"And now you need to study it?" Toki grinned, knowing him so well.

"Of course, but it can wait. I'm thinking we could take

advantage of your mother's release the way Heather and Storm are." He pulled her into his arms. "It's not every day Anseri decides to let you take care of personal needs before she talks your ear off."

"You do have a point. I keep getting pulled in so many different directions, which I'm sorry about. I had hoped I'd get a little break from work so we could have some time to ourselves, but I can't seem to get away from the job." She squealed when he scooped her up. "What are you doing?"

"Making sure you can't take off on me." He captured her lips with his before he nibbled his way to her ear. "You do have a tendency to ask for a minute or two when you realize there is something you need to do before you can relax enough to be intimate. I need to break you of that habit. You need to come first when it comes to us. Forget about the job for a few hours. If you don't, you'll burn out too fast. Doctor's orders."

"I'm so sorry if it seems I do that." Her eyes closed when she felt his lips on her ear. "I will do better because there is nothing I want more than to feel you deep inside me."

"That is what I want to hear." He took off for their rooms. "Because that is where I want to be."

Toki clung to him as he ran through the halls. He didn't let go until they were safely inside their rooms.

"Now, no quick communications. No having to check in with someone. Just you and me and that big bed." He maneuvered her toward their bedroom. "You have made a promise to me and I intend on helping you keep it."

"Really? And how do you plan on making me keep my promise?"

"Oh, let's see." He opened the seals of her top, exposing her breasts to his touch. "There's the soft caresses that make you purr for me, then there are the ones that make you growl."

"I don't growl."

"Want me to prove it?" He nibbled on her throat before he nipped on her collarbone. "Because I can." His hands slid down her stomach to slip beneath the bands of her trousers. He knew just the spot to touch to get that growl. His fingers worked their magic, and she purred. "There's the purr. It always comes first."

"You do have magic hands." A happy sigh escaped her as she worked on his clothes, peeling them off him as she spoke. "But I know how to cause you to make a few of your own noises."

"Never said I was quiet." He broke the seal on her pants as well, so they would pool at her feet. He picked her up and carried her to the bed. Placing her near the center, he touched all his favorite places on her body, watching in satisfaction as her eyes dilated with desire.

She laughed. "No you didn't."

"And I still need to make you growl." He captured her lips with his, drawing her tongue out to play with his. Kuarto stroked her core, being sure she was ready for him as he centered himself and entered her. "You are so beautiful."

Her breath hitched as he filled her. Toki wrapped her legs around him, drawing him in deeper. They both felt the heated passion race through their blood.

He kissed her as he started to move in and out of her. His pace had her arching her back quickly. She held him tight as she felt the first few ripples of her orgasm.

"See? This is what happens when you're not intimate with your mate enough. Your body screams for its release early."

"It's not all my fault." She had to pause as white hot desire shot through her. "You've been fretting over the fact that you don't look like your parents. Never seen someone so obsessed." Her last words came out as soft as a whisper, caught up in the wonderful sensations he caused.

"Hush." He wrapped his arms around her and flipped

them so she was now on top. Toki always liked being the aggressor. Her climaxes were always more powerful when she was in control, and he had no trouble with that. The way she rode him as her muscles gripped him tight had him grabbing her hips and quickening their pace. His hands cupped her breasts, gently brushing her mark, feeling her reaction by the vise-like grip she now had on his erection. He felt her shudder above him, her body reaching her climax just before he hit his release.

They lay in each other's arms, happy and spent.

"You didn't make me growl." She pushed herself up so she could look him in the face.

"I got you to purr. That is always first." He played with her hair. "You'll growl for me before the day is over."

"I accept that challenge." She touched his face. "But I do have a question. You've been going over and over those readings. Are they your parents or not?"

"They are, but there are still so many questions. I'm wondering if there was a complication with my mother's pregnancy where she had some sort of injection to save us and that was what made Heather's and my DNA mix a little. It's the only conclusion I can come up with. With the way everyone's mind was wiped, I don't know if I'll ever find out."

"We could ask Heather…"

"She has enough to deal with right now." He rolled them over so he was now on top. "Besides, it's time to make you growl."

———

Storm closed their doors and turned to face Heather. "I can't believe my mother let us off like that. What do you think possessed her?"

"How about the glow twins? Between your eyes and my skin, we do make quite a pair."

"We'll have to use that to our advantage more often." With a thought, he removed their clothes.

"Is that why you wanted to bring the computer system from the underground compound?" She placed her hands on her hips. "So you can remove my clothing with a thought?"

"I brought it because it would help keep you safe and healthy. Those adjustments it gives you when your system gets off kilter is something Kuarto can't do. The fact that I can think our clothes away or have it create my favorite chair with a thought is just a perk."

"And something that didn't even cross your mind when you decided that bringing it would be a good idea." She watched him warily as he walked up to her.

"My heart." He wrapped his arms around her. "I only wish to keep you happy, safe and healthy. If bringing the computer was going to help with that, then I want it here. I had no ulterior motive."

"Storm." She shook her head. Knowing him made her want to laugh at his outrageous statement. "I am so glad you are my heart."

"You should be." He started to nibble on her neck. "I always have your best interest at heart."

"And what is my best interest right now?"

"Seeing if I can make you moan the way that taco did."

"Are you up for the challenge?" Heather grinned when he loosened his hold enough to allow her to back up. "It was a very good taco."

"Oh, woman, you have no idea. The moment you reminded me of that picture I have been reliving the moment when we made it in my head. We're not leaving this room until I get a moan, but my goal is a scream. I have been able to cause you to scream a few times, and it was beautiful." He started to stalk her then. "And I'm still waiting for the moment when I touch you and you supernova."

"Oh, the supernova is coming, just don't know when it will happen." She couldn't help but continue to grin at him. Every time she took a step to the left or the right he copied it. "But that is part of the excitement, isn't it? Never knowing when it's going to happen."

"You and your beautiful body are what excite me, in case you haven't noticed." He maneuvered her toward the large door that led to the balcony.

"Where are you herding me?"

"To that hottub. If I remember correctly, the last time we were interrupted by my mother before we could get too far, and since she is the one who gave us permission to have this time to ourselves I was thinking it would be a good time to see if we could finish what we started."

She remembered the moment. His fingers had worked their magic on her body. If they hadn't been interrupted, he would have gotten several moans out of her. "Still marking your territory?"

"Every chance I get." He crowded her backward until she hit the edge of the tub. The glow in his eyes set her desire aflame.

She stepped into the tub, still watching him. Water bubbled around her hips. Heather dipped low into the water, disappearing from sight for a moment. When she came back up, water cascaded down her body. Storm's gaze became predatory while he watched as she slicked her hair back, causing more water to caress her curves as it ran down her form.

He climbed in the tub with her and pulled her close. "Your hair. I wish it to remain long."

"What?" He was worried about her hair at a time like this?

"You will have to wear your uniform for these upcoming

functions, right?" He ran his fingers through her hair, which now just brushed her shoulders. "And your government has a hair length limitation."

She smiled. "My hair can't touch my collar, but I had never let my hair grow out before. There never was enough time between inspections, so I always kept it short. As long as it is long enough for me to pin up, I won't have to cut it."

"Good. I like the way you look with the longer hair." He wrapped his arms around her. Storm maneuvered her to the bench around the edge of the tub. "Now let's see if we can reset the scene." His lips pressed against her neck. "I believe I nibbled on your throat as I love to do, and my hands had a mind of their own."

Heather felt everything tighten as his fingers explored her folds. He found the spot that brought her to a swift orgasm and proceeded to caress it. Her head dropped onto his shoulder as desire unfurled deep inside her, racing along her bloodstream, bringing her release with it. Just as her world started to shatter, Storm pulled her toward him, burying himself deep inside her, filling her and increasing the sensations she felt.

The moan came from deep inside, like music to his ears. Lights exploded behind her closed lids. Her body had him in a vise-like grip.

"That's my girl." He said it softly next to her ear. "Now let's see if I can get you to scream for me."

"Henry was right." She slid up and down his shaft, wanting to feel those wonderful sensations again. The heat and motion of the water as she moved intensified everything.

"How is that?" Each time she came down he pushed into her, filling her as deep as he could.

"You're like magic to me." Her tempo picked up speed as she felt heat zinging through her blood. "You do things." She paused as one stroke hit just the right spot. "Oh, God." Heather sucked in her breath. "To me no one else could."

"My heart." He captured her lips with his, their tongues entwined together as she quickened the pace once more. Storm held her close but didn't restrict her movements. She changed the tempo once again, so the strokes were longer and deeper. Her body shook and her muscles clamped down on him.

Their minds touched one another, sharing everything. She was so close. Then it started. Deep inside her, unfurling like a sail, she felt like she was on fire as the little frissons of release danced through her blood and flooded her brain. She gasped at the intensity.

Storm took control then and drove into her, causing her to take off again, this time with him. Passion had them it its grasp once again. She exploded all around him, keeping her tight grip and pulling him along with her.

"Wow." She pressed soft kisses to the hard muscles of his chest when the last tremor had racked her body.

"So that is what a hottub adds to intimacy." Storm relaxed his hold on her a little. "We'll have to add one of these to our rooms on Vespia."

Heather laughed. "You do have a one-track mind."

"When it comes to you, I do."

Heather hated all the attention they were getting because of the function. Between the cameras trained on every move she and Storm made as well as a long receiving line that never seemed to end she grew frustrated. The faint glow wasn't too noticeable and she did her best to remain calm, but every once in a while Heather would look down the receiving line and wished she hadn't.

Everyone had been very nice, wishing them well and staring at Storm in amazement. The women weren't swooning over him the way they used to. Heather found it fascinating. When there was a small lull in the handshaking and well-wishing, she had to ask Storm about it. "How come I don't have to fight the women off you anymore?"

"According to my uncle, once you and I went through the mating ritual my pheromones changed." He wrapped his arms around her and pulled her close. "I'm not searching for my mate anymore, so it doesn't affect women the same, but I might be fighting off some of the men."

"What are you talking about?"

"You are so beautiful right now. This gown hugs all the right spots. And the deep violet color sets off your eyes. I have seen the way the men have been looking at you when they think no one notices." He touched her face softly with his fingers.

"But you have noticed."

"Of course. I am proud they find you so alluring, yet if one of them even thinks about touching you, he will have to deal with me." He slipped a finger inside the top of her dress. "The design is a perfect look for you. Very Vespian, but still modest enough for the people of this planet."

"I hate to disappoint you, but you're not going to find anything special." Heather smiled up at him, knowing what his fingers were searching for. "I tried but nothing would work under this dress."

"So any flash I get is going to be your flesh?"

She nodded at him.

"Oh, my heart. Just the thought has me hard." He dipped his head to capture her lips for a quick but claiming kiss.

Someone cleared their throat. They had focused on each other for a little too long again.

"We still have to talk to the people, not just each other." Kuarto leaned over to speak softly to them.

They released each other and turned to face the captain of the ship they helped when they went first met Kuarto. Storm did find out they really were doing science exploration. They had found the planet they were heading for had a mineral Earth used regularly and they were there to see how difficult it would be to mine.

"I understand you are the one I should be thanking for our rescue."

"Really?" He looked at Heather for a moment. He had told the doctor on that mission not to mention his command ship. "Who told you that?"

"Your planet's leader. I thanked her for saving my ship and she recommended I speak to you." He shook Storm's hand, then moved on.

They continued to smile and shake hands or bow when appropriate. To Heather the line seemed to go on forever.

"Oh, dear." She had just peeked down the line and saw someone she wished she hadn't.

"Something wrong?" asked Storm. He had turned to look at her the moment she spoke.

"Um, no, but you might want to ask your men to stand down."

"Why?"

"Trust me. You see that mountain approaching us? He knows me and he has a tendency to manhandle me a bit." Her attention turned to the huge man standing in front of her so she couldn't explain more. He stood before her in his military uniform. They both checked for other officers within earshot before addressing each other. "Bear."

"Pipsqueak." He grabbed her, wrapping her in a big hug.

Weapons started to move.

"Stand down." Storm tapped the man on the shoulder. "Would you mind letting my mate go before one of my men puts a hole through you?"

"Sorry." He put her down, but didn't let go. "I have missed this little piece of trouble."

"And you can't seem to stop manhandling me either,"

Heather wiggled so she could get out of his grasp. "Just like old times."

"I don't manhandle." He grinned at her. "I'm just a friendly guy." He studied Heather and Storm, noting the size difference. "So this is what you left me for?"

"Way to make a good impression, Bear. This is my mate, Storm." She looked at her mate. "And don't believe a word he says. He has been a pain in my side as long as I've known him."

"Just like family." He grinned at her. "I took you under my wing years ago and taught you everything I know."

"So you're the reason she's so stubborn?"

Bear laughed. "I like him."

The line was slowing down because of Bear, so Storm invited him to stand with them so he could talk with them a little more.

"Is this thing ever going to end?" murmured Heather as she took another peek down the line.

"Bit impatient, too."

"Yeah, but I didn't teach her that one," said Bear. "That was one she must have inherited."

"So how do you know Heather?"

"Met her when she was about thirteen. A tall stick, nothing to her but the height. Smart as a computer with a mouth that could get her into trouble."

"She still has that problem."

Heather glared at her mate, but kept quiet.

"I was the head instructor of the security classes. Heather hated my classes, but she had a knack for them. Never seen anyone like her. She has this uncanny ability to know what people are going to do before they do it. Got out of more scraps because of that talent. After teaching her for a semester, I recommended she go into security. I became her only instructor and watched as she excelled to the top of her class." He wrapped an arm around her and squeezed. "She was the best."

"Then I have to thank you. If she hadn't been in security, I might not have ever met her."

"Don't know about that." He looked from Heather to Storm. "Something tells me you two were destined for each other. One way or another, you would have found each other."

"What makes you say that?" asked Storm.

"He has this weird ability to notice things. Things no one else would possibly see." She realized what she said and looked up at Bear. Had he figured out her little secret?

"It is something I have learned to use to my advantage. In the past, I would just blurt out what I suspected, but now I wait for the crowd to die down a little and wait for the cameras to be focused elsewhere."

"What are you getting at?" Storm's brow dropped and his eyes narrowed.

"Storm, please." She tried tugging on his arm, praying she'd stop him before the whole thing got out of control. Bear didn't like being pushed into a corner any more than she did, and he was about to prove how good he was at figuring out things.

Bear squared off with him. "Like why are you two hiding her pregnancy."

THREE

"What are you talking about?" Storm took a hold of Heather's arm so she couldn't take off and glared at Bear.

"Cameras." Heather knew the longer they stood in one place the bigger chance they had of being captured on video. Especially with the thunderous look on Storm's face. "Cameras." No one seemed to be paying any attention to her. "Cameras, cameras, cameras."

"Heather, relax. Bear, you and I need to talk about this in detail after dinner." Storm spoke to one of the servants and had Bear join them at their table.

Once they were finished with the receiving line, dinner was served. Heather was escorted to their table by Storm and found herself sitting between Storm and Bear. Her brother and his mate sat opposite them. The rest of the table was made up of dignitaries from Earth.

Being sandwiched between these two annoyed her. It was bad enough to feel small next to her mate, but with the two of them on either side, she felt like a child. She couldn't see much either with the two of them blocking her view.

Small talk filled the air as the salads, then the main meals were brought out. She did find out from Bear that although Henry was honored to be invited, he declined. Something about not fitting in with all those highfaluting dignitaries. Sounded just like him.

There was one good thing about the two men. It kept several people from asking too many stupid questions like they did at the reception on Vespia. There were so many who wanted to ask, she could see it on their faces. But Storm was intimidating on his own. Add Bear to the mix and it kept a lot at bay.

Storm must have noticed her smile. He leaned over and whispered in her ear. "I wouldn't be too happy right now. We need to talk about your friend Bear and this ability of his."

She looked up at him, her eyes overly bright. 'I tried to warn you.' She mouthed the words so no one would hear her.

The glow of her skin was subtle up to that point. Heather could barely see it, but it was getting brighter. She watched as Storm looked over at Kuarto. He had noticed it, too.

"My heart, you're starting to glow," he whispered in her ear. She wondered how everyone would react to the passionate kiss it would take to break the glow.

She looked at her hands and nodded. "Have been for a while. You're going to have to do something about it, aren't you?" she asked, her voice soft.

"We could make an excuse and go outside if you wish." He still spoke softly to her. The news people watched them like they were prey.

"No. They think I'm being abused. Maybe we should show them how you abuse me." She gave him a brave smile, but she hated all the attention.

"I'll try to be quick." He touched her face with his fingers before he captured her lips with his. There had been times when a quick, deep kiss stopped the glow, and that was what she hoped he would do now. Her mouth opened for him, allowing his tongue to sweep in. Heather felt him tighten his hold on her, loving the taste of her, but knew they couldn't continue for long. Several people were clearing their throats. He broke the kiss, a satisfied smile spread across his mouth. The faint glow must have been gone. He looked around the table apologetically. "Sorry, sometimes I can't help myself."

"At least it put a little color in her cheeks," commented Bear before he picked up his drink. "To Heather and Storm. May every kiss be as heated as that one."

Heather picked up her glass and looked at her mate. There was no problem with that. He gave her a wink before he drank from his glass. She sighed in relief. One disaster averted for the time being.

The kiss seemed to relax everyone at the table because the conversation became focused on them.

"How do you like Vespia, Heather?"

"It's a beautiful planet and the people make me feel very welcomed."

"I'm not sure I could leave Earth the way you did, but I've never been off-world before and I understand you practically lived on ships and space stations."

"I did spend a lot of time on them. Have to go where the job takes you." Heather looked up to find one of the cameras trained on her. If only she had her weapon on her. She could take it out in one shot.

"I am grateful because that job brought you straight to me," Storm commented. He looked at her like she was the only thing in the room.

She leaned her head on his shoulder. "Living on Vespia is actually the first time I've spent a lot of time on one planet."

"What do you do all day?"

Heather looked at Storm and smiled. She could say she had sex all the time, but wasn't sure if it was appropriate, even if it was true. She caught the smile on her brother's face and knew he was thinking the same thing. "I work with their security force in the morning and with the ruling council in the afternoons."

"Really?" The woman who had been asking all the questions looked at Heather in surprise. "I hear there will be a security demonstration in a few days. Will you participate?"

"Honestly? We just learned about it as well. We haven't even had time to assemble a team yet, but it is a possibility."

The plates were cleared and people started to mingle.

Storm stood. "It was a pleasure meeting all of you, but we must pay our respects to the rest of the guests." He led her away from the table. "Please tell me you were joking about the exhibition."

She looked around to make sure no cameras were on them when she turned to face him. "It would make sense."

"Heather."

"She is right, you know." Bear had caught up with them again. "And as head of security, I have a suggestion on what we should do to make these people realize what makes the elite teams so special."

"We need to talk, anyway." He looked at Heather. She could see as much as he wanted to keep her with him, he knew too many people were watching and it could come across wrong in the eyes of the Earth people. He escorted her to his sister. "Please keep her out of trouble."

He gave her another kiss that could melt any ice cubes in glasses nearby and headed off with Bear.

———

"So what did you wish to speak to me about?"

Storm gave him a bored look. "Like you don't know."

"Ah, my question earlier." He walked out into the gardens with Storm. "I could feel it when I hugged her. The cut of the gown looks deceptively formfitting, but you can't miss something like that when you hug someone."

"Heather said you had an uncanny ability to know what people were thinking."

"There were other things. The way she kept brushing her dress. Her face has that look, too. So does yours."

"What look?"

"The 'look what we did' look. The pride in the accomplishment." Bear dropped his voice. "How did you manage it? Heather has always been sterile."

So that was common knowledge. "It was a miracle, and that is why we aren't broadcasting it. How do you explain something like that?"

"I would have thought it could be because you're from two different races."

"Our race has the same problem."

"Is that why your planet asked for DNA from our population? To combat that?"

Was that common knowledge too?

"Now I see your dilemma," commented Bear.

"Let's talk about the exhibition." Storm wanted to change the subject. "I have an idea that just might help both our planets."

———

"Now why would he say that?" asked Toki.

"Remember the two times when we were in this type of setting and he left us alone? I believe the first time my dress became demagnetized, and it took the two of you to keep me from falling out of it. The next time I ended giving a peep show to half of the Vespian security force."

She started laughing. "You're right."

"Peep show?" asked Kuarto.

"Never mind," said Heather.

"She bent over to help someone and her dress gaped open. Anyone who was looking at her got quite a show. Made most of the men speechless." Toki took his hand. "It was priceless."

"Thanks. That is a news clip I hope doesn't make it to the air." Heather looked around. She knew the news people had to be somewhere. She could feel them ready to pounce.

She felt a tap on her shoulder. There they were. She turned around with a smile on her face. Mentally, she asked the computer if it could block all electronic equipment so no feed was going out, coming in, or recording for later release. The moment she received confirmation she dropped her smile. "You might not remember me, Susan, but I haven't forgotten you. You made sure I had a nickname I could never shake. You didn't like the fact that I was smarter than you, so you found things to make fun of, like my height, or how thin I was. Now you have to hope you don't anger me so much I switch reporters. Karma can be a real bitch at times." She pointed to Toki, Kuarto, and Anseri as well as a few other Vespians. "These people are my family. They accepted me with open arms, and I don't want you harassing them."

"Heather."

"Not done." She shook her head and smiled. "Your video feed isn't working right now. Nothing is broadcasting. That camera isn't recording because of me. If you want to keep your special interview, you will leave the Vespians and their guests alone. Understood?"

Susan looked at her cameraman who nodded, informing her Heather was telling the truth. "Yes."

"One more thing. I saw the feed from Ialog and I can't understand why you have taken what he said at face value, yet you have been around my husband and me for several hours and you still think I'm being held against my will." Heather watched her for a moment. "Personally, I think you're jealous." With that, Heather walked away. Once she stepped out the doors to the gardens, she had the computer release all the equipment so the newsfeed would start going out again.

Susan and her assistant stepped out into the garden right behind her. Heather assumed they were probably looking for her, so she ducked into the shadows and hoped they wouldn't see her.

"She read you the riot act." Her cameraman lowered his camera to a nearby bench.

"Shut up, Gavin." She looked around.

"And she's right. Did you see that kiss? Wow. If there is no sexual attraction between them, they know how to act like there is."

"I don't know." Susan scratched her head. "That man sure was convincing."

"What sort of proof do you need to see to get you to switch your angle? We could do so much with the sex angle. I have lots of footage showing how they can't keep their hands off each other. Very little of him treating her badly."

"But you do have some footage."

"No, just caught him frowning a few times, but she is in every shot and you can see his anger wasn't directed at her. They have a very strong bond and you, Susan, are being stupid in ignoring it."

Heather agreed. She sensed Storm looking for her, so moved to intercept him.

"There you are." He pressed his hand against her heart.

"Just needed a few moments to myself." She mimicked his move. "I spoke to the news people."

"I heard." He wrapped his arm around her and walked her back into the main ballroom.

"Perhaps we should release the news video from Vespia on the mission. Let the planet see what really happened."

"You think that will help?"

"I don't know, but it wouldn't hurt." She wasn't sure if

releasing the real video would help, but at least the people would know they were trying to show what really happened.

He nodded. "I'll get it together now."

"Give it to the cameraman. Gavin is his name. He's the one to trust to use it properly."

"Has my mate been spying while she was outside?" He squeezed her waist.

"Maybe a little." She approached Anseri and the president of the planet while Storm went to gather the videos together. It didn't take him long before he was back by her side. "All done?"

"We should be seeing it momentarily." The large screen above their head showed live footage from the banquet. The image switched to Susan introducing new footage and the real information on the mission where Heather was hurt came onto the screen.

Heather just hoped it would be enough. She didn't pay much attention to the screen until the room went silent and she heard several sharp intakes of breath. Looking up at the screen was her picture from the grotto where Storm caught her just as she started her orgasm.

"My heart, I didn't release that." Storm had stepped up to her side and stared at the huge picture as well.

She looked up at the image, still amazed it was her. Her dress pooled around her hips, her naked body held in Storm's embrace. The look of ecstasy on her face was impossible to miss. "I know."

He looked at her. "Did you release it?"

"No, but I think I know who did." She tapped the side of her head. "If they don't see how it is between us with that picture, then we'll never convince them."

Storm pulled her against him. The picture always aroused him. She could feel the evidence pressing into her.

"It definitely paints me in a different light." She wasn't

sure if she wanted it released now, but it was better at this point than during one of the military functions.

"You know it doesn't matter what they think, right?" He gently touched her face. "Only what we think."

"Heather, that is a lovely picture of you," said Bear, who had joined them. "But don't you think you should move on to another picture, one not so, um, arousing?"

"Not our doing. That is part of the live feed from the crew here. You're head of security, right? Here to protect the president?"

"Figured it out, huh?" he grinned at her.

"Simple deduction. Although I don't know why I didn't see you before." She was referring to when she first met Storm. The president was at several functions, including her wedding.

"Just been assigned in the last three months."

"Ah." Heather looked up at the image. "Anyway, we gave them the footage of my injury, since that was the reason everyone was up in arms over my treatment. Somehow, that got snuck in."

"You saying it shouldn't have been released?"

"Do you honestly think I would want the world to see me that way?"

"Good point." He looked at Storm. "But your husband might."

"I would never do anything to make her uncomfortable." Storm looked back at him. "She is my heart and I want her happy."

"I'll go speak to them."

It wasn't long before the picture was replaced by live footage again.

Heather was happy to see the image gone, but she found it had done its job. Every man or woman was either eyeing her or checking out Storm. They all probably wondered what it would be like to have either one of them as a sex partner.

"How did you know he was head of security for the president?"

"The fact that he's here was the biggest clue. He knew to speak to you about the security exhibition, too. I also noticed that he has been very close to the man all evening. He was a very good trainer."

"Really? The best?"

"Maybe on Earth." She looked up at him, knowing what he was trying to find out. "But not the best. I'm mated to that."

"Now that is a good answer." He dipped his head to nibble on her throat.

She felt it to her toes. He held her close as he continued to focus on her mark. "You know that isn't fair."

"What?"

"You—oh dear."

Heather felt disorientated. She was just in Storm's arms, yet now she found herself surrounded by guards and speaking to the president of Earth. She lost her words when she found herself in the wrong place. How did this happen? She looked around and saw Storm holding her body. She looked down at her hands and stared at them. They weren't hers. She opened her mouth, maybe to scream, when everything went black.

———

Storm loved the way Heather reacted when he focused his attention on her mark. She always came alive in his arms, so when she pressed her hand against his chest and pushed him away, he didn't know what to think.

"Please."

"Heather?" He then felt her confusion.

"I'm sure your mate cares for you very much, but she isn't in this body right now. Your mother is."

He let go immediately. "Mother?"

"Sorry." She smiled at him.

Storm watched in confusion as she crumpled at his feet. He grabbed her before she hit the floor and turned to look at where his mother stood and noticed she had fainted too.

Heather's eyes opened but he wasn't sure who was in control of the body.

"Heather?"

"I'm here, my heart." She looked up at him.

"What just happened?"

"I'm not sure. One moment we were, um, engaged, and the next I was standing over there." She pointed to where Anseri stood. "It was very strange."

"Imagine holding your mate one minute and having her turn into your mother the next."

"Sorry about that. I'm assuming we switched because of my contact with her mind." Heather touched his face. "Perhaps we should start from the beginning?"

"Your mind is expanding again, isn't it?"

She nodded.

"I hate to sound selfish, but why didn't it happen between us first?"

"Who says it hasn't. We share so much now how would we know if we switched bodies when we're intimate?"

"You have a point." He helped her to her feet. "But please don't do that anymore."

"I'll try not to."

———

The night finally ended without any more trouble. Heather was glad when it was all over. One thing done.

Storm had a few things to check on before he could join her.

Heather found she finally had a few minutes to think

about what had happened. How did she switch minds with Anseri? Her mind had moved from one body to another without her direction. Nothing like that had ever happened before.

Storm hadn't been right since she switched with his mother and that upset Heather. He deserved a special treat. Something to make him happy and relaxed. There was only one thing she could think of that would get him to be his old self again.

She pulled up the images from a local store to see what might have been created since she left. This was the main site she found most of the outfits he loved so much.

"What are you doing?" The heat of his arms around her filled her with joy. He had come back a little early. She had hoped to find something that would set him on fire and have it on before he showed up. He looked over her shoulder at the site she was scanning.

"Looking for something you might enjoy." She worked her way through some of the pages to get to what she was looking for. She could have stopped, but perhaps he would enjoy seeing all the different designs.

"Is this where you get those outfits from?" He perked up when he realized she was looking for something for him.

"Most of them." She leaned into him, enjoying the warmth his body gave her. "Since I didn't see a need to bring any of the ones I created with me, I'm finding a need to create something special."

"You didn't bring any of my favorite garments with you?" He sounded disappointed.

"No. Why should I when this is where they came from? Most of the images I have are old now and I thought I might find something new. Something that might excite you more than the ones I already have."

"Well." He didn't sound convinced. "Let's see what you have come up with."

"You sure?" She turned to look at him. "You have always enjoyed the not knowing. You will lose this if you help me pick it out."

"It's only this one time."

"True." She leaned against him as she brought the outfits up onto the main screen. "But if I give you this power now, how will I keep you from trying to control this aspect of our intimacy in the future?"

"Because I enjoy you doing this for me." He touched her so she would look at him and not the screen. "The very first time you did this, why did you do it?"

"I don't know." She looked away. "I guess I am a bit like you. I had lost control of so much of my life then it was one thing I could control."

"That I understand." He slipped a finger under her chin and made her look at him again. "But out of all the areas of your life where you could have worked for more control, why this? Why our intimacy?"

"I remember your reaction to the foundations I had on under my formal military gown. And those were simple garments. I guess it filled me with a power I didn't know I had, and I wanted to see what other outfits would do to you."

"About that." He watched her. He knew there was more to it. "I thought feminine support was built into all of your clothing."

"In our day-to-day wear of course, but the formal uniforms aren't as form-fitting, so the support isn't quite there. Although it isn't required and a lot of women don't wear anything under theirs, I always have. I wanted men to respect me because of my skills, not my body."

"Which is why you continued to use the Ice Princess persona."

She nodded. "It worked for me. Kept men at arm's length and allowed me to keep to myself. I watched other women in relationships and it was a mess. Both sides were so fickle at times I didn't want anything to do with it."

"Then I came along."

"And turned my world upside down." She smiled at him. "My commander explained about the pheromones your race exuded and that I had some sort of immunity. Yet that first night when I saw you I knew I was in trouble. I wasn't immune to you."

"For which I am very grateful." He pressed his lips to her mark. "You looked so prim and proper that night, but what I noticed the most was how expressive your eyes were. Those beautiful violet eyes."

She tilted her head so he could have easy access to her throat. "You want to get back to looking for an outfit? Or shall we continue to talk about what happened that night. That kiss we shared."

"The one that made my blood boil? Never had a woman come alive in my arms like that." His tongue lathed the side of her neck. "I knew you were special then."

"And I was embarrassed. I had never lost control like that before. The evidence of that kiss was on your leg and crotch, and it was all I could think about."

"Me too, but for an entirely different reason. If a kiss could do that to you, I wanted to know what would happen if we were intimate." He started to work on the seams of her outfit. "All this talk about that kiss has my mind going in one direction."

"My heart, it doesn't take much for you to be focused on sex." She felt the heat of his mouth on the soft tissue of her breast and she lost all desire except to feel him deep inside her. The outfit would wait until later.

"You are just as bad as I am." He had finished working on the top of her outfit and was working on the bottoms, allowing his fingers to linger in places he knew heightened her arousal. "You want me as bad as I want you."

"I don't deny that." Storm had utilized the computer system in removing her clothes a lot so Heather was surprised he didn't do it this time, but she wanted to. One thought later and she could feel his skin under her fingertips. With another thought, she had Storm's chair appear in the room.

"I need you, my heart. I need to feel your body take me as deep as you can, feel your muscles hold me inside you." He picked her up and turned to head to their bed. In its place stood his chair. "You have been busy."

"Just anticipating my heart's desire." She wrapped her legs around his waist, her core pressed against his length. "Just like he would do for me."

He hugged her close and took the two strides it took to make it to the chair. Heather was already drawing him into her body and didn't care if they made it. She needed to feel him inside her now. Her desire for him had always been strong. Every time he wanted her she was ready and willing. But since she had become pregnant she found that desire stronger.

Once he had them seated, she felt him slide in all the way. He filled her perfectly. Her muscles clamped down on him, causing an exquisitely tight sheath for him to move against. Storm placed his hands on her hips as he shifted them so she could straddle him the way she liked. He helped her set the pace for them.

She found every stroke more intoxicating than the last. Each time he filled her, it was deep and satisfying. Little spasms took hold when she took him in all the way. Lost in the sensations, she moved faster, wanting to feel him deep inside her more. Her head dropped back as she felt her release race up on her. It started in her center, spiraling out of her to encompass all of her.

Storm felt everything as intensely as she did. He was

close to his release, but not quite there yet. Did he hold back so she could have more than one powerful orgasm?

He eased her back and took control as her release was upon her. Pushing her over the edge with each deep drive. She quaked in his arms as it started. Overwhelming heat filled her veins. And he wasn't done yet. As he continued to push into her, she tightened her muscles against him, causing more friction between them. This time, his breath hitched as he got closer. His tongue found her mark. She arched her back against him as she hit the heights she was reaching for. "Oh, God."

Storm pounded into her twice more before he joined her in the freefall they felt every time. They reveled in the mind-meld as their bodies escaped reality for a long moment.

"We forgot about the outfit." Storm brushed a few strands of her hair out of her face.

"We can go back to the computer to look." She stretched against him still buried deep inside her. "Unless you're ready to go again."

"All you have to do is touch me and I'm ready to go, my heart." He pressed his lips to her mark. Her body pulsed around him. "And you're definitely touching me right now."

She couldn't help but smile. "You are incorrigible."

"And you have become insatiable."

FOUR

Heather woke up screaming. Storm had her in his arms, trying hard to calm her down. It took a few moments before she was aware of her surroundings. By the way she was behaving, she had had another vision. Tears streamed down her face as she looked up at him. She touched his face softly, stark fear in her eyes.

"What did you see?"

"Me shooting you at point blank range."

———

That vision still had a hold of her when she planned the awards ceremony. Bear worked with her to make sure everything would run smoothly.

"You have your uniform ready, don't you?" he asked.

"Yep." Heather hit a few keys on the pad she held. "I assumed they will want to give me some sort of citation because of the treaty, so I brought it with me."

"Have you tried it on?" He said it nonchalantly, but she could hear an undertone in his voice. What was he getting at?

"No, why?" She gave him an odd look. "It fit perfectly when I went through my wedding ceremony."

"Okay, just thought you might want to since your body has gone through a few changes since then." He gestured up and down her form.

She looked at him, realizing what he was getting at. "Crap."

"See you in a few minutes?"

"Yes." She took off down the hall. Once she was in the room, she spoke to the computer. "Does this garment you created to hide my pregnancy also hide any weight gain?"

"It will disguise it, but not remove it."

"Great." She pulled her uniform out of the closet and laid it on the bed. She removed her dress and slipped on the skirt. It was tight, but she could fasten the skirt.

She heard the doors slide open just as she heard Storm's voice. "Problem?"

She turned to look at him. "Just figured out my uniform might not fit."

"You look good right now." His eyes held that glow she knew so well now.

"To you, but my government might frown on me going topless." She pulled the jacket on and sealed it. "Wow, they have grown, haven't they?"

"Told you." Storm stepped up to her to see if he could help close it better, but there was no give in the jacket and she was exposed.

"I'm going to need a whole new outfit." This couldn't have come at a worse time. She didn't have time to go and get one.

"Have you tried thinking a new uniform on? One that fits?"

"I keep forgetting the computer can do something like that." She closed her eyes and spoke to the computer.

"Why are you closing your eyes?"

"Because yours are glowing again and I have to get this right." In seconds, she found a perfectly fitting uniform on her. "You are wonderful." She kissed him. "Now I have to get back to Bear so we can make sure everything is ready for the ceremony tomorrow."

"Is that your way of saying the glow in my eyes will stay there for a while?"

She wrapped her arms around him and rested her head against his chest. "I promise I will take care of your problem as soon as I can."

"It's never soon enough." He nibbled on her neck. At least what he could get to. "The collar on this uniform is too high."

"I'm sorry." She took her jacket off, and he was right there with her. His hands cupped her breasts. "My heart, really. I need to get back to Bear. He is waiting for me and will know what delayed me. We have to get through the lineup for the ceremony to make sure everything is done."

He continued to focus on the now very accessible throat he considered his. "How am I stopping you?"

"By making my body want you when my mind knows I need to go back and take care of one of the most boring assignments I've had in a long time." She tilted her head to one side so Storm could have total access to her mark. "It's not fair."

"I know." He lathed her mark a few times before he let go of her and backed off.

"What are you doing?"

"Letting you get back to work."

"Oh, that is evil." She pulled her dress back on. "Truly evil."

"You don't know evil yet. I'm going to join you." He gave her a devilish grin. He slipped an arm around her and escorted her back to Bear's side.

"About time. I thought I'd have to send a search party after you," said Bear when he saw her come in the door.

"Well, my uniform does fit, so that is one headache I don't have to worry about anymore." She gave him a bright smile. "And I hope you don't mind, but Storm is going to join us."

The two men nodded to each other.

"Now, we need to get the seating arrangement down," said Bear. "Normally, we would just put the seats in a row, facing the ceremony, but someone got this bright idea to put the first ten rows facing out so they are watching the people go down the line instead."

"You mean like a runway? Where they're facing the people on the other side?"

"Yes."

Heather shook her head. She glanced over to where Storm had taken a seat. He was intently watching her and she found his undivided attention arousing. Time to focus. "I guess you take care of the Earth side and I'll take care of the Vespian side."

"They want it highest ranking down."

"I know that." She wanted to smack Bear. She hadn't forgotten any of her training. "But you have to make sure they understand that the highest rank isn't the ruling council and spouses are considered equal in Vespian society."

"What do you mean?"

"The highest ranked person is Storm's sister. Her mate would sit next to her, then Storm as head of security and me as his mate, then the ruling council would be seated."

"You won't get to sit with Storm, though, because of your certificate."

"Are they going to wait to the very end to give it to me?" She couldn't believe they would make her wait to last, all because of a stupid certificate. "You know how much I love wearing that uniform."

"No. But you will be in the ceremony several times."

"Why?"

"You're receiving rank, too."

"Rank? Bear, I'm not even part of Earth's military anymore."

"As long as you receive payment you are and they have been paying you the whole time you've been on Vespia. They fear the Vespians could go back on their word since no one has volunteered to donate DNA yet."

"And I'm sure the government had something to do with that." Heather looked over at Storm. He hadn't moved, although the glow in his eyes was still strong. "That might be something I'll address when I have to do that stupid interview."

"Interview?"

"I am supposed to speak with the newswoman who was there at the banquet last night. President's orders. They want me to clear up the mess caused by her." She felt something caress her leg, but when she looked down, there was nothing there. Her first thought was Storm. Somehow he had done that. Well, two could play that game.

She worked on the small handheld electronic pad she had while using her mind to caress Storm. A loud bang came from his direction, which made her smile. She had mentally wrapped her hand around his erection and caused him to kick a chair nearby.

"Is he okay?"

"Storm? Sure. He has already finished his part in the security exhibition as well as security for this function here, so he has a little time on his hands."

"Well, he keeps staring at you like he's going to devour you the moment we're done." Bear hit a few keys on his pad. "It's a little unnerving."

"Don't let him get to you."

———

Storm felt something wrap around his erection and squeeze. He jumped at the sensation and banged the chair next to him. His mate was taking advantage of her mind again. He had wished he could touch her earlier and imagined himself caressing her leg. Had she felt that? If she did, he could tease her until she gave up and came to him.

Kuarto plopped down in the chair next to him. Now what?

"You do enjoy just staring at her, don't you?" Kuarto pulled out his scanner and rolled it in his hands.

"What do you want, Kuarto?" Storm turned his attention to Heather's brother. The man could be very annoying when he wanted to be.

"Just checking on you. Your readings went through the roof a few minutes ago, and I was concerned."

"And Heather's?"

"Just yours." He leaned back in the chair. "Noticed anything new?"

"No." Storm turned his focus back to Heather. She was bending over while she faced them and he was enjoying the view. It surprised him when Kuarto didn't say anything. He glanced at him and found him watching Heather and Bear. Didn't he see what Storm did?

"If I didn't know better, I'd say you could actually see down the front of her dress."

"I can." Storm turned to look at Kuarto for a moment. "Can't you?"

"She's too far away from us to really see anything. Twenty/twenty vision only gets you so far." He leaned his arms on his thighs. "So your vision has changed a little. How clearly can you see her right now?"

"Like I'm standing right next to her." Storm found

Heather mesmerizing. He sniffed the air. "I can smell her too."

"You want to explain that one?"

"Her unique essence, her desire for me. It's so potent. You can't detect it?" Storm stood. "It calls to me."

"Whoa, big boy. I think you need to wait a moment." Kuarto grabbed his arm as he took a step toward Heather. He was greeted with a menacing sound from the back of Storm's throat. "Did you just growl at me?"

Storm turned to look at Kuarto. Part of him recognized the man was trying to protect him, but another part, a more base instinct, saw him as a threat, trying to keep him from what was his.

The heat of Heather's hand on his arm brought his attention to what he desired most.

"Perhaps you could keep Bear company for a few minutes?" She looked at Kuarto for a moment before turning her attention to Storm. "My heart? I sensed your stress from over there."

"I need you so bad." Raw desire burned in his eyes. He pulled her into his arms with more force than what she was used to. He could sense her nervousness toward him. "I don't want to hurt you." Words were getting harder to form.

Heather looked at him with fear in her eyes.

———

Heather didn't know what to do. Storm was beyond reach. She had tried to brush her mind against his, but whatever was going on with him now had too strong a grip. His desire for her was almost animalistic in the way it had control of him. Somehow, she needed to get through to him.

She prayed Kuarto had taken Bear out of the room or he might get an eye full because she didn't think she could stop

Storm from his goal of taking her right there and then. His desire was the only thing he could think of.

Heather felt his hands in her hair, moving it aside so he could have access to her mark. His teeth scraped across the tender skin before he sucked it into his mouth, swirling his tongue erotically against her flesh. She closed her eyes at the white hot arousal shooting through her blood. Everything tightened inside.

Cool air hit her skin, and she knew one of them had thought their clothes away. Storm lowered her to the carpeted floor and drove into her, burying himself deep inside. He groaned as her muscles contracted around him. He started pounding into her, instinct in control. Each time he filled her to capacity. If she didn't know any better, she'd swear he was bigger. Each stroke pushed him in deep. She could do nothing but cling to him.

Her body shook with each invasion. He pumped into her, bringing her along with his out of control desire for her. She felt his need, his want. He slowly started to regain control of his mind. She felt his thoughts blend with hers.

"My heart, I am so sorry." He was close, and too late to stop. He continued to drive in and out of her, now working to make sure her body sang for him the way it always did. "I will make this up to you."

Her body responded to his constant pounding, clenching against him. Her back arched. She wasn't sure if she could take anymore.

Storm angled his body so his mouth covered her mark. His tongue lathed the soft tissue, and it sent her over the edge. She moaned as her muscles clamped against him. The powerful orgasm had her in its hold. He followed her release with his.

Once they were able to breathe normally again, he pushed himself up on his elbows.

"You okay?"

"Yes." She looked up at him, seeing the concern in his eyes.

"I don't know what came over me." He pressed soft kisses all along her face. "I just found this uncontrollable need to be with you. I didn't mean to frighten you the way I did."

"I wasn't frightened of you, more frightened for you." She brushed his hair out of his face. "Not knowing what was going on with you worried me. I tried to touch your mind and couldn't. Promise me you'll let Kuarto check it out."

"Where is he?" He looked around.

She looked around to see if anyone was in the room and found it empty. "I'm hoping he took Bear out of the room before this started, but I don't know for sure."

"I don't see either one." He pulled out of her and helped her to her feet. His first thought was to clothe them. "Again, I'm sorry."

"Well, now we have one person who knows the passion is real." She smoothed out her dress.

"After that? I sure hope so."

"Let's go find them and allow the awkwardness to start." She wrapped her arm around his waist.

"Awkwardness?" he put his arm around her shoulders.

"A human thing. Everyone knows what happened. They would have to be blind to not know, but no one will talk about it. Instead, there be a lot of throat clearing and strange glances."

"I will talk to him."

"You could possibly make it worse."

"Trust me." He gave her a quick kiss and headed out the doors.

———

Heather brushed her jacket one last time before she was ready to pin her medals on. She was amazed at how well Bear had handled what had happened. She didn't know what Storm had said to him but he looked her in the eye and said, 'I knew you had it in you'. When she asked what he was talking about he said, 'the ability to drive a man to distraction'. Then never said another word about it.

Once she had her medals pinned on properly, she slid one arm, then the other, into the sleeves and sealed the jacket. She slipped her heels on and opened the door. To her surprise, Storm stood there, in his dress uniform, waiting for her. His broad shoulders looked bigger in the black jacket he wore.

"Mother thought it would show proper courtesy." He had been very attentive since the ballroom. She knew he still felt bad over what happened and she didn't know what to say to make him understand it was okay. Not every woman can say they literally drive their men wild. He held out his arm for her.

"You know this will be as bad as the ceremony we sat through when your sister became religious leader." She took his arm. "They are the worst."

"I've been through so many one more won't matter." He guided her down the halls to the main ballroom. When they reached the rest of the recipients, she pressed a soft kiss to his lips and sent him to his seat.

It went by pretty quickly. She received rank and a special medal for her work with the Vespians. Once the ceremony itself was done, everyone was ushered into another section of the ballroom for dinner. She had no control over how the seating arrangement was done and wasn't happy when she found herself separated from Storm. All the recipients sat at three tables in the center of the room near a dais while the dignitaries were seated at the eight tables surrounding them, then guests were at ones further in the back of the room.

She hadn't been able to say much to Storm. A quick touch and a kiss, and they were separated again. At least she could see him from her seat. The chairs were angled just right so they could look at each other whenever they wanted to. Storm sat with his sister, Kuarto, the President, Bear and a few other dignitaries from the planet. Anseri and the ruling council were at a separate table with the second half of Earth's rulers and a few more dignitaries.

"He's gorgeous, Heather," said one of the women at the table. She knew some of the people since they'd had an assignment or two together. They weren't anyone she would have kept in touch with, but at least she didn't have to sit amongst strangers.

"Thank you." She looked up to find Storm watching her. She smiled at him and gave him a silent toast.

"What is it like?"

"What?" She nodded to the waiter who placed a salad in front of her.

"Being with a man like that? He's huge."

Heather had started to eat her salad before the woman made her comment and choked on the piece of lettuce that wedged itself in her throat. She couldn't be asking about sex. Could she?

"I mean, I'd be afraid he would crush me."

Yep, she was talking about sex. "I'm guessing everyone has seen the picture?"

Nods all around the table.

"And you want to know if it was real?" More nods. She gave them all a catlike smile. "Have I ever been known for faking anything?"

They shook their heads as one to that question, too. She never lied. That was what got her into trouble with the government as well as some of her fellow soldiers.

"Then believe me when I say it is very real."

"Damn, Heather, how did they get you to pose for that?" asked one of the men.

"If you look at the image closely, you'll realize that isn't a pose." She speared a few smaller pieces of her salad and put them in her mouth. Let them chew on that for a few minutes.

"So what is it like?"

"What is what like?" She couldn't believe they were going to get into this at the dinner table. None of these people were close friends. Why would they want such intimate details?

"Being with a Vespian? I mean, compared to a human."

"Considering the men I have been with from Earth didn't really care whether I got any pleasure out of the act or not, I'd have to say better. Much, much, better. He's attentive, caring, and a master at the art." She looked at everyone at the table. They asked for it. "Oh, and won't stop until I have my orgasm."

The table was silent for a moment. Heather turned her attention back to her salad.

"You are so lucky."

Heather couldn't remember the woman's name, but they had been assigned together for a few missions. "How so?"

"So many of us would die for a chance to marry a man like that, and he seems to be in love with you." She stabbed her fork into a big piece of lettuce. "You were lucky you won that little lotto."

"What?"

"Oh, nothing." She looked at several of the others, who gave her that you said too much look. She ducked her head and didn't say another word.

This time someone else spoke. "We heard you weren't the only one up to be working with the Vespians. There were several women in contention. All of you fit the parameters, whatever that means. Susan, you remember Susan, don't you? The newscaster? She was one of your competitors. And she thought for sure she had it."

"Yeah," responded another. "Remember hearing her brag about it just before we all heard you were assigned to protect him."

"Now look at you. Married to a very powerful man and living on another planet."

This changed everything. No wonder Susan didn't want to change the angle of the story. She was jealous. She thought she'd be Storm's mate instead of interviewing the one person she never liked. That had to hurt.

Heather needed to speak to Anseri, though. She had never thought to ask how many other candidates they had thought was the child they sent away.

Once the meal ended, she found Storm right by her chair. He kneeled down so they could be at eye level. "I have been informed I have been remiss in my duties as your husband."

"That's not what we have heard," said one of the men at the table.

"Shut up, you idiot. Let him talk," demanded another.

Storm arched a brow at her. She just smiled and shrugged her shoulders. He held up a small velvet box. The last time he showed her one of those it held her engagement ring. He opened the lid and pulled out another diamond encrusted band.

"Your friend Bear, informed me that I should have given this to you during our wedding ceremony. And as I think back when you explained the reason of the rings to some people on Vespia you did mention a second one."

"You didn't have to." She touched his face. "I have proof I belong to you."

"True." He ran his finger down the side of her neck where her mark was, watching as her eyes dilated at the sensation. "But you know how I like to follow tradition."

Her eyes widened at that remark. She wanted to make a

comment so badly, but being the good little mate she didn't. Heather pulled her engagement ring off so he could put the ring on her properly. His eyes sparkled as he slipped it on her finger then added her engagement ring, putting it back where it belonged. He must have felt her desire to laugh in his head.

"It is beautiful, my heart, but I fear I will blind people as the light catches these two rings."

He offered her his hand. "We'll just have to take that chance."

"Ladies, gentlemen, it has been fun, but I am needed elsewhere." Heather smiled, grateful she was getting away from them. The questions about her sex life were a bit much.

"And what did you tell them that made the women look at me with a gleam in their eyes?"

"The truth." She knew he'd be combing through the security videos to see what she said. Maybe that would be what it would take for him to believe she wasn't flustered over what happened in the ballroom the other day. "I need to speak to Anseri."

"I believe she is talking to your President." He escorted her over to his mother's side.

"Commander." The president smiled as she stepped up. "We're looking forward to seeing the security exhibition tomorrow."

"It should be exciting, sir. Two of the best security leaders I know are putting it together."

He said his goodbyes and headed for another group of people wishing to speak to him.

"Anseri, it was brought to my attention that there were other women who fit the criteria you used to help find me. Do you know who they were?"

"Not offhand, but I do have it in the files. And they really weren't in contention, Heather. We didn't have all the family history on one. The moment we learned she was born to

Earth parents it removed her from the list. There were a few others, but they were removed pretty early. I will send the information to your room so you can look at it later. Why?"

"Just curious." She smiled at Storm's mother. "Nothing to worry about."

Anseri had been called to another group, which left Heather and Storm alone for a few moments.

"So what is the real reason you wish to see the list of women they thought would be you?" Storm knew her too well.

"You remember the young woman who was recording the party the other night? The same one I'm to have an interview with?" She entwined her fingers with his. "She was one of the candidates and from what my cohorts at the table were saying she thought she was going to be one who would be working with you to get the treaty signed."

"So you think she's jealous?"

"I'm positive she is." Heather continued to smile as they walked around. "That interview just got more complicated."

———

She sat on the bed, reading the file Anseri sent her. She had peeled off her uniform as fast as she could. Now she rested against a stack of pillows in a silk robe.

Storm said he had something he needed to take care of before he came to the room, which gave her a chance to see who was listed as candidates. Most of the names she had never heard of. And she saw how quickly the list had been narrowed down. Ultimately, there were four women who could have been what they were looking for. The first woman was already married with three children. She wasn't sterile, so that took her out of the running.

The next candidate was a young woman working at the science academy. Her file did have a lot of the same things

Heather's did, she also was an orphan, but further digging showed her parents died when she was a child, so that took her out.

Then there was Susan. Her file didn't show any of the information that the other files did. How did she even get considered? No parents were listed, but it didn't show her as an orphan either. She was two years older than Heather, but no age was listed for her. None of it made sense.

The doors opened, making her look up. Storm came in and walked straight for her. He shed his clothes as he reached the bed. Pulling the small pad out of her hand, he leaned down and captured her lips with his for a quick kiss. He pressed his weight into her as he wrapped his arms around her. "So, I'm the best you've ever had, huh?"

"I see someone couldn't wait to see what was said at my table tonight." She couldn't help but grin as she wrapped her arms around his neck. Heather had wondered if watching the tape was what he wanted to do. "And I'm pretty sure those words never came from my lips."

"Had to make sure no one insulted or made rude advances toward my mate." He nibbled on her neck. "Need to protect that which is mine. And I might have paraphrased, but I did get the gist of the conversation."

"And was I insulted?" She tilted her head so he could nibble to his heart's content.

"They sure didn't waste any time asking about our sex life." He pulled up to look her in the face. "But I do love the way you defended us. And every Vespian male will thank you for the vote of confidence." He ran his hand over the silky material of her robe. "I do like this. It is as soft as your skin."

"Thought you would. That picture really is a conversation starter." She ran her fingers through his hair. "And people are definitely treating me different. The women think they can ask me anything now."

"What about the men?"

"They are keeping their distance. Not sure if they're intimidated by the picture or by you."

"As long as they stay away from you, I don't really care." He touched her face. "You are mine and I don't share."

She returned the gesture as she smiled. If another Vespian heard him, they'd think he was out of his mind. Even mated, they could have other partners if they wished. But she didn't want to share him with anyone, either. "Is that the reason you made my left hand so heavy? So all the human males will know that I'm off limits?"

"After they've seen that image of you?" He nibbled a little more. "I know how that picture makes me feel every time I see it."

"You must look at it all the time."

"Have it burned into my memory." His tongue lathed her mark, making her arch up against him. "See it every time I close my eyes. The only thing better is seeing it live, which should be soon now."

"Have a plan?"

"Yes." He kissed his way down her throat to her collarbone. "I plan on working my way down this luscious body of yours with my lips. Show you how much it means to know you defended me the way you did, especially after the way I attacked you in the ballroom."

"You didn't attack me."

"Could you have fought me off?" He pushed himself up so he could watch her as she answered.

"Well, no, you were a little focused. But you are my mate, so why would I want to fight you off?"

"You were afraid. I could smell it."

"I wasn't afraid of you, but for you." He didn't look convinced. "Storm, would this have bothered you as much if it had happened here in our room?"

"Probably not. But that isn't the point. I could have hurt you."

"Overprotective? A whole lot, but violent? Never, not with me. You wanted to be gentle, even at the height of it. It came through in the way you touched me. Your grip was sure, but not menacing. And as you claimed me, you came back to me. Your mind started to merge with mine. You regained control. My only concern when it all started was how much of an eyeful did Bear see before he left the room?"

"He told me Kuarto walked him out of the room the moment I started moving toward you." Storm brushed his fingers along her jaw line. "He didn't embarrass you, did he?"

"No." A slight blush filled her cheeks as she remembered their short conversation. "He only said he knew I had the ability to drive men wild, then we went on to our seating arrangements. Normally, I just drive men crazy."

"You do that too." He chuckled. "Bear knows you well."

"I was his favorite annoying little pest, as he put it." She touched his lips.

"You sound proud of it."

"You know how Toki liked to interfere all the time? Before Kuarto? I had a knack of ruining Bear's favorite plans."

"Favorite plans?"

"He would come up with security scenarios and I'd be the one to find the flaw in them. Sometimes before they were executed."

"So that is why he wanted you to go into security."

She nodded. Heather watched his beautiful golden eyes as they studied her. She caught the slight upturn of his lips as he lowered his mouth to hers. The moment they touched, his tongue searched for hers, drawing it out to dance with his. A sigh escaped her when the kiss ended.

"Now, where were we?" He pressed his lips to her collarbone. "Right, first I'm going to work my way down one side of your luscious body, maybe focusing on each side except in certain places, and one spot in particular will get my attention as I work my way down one side and back up the other."

"And what if I'm ready now and need to feel you inside me, where you belong?" Her hands caressed his chest.

"Then you will have to deal with the fact that this is something I want and my desires come first right now." He captured her hands with his. "But I've been ready for this." He reached off the side of the bed and pulled up a soft fur strap. Storm wrapped it around her hand. "I did a lot of research on these. They are very soft and won't hurt you, but they will keep those willful hands of yours still. There is also a set for those wicked legs of yours."

"Storm, you don't have to tie me down."

"How long have we been mated?" After securing the first hand, he worked on the other, then her feet. He sat back on his heels when he was finished. "You might not say much when we're intimate, but you are very good at making sure I know what you want. Your body is my favorite playground and you know it, but you won't let me play to my heart's content and I think that is wrong, so I found a way to fix that problem."

He opened the sash that held the silk robe around her and revealed her body to his gaze. His hands skimmed across her stomach and breasts to touch her mark gently with his fingers. She sucked in her breath with the caress. "This seems to be more sensitive."

"Only when you touch it."

"Really?" He ran a finger over it again.

She nodded as she bit her lip. "Clothes don't bother it. If someone else inadvertently touches it doesn't bother it, but your touch seems to make it come alive."

"I noticed it earlier when I touched you. Your eyes

dilated. Never noticed that before." He rested his finger against her mark, wondering what the prolonged contact would do to her. "It has always been a direct line to your arousal, but never to this extent."

"I know." Her legs shifted, and she arched her back. "Please, Storm, if you wish to use your playground the way you planned I wouldn't leave your hand where it is for very long, or I just might rip these silly restraints off of whatever you secured them to and have my way with you."

FIVE

"There is a part of me that would love to see that." He smiled down at her. "But you're right. There are lots of places I wish to show my attention to and pushing you to see what you would do wouldn't be fair to either of us."

She sighed in relief when he moved his fingers to a safer spot. At least for the moment. Storm took his time. Kneeling between her secured legs, he slowly moved her robe, which had slid around as they talked, revealing all of her body to his gaze, barely touching her as he did so, but she felt every accidental brush deep inside. His large hands skimmed across her upper torso, the simple movement causing heat to pool in her core.

If something so simple was causing such a reaction, what would happen when he focused on the sensitive parts of her body? Storm smiled. He knew every spot that aroused her.

His mouth replaced his hands, and she knew she was in trouble. Her desire spiraled out of control. He placed soft wet kisses on the inside of her arm and palm before he moved to one of his favorite places. His mouth closed on one breast and she moaned. Everything tightened inside. She could feel her orgasm just out of her grasp. The delicious tendrils of arousal snaked up her legs and into her core.

He focused on one, then the other, but not long enough to cause her pain. The last few weeks they had become sensitive so couldn't take too much attention. He then nipped at her hip before working his way to her mound. He lathed her mound, and she moaned again.

"Two moans, my heart? And I'm not even halfway done with your body yet. Maybe I'll get my elusive scream tonight."

The heat of his mouth and the pressure of his tongue sent the first wave of release crashing over her. The strength carried her away for a moment before he began to build her back up. Storm worked his way down her left leg. Nipping in all the right places. She found herself squirming as the tickling sensations brought pleasure.

He kissed the inside of her knee, nibbled on her ankle bone. Then he worked his way up her other leg. Anticipation built as he grew closer to her core again. Her body tensed, knowing this orgasm would be more powerful than the last. The heat of his breath teased the fine hairs of her mound, and she was already quaking. His mouth closed over her and her body shook as a strong release grabbed her and flung her into ecstasy.

"Oh, God."

Storm continued up her body at this point, paying homage to the children she carried in her womb before focusing on her breasts once again. By the time he had worked his way back to her mark, she was ready for round three.

His teeth scraped the delicate tissue there, and she arched up against him once more. She was beyond begging at this point. If he didn't enter her soon, she was going to scream, but it would be in frustration, not joy.

He licked her mark one last time before he filled her. Her

third orgasm started immediately. Her muscles tightened on him until they were vise-like, doubling the wonderful friction between them. She felt the heat deep inside, bubbling up through her bloodstream. The power of the release made it hard for her to breathe. The things this man did to her.

Storm leaned back as he continued to drive into her so he could watch as she felt the orgasm take control. Her climax brought him a joyful satisfaction. He was the only one who did this for her and he was proud of it.

"My heart, you are so beautiful." He leaned down to capture her lips with his. He moved faster within her now, getting closer to his own orgasm. She could feel his release coming. It would only take a stroke or two more. Something deep inside her wanted to control his release. She broke her bonds, flipped him over, and climbed on top.

———

Storm watched in amazement as the bonds he placed on her removed themselves. He felt his body moving, having an almost weightless feel to it as he turned over. When Heather impaled herself on his staff, he couldn't help but grin. He had driven her to this. He sat up and wrapped his arms around her, holding her in her favorite position. Having her a little higher also gave him better access to her mark, which he wanted. She wrapped her legs around him and began to move against him. Her head tilted back as the friction between them built again. His mouth covered her mark, and she squeezed him with her muscles. As he sucked on the soft skin, she trembled. He loved the way she came undone in his arms. Her modesty disappeared every time they were intimate.

He could feel she was very close, as was he. Their minds touched and shared each level of arousal reached. Her breath hitched, and she was caught up in the sensations racing through her system. He held her close as he guided her mindless body up and down a few more times so he could join her. They soared together as their bodies hit their release.

Afterwards, he held her close, waiting for her mind to come back to him. It was like an out-of-body experience for her sometimes.

"Wow." She snuggled against him.

"Wow indeed. You were an orgasmic machine, my heart. That was almost like the time when you and your brother created the wall in your mind and you just kept having one orgasm after another. Do you realize you broke your bonds?"

"I did?" She lifted her head up to look at him.

"I didn't release you."

"How did I do that?" She rested her head back on his chest. "I remember thinking I wanted to, but don't remember anything past that."

"I saw it happen. They just fell off like an invisible hand took them off you." He hugged her. "If you're going to start using your mind to get the upper hand during sex, I'm going to have to come up with better ways to restrain you when I want to get my way."

"And what about when I want to get my way?"

"Don't you always?"

———

The next morning, they worked in the gym putting the final changes on the routine for the security demonstration. Heather found out she was to be part of both teams at different stages of the competition and now had to make sure she had both sides down. There was a lot for her to memorize but she was excited about the chance to show off what she knew and what she had learned.

Storm was giving her some instructions about one particular section she needed to master when she started to feel a little lighthearted again. He was speaking to her, but it seemed to be from the long end of a tunnel.

Her head spun, making her feel disorientated. She shook her head to clear the cobwebs and looked around in confusion. What just happened? One minute she was listening to Storm explain what he wanted her to do during her part in the routine, then the next thing she knew, she was here. Heather looked around, wherever 'here' was. Trying to figure out where she had ended up, she moved about the room. Where was she?

Who was she?

The room was empty. No furniture or windows. There was a door in front of her, so she walked to it and tugged, only to find it locked. The smooth metal surface of the door caught her eye, and she felt ill. The face staring back at her wasn't her own, but Ialog's.

Her mind reached for Storm, but he wasn't there. Heather screamed.

———

Heather seemed to be miles away when Storm needed her to pay attention. Her lack of focus annoyed him. "Are you listening?"

Their mindmeld always allowed him to get her back when she drifted away on him like this, but this time Storm couldn't reach out and touch Heather's mind. It was like she wasn't there.

Something was wrong.

Heather turned to look at him and smiled. It was a cold, calculating smile that sent chills down his back. He knew that smile. It belonged to Ialog.

His mate lifted the weapon she had in her hand and aimed it at his heart. Her vision! He realized what was happening and dove. Storm felt the heat of the blast graze him as he tried to get out of the line of fire. Thank God the weapons didn't have a higher setting than stun or he could have been killed. The blast still hurt like hell.

Not knowing what happened had him acting instinctively. He tackled Heather, knocking her to the ground. His height allowed him to sit back far enough on her so she couldn't use her legs and he pinned her arms with his knees. How Ialog took over her body was something Storm wanted answers to.

"Storm?" Frightened violet eyes stared up at him. "Why am I pinned to the ground? What happened? What did I do?"

"You shot at me." He wasn't sure who he was talking to and he wasn't taking any chances. Ialog couldn't be trusted. "How the hell did you take over my mate's body?"

"Oh, God." Her eyes became glassy with unshed tears. "I don't know how it happened either, my heart, but he's gone now. It's me."

"And how do I know it is you?" Storm wanted to believe it was Heather, but he wasn't sure if he should trust her. Perhaps Ialog was still in control and pretending to get him to lighten up so he could try again. He watched the expression on her face as a myriad of thoughts raced through her mind.

The first sign he received that it was Heather beneath him was her mind reaching for his. He relaxed, knowing it was his mate.

"You got two moans out of me last night and four orgasms. No matter what, only I would know that." She looked up at him, fear filling them. "It was my vision, wasn't it? I looked at you, smiled and shot you."

"You did look at me and smiled, but you shot at me not shot me. There is a big difference." He climbed off her and helped her to her feet.

"Did I hit you?" Her voice was a little shrill as she searched his body for signs of damage.

"Grazed me, that's all." He showed her the burn mark on his shoulder where the blast cut through his uniform.

Ten guards entered the room with their weapons up.

"Sorry." Heather held her hands up. "My weapon went off while I was practicing." She pointed to the weapon she had dropped on the floor the moment Storm tackled her. "I should have contacted you the moment I did it."

"And it is my fault she didn't contact you. I was too busy berating her for making such an amateur move."

"Yes, sir." One of the guards picked up her weapon and checked it. After looking at her, he nodded to the others, and after handing her weapon to Storm they left the room.

"Amateur move?" she asked quietly as she took her weapon and reholstered it. "Really?"

"Can he do that to you again?" He touched her face.

"I don't know." She wrapped her arms around him. Storm could feel her shaking as she held him.

"We need to speak to your brother." He eased himself out of her hold, grabbed her by her arm, and led her out of the room and down several halls. "He might be able to help."

They found Kuarto in his room, working on a file while Toki sat next to him working on something as well. He stood when they entered, surprised to see them. "Is there a problem?"

"Al took over her body for a minute."

"What?" Kuarto and his mate said in unison. He grabbed his scanner. He looked at Storm as he ran the scanner over Heather. "Did that little device activate?"

"Device?"

"Remember? I created a mimic of that security camera we found in Heather's mind and put a link to your mind." He looked at his readings, then looked at Storm.

"No. At least I don't think so. It happened so fast."

"What do you remember, Heather?" He used the scanner on Storm as well. He must have noticed the hole in his uniform.

"Storm was going over something in the routine that needed to be addressed. As he was talking, it was like he was carrying on this conversation down a long tunnel, then I was in a room void of furniture. There was a door but I couldn't open it. Then I was back here in my body." She looked from her brother to her mate. "I remember noticing my face in a shiny surface and it was Ialog's. I was frightened for Storm and knew I had to get back here."

"That's what I wondered. You probably forced your way back into your body." He pressed a hypo against Storm's shoulder. The shot would help him heal faster as well as clean the wound. "I'm not finding anything out of the ordinary with you. Do you know if this has happened before?"

"I'm aware of one time so far. I switched places with Anseri, but I thought that happened because I have been in her mind."

"Probably." He gestured for Heather to sit. Storm joined her on the couch. He moved his shoulder as the medication healed the pain there. "I would expect that as your mind continues to grow and expand you're going to find new things you can do and it will start with familiar things. Switching bodies is a bit unique, but it would make sense you could switch with Anseri, Storm, or me since you have a link with each of us."

"Can you stop it from happening again?" asked Storm.

"There are a few things Heather can do to protect her mind, but I have a feeling she has already done that since she bounced back into her body so fast." He pulled up a chair to where she sat and took her hands in his. "You ready?"

"I guess." She found closing her eyes helped her focus. "What am I supposed to do?"

"Go to the door. Let me in."

She opened the door he spoke about and allowed him into her mind. "How am I to stop Ialog from taking over my body again? I don't know how he did it in the first place."

"That's why I'm here. I just want to look around and see what you have done."

"Okay. But not sure what you're looking for." They walked side by side inside her mind.

"Ah, but I do." He looked up and noticed there was now a golden grid over their heads. "And it looks like you have built your own protection against any type of attack."

"Ialog has ways around something like this, we both know that." She looked up, seeing it for the first time. "Is it enough?"

"Only time will tell."

———

Heather waited in the wings with the rest of the Vespian security squad for the signal to begin. How Storm and Bear were going to pull this off she wasn't sure, but it should be a beautiful, visual show. The goal was to work each group together so in the end no one would know which person was Vespian and which one was human. No one would be able to say one was better than the other.

The hall grew dark and the participants walked out one by one. Everyone carried their helmets so the audience could see their faces. They took their place along the floor. Heather was the center person, bridging both teams. Once everyone had been introduced, helmets went on and the place went black. Using their helmets, they all found their marks and waited for the cue to start their presentation.

Heather felt excitement race through her. She wanted this to go perfectly.

Spotlights illuminated the floor.

It was time to start.

The two teams began with acrobatics. Fast-paced flips across the floor, tumbles, and dives as well. Perfectly timed moves that brought one person inches from another. They flew by each other, sometimes touching, other times pulling glowing markers off the uniform they were passing. Streaks of color filled the air as more and more held markers as they seemed to fly across the floor.

They also did hand-to-hand combat. Their movements lightning-fast and hard to follow. The lights would switch from group to group, keeping the audience guessing who they were watching.

All the uniforms were Vespian in design, created for this type of show. The helmet hid the faces as well and the uniform blended all the heights so you couldn't see who was shorter or taller. All designed to keep everyone's identity secret.

Then the uniforms switched from black to white, synchronizing with an outside source. One minute the audience would be watching one person in a white uniform sparring with someone in a black uniform then suddenly they would both be wearing the same color. They kept switching, making it hard for anyone to follow the groups.

Most of the routines were easy for her: joint lock manipulations, flying sidekicks, what she considered pretty standard stuff. But her team was able to do one routine different from the others. A triple back flip off the back of a speeding air bike. She had done it before to save her life, but now was trained to do all sorts of maneuvers off the bikes. Knowing how to do this was something she had spearheaded. The space was a little tight, but they were trained to do just this sort of thing. Heather and her team were the best trained and they got to show off their talent to the amazement of the crowd.

Once everything was done, all the teams assembled

together. All the uniforms were now white. The announcer spoke.

"How many of you believe you know which member belongs to which team?"

There was a show of hands. Not too many raised them. Good, they wanted to confuse the audience on purpose. Make them understand that they were all good at their jobs no matter what planet they represented.

"How many believe you know which one is the ambassador's wife?"

More hands came up for that one.

"Well, we thought we'd give you a chance to see how well you were able to follow her. Under your seats, you will find a keypad. You'll see images corresponding with the security people now lined up on the stage. Just touch the figure you think is the commander, and we will reveal the top three picks."

There was an excitement in the room. Heather wondered if they could tell which one she was. Of the fifty people in the line, she was number thirty-two.

It didn't take long for the audience to make up their mind.

"Now, this is interesting. More than fifty percent of the crowd believes it is number thirty-five. Will that participant please step forward? And remove your helmet?"

When the helmet came off, there were quite a few gasps. The person behind the mask was her mate, Storm. Heather couldn't help but grin. Now she only had to dodge two more guesses.

"Since your guess wasn't quite accurate, we'll move on to the next guess. Number twenty-four. Please step out and reveal yourself."

The person in question took one step forward and pulled off their helmet. It was Fridon from her team. One more to go.

"Goodness, you've picked two males, thinking it was the commander. Those uniforms do a good job hiding the identity of the person wearing it, don't they? Okay, the final pick is number twelve."

That person stepped forward and removed their helmet. Another male. Heather didn't know him, but he was a newer recruit for Earth.

"Well. It looks like we can do this all night, but I'm sure you have better things to do, so we'll have the participants pull their helmets off one by one."

Each person stepped forward and removed their helmets. They did it pretty quickly and went straight down the line. Heather stepped forward, pulled her helmet off, and was greeted with laughter and a strong round of applause.

Once everyone had removed their helmets and been dismissed, she walked up to her mate. "They thought you were me?"

"You think it's funny, don't you?"

"Of course not." But she couldn't fight the laughter bubbling up inside. "Perhaps I should go change before we all move into the ballroom for the buffet?"

"Might be a good idea."

———

Heather stood next to Storm as people came by and showed their appreciation of the demonstration. Having the two teams working together really helped with planet relations. People weren't treating the Vespians as the interlopers anymore and that made Heather happy.

The uniforms were a big hit. Several people approached Storm about acquiring a few for Earth's security, but he politely recommended they follow protocol and have their government request them in writing.

Susan was back, with her cameraman, who was recording

everything he could. Heather noticed she kept her distance from the two of them. Her threat from the other night seemed to have worked.

"It seems that our demonstration was a hit, Storm." Bear had walked up to them a moment ago.

"It does." He smiled at Bear and shook his hand. "Glad the uniforms did what they were supposed to. Been working hard at perfecting them."

"The government loved them, and of course wants to have some of their own. I have asked them to put it in writing."

"Me too." Storm laughed. "I've been approached a couple of times now. You think they went to you, didn't get the answer they wanted, and decided to see if they could get a different answer from me?"

"With these people? You never know. I'm just glad it's all over. And Heather, you were phenomenal. Loved the bit with the bike. Felt my heart in my throat when you launched off the back of that thing like it was nothing."

"Thank you, Bear."

"I must ask. Your race is very big on the rank. How do you two get away with not using it?"

"We only call each other by name when we're alone or out of uniform." Heather leaned her head against Storm's chest. "The government knows him as Admiral Archibald Barrister."

"So that is where Bear came from."

"Yes. Heather was the first one to use it, and it stuck fast." He gave her a wink. "What were you, thirteen? Fourteen?"

"Thirteen and a half. That's when I learned my first lesson in security. If you just stand there, you can get hurt."

"I can't see you as a passive person," commented Storm. "You have been the exact opposite as long as I've known you."

"What can I say? I was young and naive."

"And a fast learner. She only stood there like a frightened doe the one time. After that, she was the one who normally struck first. That was one of the reasons I felt she'd be good at security."

Kuarto walked up to them. Looking at Storm, he asked, "May I borrow your mate for a moment?"

"Sure." Storm's brow furrowed. "Is there a problem?"

"No. Just need to speak to Heather for a moment."

She got up on her tiptoes and kissed Storm on the cheek. "I'm sure everything is fine."

He touched her face. "Don't be long."

"Promise." She walked away with Kuarto. "So what am I doing now?"

"You look a little tired. I wanted to give you a boost to help you through the next few hours." He walked her into the medical center. "Have a seat."

She parked herself on the table.

"You're starting to get the dark circles under your eyes again. Don't need that to end up on a planet wide news-feed." He gave her a quick injection at each temple. "That should fix the problem for a little while."

"But you still haven't figured out what is causing it, have you?"

"No." He watched in satisfaction as the slight discoloration faded. "You're having some sort of deficiency, but I can't figure out what is causing it. I've been diligent in keeping your minerals and vitamins at the highest level possible, so whatever is causing this isn't something so simple. But I bet it is something that is staring me in the face and I can't see it." He patted her on the leg. "You're good to go."

"Thanks, Kuarto." She slid off the table. "Better get back and make sure everyone is still playing nice." She felt aggravation coming from Storm. Something was brewing and she needed to get back before it got out of hand.

She reentered the ballroom to find Storm standing in front of Bear, glowering at Susan.

"Hello?" Heather stepped up to Storm. "Everything okay?"

"This woman is insulting our friend."

"I'm not surprised." She placed her hand over his heart. "She's just jealous."

"Why?" He looked at her with curiosity.

"Because she was also up for the position that brought us together."

"Really?" He looked at Susan, then shook his head. "But she wouldn't have been able to fulfill the position properly." He placed his hand on Heather's heart. Storm also gave her a heart-stopping smile because he knew Susan would have ended up in the hospital over his libido. She never would have been able to keep up with him.

"I know." Heather felt that smile all the way to her toes. "I'm not real sure how she was even considered since she came from Earth parents who wouldn't have wanted their daughter to leave the planet. Especially to marry an alien if that had been offered to her the way it was offered to me."

He wrapped his free arm around her waist and pulled her close. "The elders never make a mistake. You were the perfect choice."

"Thank you, my heart." She looked around him and made eye contact with Bear. "May I speak to the president?"

"Of course." Bear stepped away to make sure she could approach the man.

"My heart?" Storm gave her a confused look.

"I asked Susan to not accost my family and she did." Heather pointed to the woman who still stood a few feet away. "That violates my trust and I don't feel she should be able to do the interview."

"I disagree."

"You do?" Now she felt confused. "You are a very big

proponent of truth and honesty. What she did was the opposite."

"True, but the camera has been on us since you came back. The whole planet is watching and wants to know the truth." He pointed to the live video of them on the screen. "Even now they are watching. She won't be able to slant the interview her way now. The people of this planet will know. You have said you wanted this world to know how it is between us, and now you truly have your chance."

He had a point. Bear came back with the president right at that moment. "You wish to speak to me, Commander?"

"Yes." She looked at Storm once more before she looked back at the President. "The interview time hasn't been set yet and I wish to do that, but I would like to ask one favor. I'd like it to be live if possible."

"Perfect. People have been weighing in and asking for a live interview. When do you wish to do this?"

"Tomorrow," said Storm. "Have Susan come to the embassy around eleven in the morning."

———

Heather sat on the couch for a few moments before she got up and started walking around.

"My heart, please relax." Storm stood in her way. "You are making me nervous and I'm supposed to be your moral support."

"I'm sorry." She wrapped her arms around him and rested her head on his chest. "I just hate the whole idea of this interview."

"Heather." He wrapped his arms around her and held her close. "You are so strong. I can't believe something like this has you so upset."

"I hate talking in front of crowds and I just don't trust Susan." Heather sighed as she let his heartbeat calm her.

"And with all the crazy stuff going on with me I worry about the darnedest things going wrong."

"Stop fretting. All of Vespia has gotten to know you and love you. These people will do the same. How could they resist such a wonderful, honest, beautiful woman?"

"You are so good for my ego."

"I know." He grinned and led her to the room where the interview would take place. "Now, remember I'll be right there. Don't let her get to you."

"Okay." She took a deep breath and entered the room. The moment the doors opened she found herself surrounded by people. One was checking her outfit to see how it would do in front of the camera. Another was checking her face to make sure she wouldn't have any type of weird shine that would make her look funny. A third checked her hair. "My goodness. Is it alright if I sit down before you attack like that again?"

Storm had come in behind her, a frown on his face over the way they swarmed around her.

They all stopped when she spoke.

The cameraman from the other night stepped up and shooed everyone away while he spoke to her. "Sorry, Heather. They forget not everyone is used to being in front of a camera. Why don't you take your seat and then they will have a chance to do their job."

"Thank you." She walked to the couch that had been placed for the interview. The different people who had tried to approach her earlier were now taking their time, making sure she was camera ready. Heather pulled out the pad that held the questions Susan was supposed to ask her. She had rehearsed her answers over and over so the words would flow naturally.

She also had been watching the newsfeed on the upcoming interview and saw the list of questions the population wanted to have answered, so she was ready for that as well.

A screen had been placed in front of her so she would know when they were live. She didn't really want to watch herself on screen, but she wanted to have as much control of this situation as possible. Heather grinned as she looked at Storm. She was acting like her mate.

Susan sat down opposite her on a straight back chair seconds before they were to go on air.

"Glad you could make it, Susan," said the cameraman sarcastically. "I thought I was going to be the one asking the questions there for a few minutes."

"Shut up, Gavin." She made herself comfortable, but Heather noticed she wouldn't look at her. Something was up.

He signaled silently when they went live.

"Good morning, Earth. Glad to have everyone with us today." Susan looked right at the camera. Heather read the tally of people tuning in and felt a little sick. More than half the planet had tuned in to hear her side of the story. "We hope everyone is ready for the interview of Commander Heather Drexel, ambassador to Vespia and treaty negotiator. Thank you for joining us today, Heather."

"Thank you for allowing me to speak to Earth, Susan. I hope this will allow me to clear the air about some of the concerns everyone is having."

"Of course." Susan leaned forward. "So what is it like to have sex with a Vespian?"

Heather just looked at her. "Really? That is the way you plan on handling this interview?" She shook her head. "I have a list of what your questions were supposed to be." Heather touched a spot on the pad she held and the questions Susan had submitted for approval loaded on the screen so the audience could see them as well. "And I know what the public wanted to find out." She brought up the top ten questions the viewing audience wanted to know based off the requests posted on Susan's web page. "And that question isn't there." Heather stood. "This interview is over."

"Can you hang on a minute, Heather?" asked Gavin.

Heather nodded.

"Excuse me, Susan." Her cameraman spoke to her. "You're wanted in the remote studio. The big man wishes to speak to you. Now."

She glared at him before she touched her earpiece and nodded.

"Ladies and gentlemen." Gavin jumped in front of the camera. "We're going to take a quick break while we have a change of venue. You will get your interview with the commander in just a few minutes."

The moment Susan left the room Heather watched Storm walk over to the guards at the door. She could bet that Storm told them to block Susan from reentering the room.

Images Heather had never seen of herself and Storm started to stream across the screen. They showed Heather and Storm as a couple. Small moments caught on screen. "These are wonderful. Who took them?"

"Thank you. I did," said Gavin. "I know you wanted to end the interview because of Susan and her unprofessional question and my bosses don't blame you. They have removed her and are hoping you will allow me to continue the interview."

Heather wasn't sure if it was a good idea, but she never wanted to do this in the first place. She looked at her mate for guidance, who gave her a slight nod. "Alright, but understand another question like that and it's over with."

"I promise to stick with the questions submitted. In fact, how would you feel if I let you pick the questions?"

"It would make me feel a whole lot better."

"Done, then." He went to stand in front of Storm. "I'd like you to join Heather on the couch."

"Okay." He moved to her side. Heather knew he'd rather

be at her side, anyway. Storm had told her that earlier. "Why?"

"Because you're the real reason everyone is watching. They want to know about you, about your relationship with the commander." He gestured for Heather to stand. "Storm, you sit first, then Heather will sit between your legs."

"I like that." He gave Heather one of his heart stopping smiles.

"You see? That is what the audience wants to see. We humans are suckers for love stories and yours is one of the best. Be yourselves. We're coming back." He went silent for a moment. Once the camera went live, he spoke again. "Sorry about that folks. It seems we're going to make a bit of a change here. Since Susan has been called away, I'll be taking over the interview.

"Heather, since you have that wonderful list of questions why don't you pick out the ones you think the audience would like to know the answers to and we'll go from there. I'll be able to see if we're on the right track by how many viewers we have at any given time."

While he was talking, Heather sat in front of Storm so they would portray the loving couple image she wanted people to have. "Okay." She hesitated for a moment. "Not sure if I like having so many watch me. Not used to it. But I know what I would want to know if I was sitting in the audience. How different is Vespia from Earth?"

"You do have to understand I haven't spent a lot of time on Earth. Most of my life was spent on space station twenty-four. I think the only real difference between the two planets is the two suns Vespia has and the shorter days. Their people are very much like anyone else. They were extremely curious about me because they knew nothing about humans. Like everyone here is curious about Storm because very little is known about Vespians."

"Did they accept you?" asked Gavin.

"Yes. As long as I proved that Storm and I were meant to be together." She looked back at him with a smile. "The photograph did that."

"The one from Vespia?" He loaded it onto the screen.

"Storm felt a picture spoke a thousand words. That right there proved that there is something special between us." She felt something hard against her back. Heather tilted her head back to look at Storm.

'Really?' she mouthed.

'I told you,' he mouthed back.

That made her grin, and she relaxed against him. That picture did hold a lot of power. She had to focus on the interview, though, and not her mate's arousal. As much as she would like to focus on the stiff erection pressing into her back. "They were wonderful to me before the picture was released, but once that came out, everyone seemed much more relaxed around me."

Storm started drawing little circles against her arm. Heather had her hand resting against his left thigh and could feel his muscle jump from the innocent contact.

"It's beautiful. Erotic, but beautiful." Gavin had been looking at the picture, but now turned his attention back to Heather. "Why did the picture make a difference?"

"Vespians don't see sex the way we do. Their view is that it is a beautiful thing that should be celebrated. They have great respect for it but don't see a reason for it to be so secretive. They feel it is too wonderful to be kept behind closed doors."

"Which is why we've heard stories about orgies in the streets."

"Exactly." She smiled at Gavin. "A lot of people have a misconception that Vespia is one big porn movie and it's not. But it is very important to them and they wanted to be sure I was a good partner for him. That picture showed I was."

"Well, I have a question that I think a lot of the planet

would like to know. Why have you stayed with Storm and not come home?"

"Because he is my heart. I can't see my life without him."

"And the rumors of you being mistreated?"

"Do I look mistreated?" She looked right at the camera. "I saw the interview Susan did with Ialog. Or Al as he calls himself, and he lied. Was I hurt? Yes. We released the video showing the Vespian report on that, but I was on maneuvers with the Vespian security. What Al failed to tell you was he was the one responsible for that injury. He was trying to capture me. Instead, he ended up hurting me and critically wounding one other soldier in the process."

"Why did he want you?"

"Don't know." Heather shrugged. "I didn't even know the man, but now he wants me and hasn't stopped trying to get me. Storm frets over my safety every minute we're away from the embassy because Ialog can't be trusted. His interview is proof."

Heather saw Kuarto step into the room. She wondered why. His presence normally meant she was having problems. Storm perked up when he came in and it didn't take too long before he excused himself and walked over to where Kuarto stood. She watched them out of the corner of her eye as she continued to answer the questions Gavin asked.

"When did you know you were in love?"

"Wow." She sat back for a second. "I think it was when he had to go away on a mission right after the wedding ceremony. I was by myself on a strange planet and all I thought about was how much I missed him and wished he was home."

"So you never thought about coming back here until he came back to Vespia? No one would have thought wrong of you if you had."

"No. He was home to me and I wanted to be there, waiting for him." She couldn't help but look at her mate, remembering how she greeted him. Storm's big smile told her he was thinking the same thing.

There was a commotion to her right, which made Heather look away from Gavin for the first time.

"Explain to them how Al tried to kidnap you!" demanded Susan. How she got back into the room Heather didn't know. She knew the guards had orders to keep her out once she had left earlier.

"Why don't you explain how you were up for the same position I was when the Vespians had a very specific profile to fill? You were not an orphan, you were not sterile and you were a little too old." Anger rolled off her in waves. "What does the man have over you?"

Storm stepped between them, Kuarto on his heels. Kuarto grabbed Susan and pulled her back while Storm knelt in front of Heather. He touched her face softly. *You're glowing.*

Heather blinked. *I heard that.*

How about that? Now you won't be able to keep me out of your thoughts. Let's show the world how it is between us.

SIX

His mouth covered hers, his tongue delved into her mouth, searching the recesses for its partner. Their tongues touched, danced together. Storm pulled her to the edge of the couch so he could hold her close.

Heather slipped her arms around his neck, pressing her body against him as he deepened the kiss. His hold on her tightened as he slanted his head. She sensed his desire spike as her arousal grew. His tongue slid around hers, causing little frissons of excitement to race up her spine. When he finally broke the kiss, they were breathing heavy.

"Wow." She touched his face softly with her fingers, watching as he struggled to control his need for her.

He kissed her again, this one quicker, less intense, but just as powerful. "I think it is time for us to head back to our rooms."

"I can see why," commented Gavin. "Wow, that was so intense to watch. Is it always like this between you?"

"Yes." Heather still looked at Storm. *We need to finish this interview, my heart. It shouldn't take much longer.*

I don't think I can keep my hands off you if I sit on that couch again. He looked over at Kuarto who hadn't moved. *I'll wait for you with your brother.*

Heather nodded and waited until he stood before turning her attention back to Gavin. "I do have a few things to tend to, so I can only take a couple more questions." She knew people would catch the double entendre and didn't care.

"Of course." He checked the list of questions that they hadn't touched on. "Do you think you'll ever come home again?"

"For visits, sure. Storm is the ambassador. But to live? I go where my mate goes." Gavin looked at her oddly. Did she not phrase it right? Was she glowing again? She felt Storm tell her no. "Something wrong?"

"You'd follow him everywhere?"

"Oh, I see." She smiled. "I think I need to explain a few things first. There are certain words that the Vespian language can't translate from our language. Like the word love. They understand our use of it in the sexual act but not the emotion. It just doesn't translate. Love to them is a strange word for their mating. Yet we find it odd to hear people refer to their relationships as mating because we use it when speaking of animals and their mating cycle. Have you noticed that Storm and I never say I love you?"

"Yeah, I did notice that, but you do use my heart a lot."

"That's our endearment for each other. And he is a part of me. On Vespia, two people who are mated would say I will follow you. What they mean is I'll go where you go because I love you. I can't see my life without Storm. Home is where he is. It doesn't matter if he's on a ship, on Vespia or Earth."

"Home is where your heart is."

"Exactly."

———

"So how do you think that went?" asked Storm as he escorted her out of the room.

"Well, I think." She wrapped an arm around him. "It's hard to tell right now. We'll have to wait for the recap of the interview to air. That's when we'll know if this helped or not."

"I know it helped me."

"What do you mean?" She looked up at him.

"I was able to prove how that picture affected me." He maneuvered her to the left, then down the corridor that led to their rooms. "I also got to kiss you the way I like to, and we learned we can now read each other's mind."

"True, but I don't have to be a mind reader to know what you have on your mind." She gave him a sultry smile.

"Really?" He pulled her closer. "And what do you think I have in mind?"

"I think you want to make me scream in passion."

"You are reading my mind." He lifted her up so he could capture her lips for a quick kiss. "That is my next goal now that I can get you to moan for me. All I have to do is fill you with tacos."

She had to laugh. "And will you tire of me once you get me to scream for you?"

"Never." He touched her face with the tips of his fingers. "You could moan and scream every time and I'd never tire of you. It's just nice to have these little goals to work for."

"You know the pregnancy has changed sex for me."

"What do you mean?"

"It seems to have heightened my libido, and don't act like you haven't noticed." She saw the feigned shock on his face.

"I think the pregnancy is just a happy coincidence." He took the last turn before their rooms. "Personally, I think your libido was waiting for me. You said your earlier part-ners didn't satisfy you. It's just playing catch up from all that missed sex." He was working on her dress before he carried her across the threshold.

"Heather, Storm, good to see you."

Since when did the computer talk to them like that? Heather looked up and found Anseri sitting at their large table, cup of coffee in her hand. "Storm?"

He nibbled on her throat, opening the seam of her dress with deliberate slowness. Didn't he hear his mother?

"We have company."

He looked up at her. "Who would dare be in our rooms without my permission?"

"I would," responded his mother. "We need to talk, and you kept putting me off."

"Not now, Mother," he said, his mood turning sour quickly.

"Then when, Storm?" She pressed her hands against the smooth top as she used her palms to leverage herself up to her feet. "I have waited as long as I could. We must speak and it must be now."

"What is so important that you must plague me now?" He glared at his mother. "I wish to spend time with my mate."

Heather loved the way the translator sometimes used old words to try to translate the Vespian language. He sounded like some old-fashioned ship's captain.

Anseri looked at Heather before focusing on Storm once again.

Heather took that as her cue to leave. Whatever she wanted to speak to Storm about was private. Anseri would never ask Heather to leave, but she could read the cues she sent her. "I have some work to do."

Storm wrapped a hand around her arm, keeping her at his side. "Whatever you have to say you will say in front of my mate." He looked at Heather. "I want you to stay."

She nodded. Arguing with him at this moment wouldn't be smart.

"Alright." Anseri straightened her clothes as she chose her words carefully. "I have a few personal questions to ask Storm first. I have noticed that your eyes glow, like they are right now. Does this only happen when you're aroused?"

"Yes." He practically growled his response.

Storm had let go of her arm so she could sit at the table. Did Anseri know what was going on with Storm? Something she thought might upset her? She sure didn't seem to be comfortable with Heather sitting there, which made Heather wonder if she should hear their conversation. Storm would tell her what was said later. She tried to stand again and found Storm's hand on her shoulder. She eased herself back into the chair.

"And your senses? Any of them heightened?"

He frowned as he sat beside Heather. "Yes, why?"

"I'll explain later." She looked at Heather once again before she studied her son. "Have you been overwhelmed with a primal drive to have sex with your mate?"

"What?"

"Yes." Heather answered for him since she could feel his shock at his mother's question in her mind. "Do you know what is happening to him?"

"I think so, but I can't be sure until you answer a few more questions." She looked at Storm. "Have you had any blackouts?"

"No." He stood and moved behind Heather's chair so he could keep his hand on her shoulder. She laced her fingers with his to give him physical support.

"I'm sorry to interrupt, but Heather has a call coming in from Earth headquarters. It is your old boss."

"Thank you, computer." She stood and touched Storm's face. "I need to take this." She headed into their bedroom to take the call. She wondered what Anseri would say about the computer. She should recognize the voice, since she had heard the underground system before.

She was glad to get out of there.

Heather wondered what Storm's mother was telling him. Too bad she didn't know how to use their link to eavesdrop on the conversation. She dragged her thoughts away from Storm and his mother to face her commander. "Sir."

"Good afternoon. Wanted to let you know the interview was a success. Your passionate kiss is all over the news and although the president wished you could have refrained from something like that it did do the job."

"Thank you, sir." There had to be another reason he was calling. He could have sent a message otherwise.

"It also seems that Susan wishes to apologize to you for her behavior."

"Well, good for her." Heather really didn't care. "Have her write a letter."

"She wants to do it in person, in front of her boss," he said. "It's the only way she'll get her job back."

"She doesn't deserve her job back, sir." Heather could feel frustration taking over. She looked at her hands to make sure she wasn't starting to glow. "You know that."

"Heather."

"No, sir. I have been a good little soldier until this point, but I refuse to be in the same room as that woman and you can tell her that. If she wants to apologize, she better come up with something better than that." Heather took a deep breath to calm herself. It wouldn't be good to start glowing in front of her old boss. "I will resign my commission and my post if you try to force me."

He didn't say anything for a moment or two. "I'll pass your message on."

"Thank you." She closed the transmission before she could change her mind. When she turned, she found Storm standing behind her. "How much did you hear?"

"Enough." He stepped up to her. "You would really give up your position here?"

"This isn't home to me, being with you is." She placed her hand against his heart. "But they won't let me quit. As long as they have me listed as active duty, they feel they have eyes and ears in Vespian society."

"So you think they will continue to push until this Susan gets her way?" He returned the gesture.

"Sure do." She pulled her hair back from her face, using the motion to cleanse her thoughts. "So what did your mom want to talk to you about?"

"Oh, it's a little crazy and not worth mentioning." He slid his hand up to her collar, working to free her of the gown once again.

"Really? Any crazier than what we have already been through?" She looked at him, watching his face. He couldn't hide anything from her with the mindlink now.

"To me it was." He smiled at her. That wonderfully bone-melting one that had a way of distracting her. "She told me that it was possible I could develop three different talents and told me what to look for with each of them. Once I know for sure which one is developing, I'll let you know."

"Promise?" She closed her eyes as she felt his fingers glide along the edge of fabric, caressing her skin as he broke the magnetic seal.

"I still find that so strange to say. You know I would never keep anything from you." He eased the dress off her shoulders, trapping her arms, yet exposing her breasts to his gaze.

"Now I see why you decided to do this by hand instead of having the computer remove my clothes. You want to cheat."

"I never cheat. Use things to my advantage, always." He cupped them gently, taking their weight into the palm of his hands.

"And trapping my arms so I can't touch you?"

"Leveling the playing field, since you can do things with your mind that I can't do."

"I don't know what you're talking about." She tried to act indignant, but it was hard when he touched her so gently. Heather wanted more.

"You got out of those restraints."

"It was a fluke." She smiled at him, soft, seductive. One thought and she stood before him naked. The next moment he was too, thanks to the efficiency of the computer. Heather pressed her palms against his skin, allowing her hands to wander his chest. Her fingers brushed against his mark. She smiled in satisfaction when his body shuddered. "I see your mark is as sensitive as mine."

She pressed her lips to it, sucking on the soft tissue before lathing it with her tongue.

"Heather." Placing a finger under her chin, he lifted her face. "That goes right to my groin."

"I know." The gleam in her eyes warned him there would be more.

"I'm already so hard for you I can't think straight." He wrapped his arms around her, pulling her against his body, angling hers so she could feel his rigid staff.

"I don't want you thinking right now. I want to feel you deep inside me, filling me the way only you can." She had been inching him back to the bed, and now she gave him a gentle push so he would sit. Heather placed her knees on either side of his hips and eased herself down on his hard member. "God, that feels so good."

"My heart." He wrapped his arms around her and held her close. They clung to each other, allowing her body a chance to accept his invasion. The moment she mounted him, her muscles contracted around him. The intensity of her vise-like grip taught them to remain still until her body relaxed. It helped prolong their joining.

"I swear each time we're intimate these first few seconds get more intense." Heather's voice came out soft and deep for her. She tilted her head back as a frisson of delight raced up her spine. The sensation made her shake, which set off another series of her muscles tightening against him. "I may never move again."

Storm chuckled. "As much as I enjoy our intimacy you know we can't stay like this forever."

She leaned back to look at him. "We could try."

"True, but we'd never get any work done." He placed his hands on her hips and helped her set a nice, slow pace for them.

Heather bit her lip as a new wave of desire swept over her. Each time she descended on him and he filled her completely she felt the little swirls in her stomach that triggered her orgasm. It grew with each plunge. She was close, but not quite ready to climax. Then she felt Storm's fingers slide into her folds. "My heart, if you do that I might just explode."

"I know. My goal is to make you explode each time."

His fingers found her pleasure point, drawing a shudder from Heather. She picked up the pace, wanting to increase the friction between them. Her head dropped back as she felt the first tendrils of her release wrap itself around her spine. It built slowly, encompassing her whole body before she felt the joy of the freefall she experienced. Once she could find her voice again, she commented, "I thought it was to make me scream."

"Oh, that is a goal too, my heart, but I want to be sure you never tire of me."

"That won't happen." She opened her eyes to find him watching her.

"Ready for more?" He held her close as he shifted their positions. Once he had her lying on the bed, he buried himself deep within her, causing her to suck in her breath at the exquisite sensation.

She touched his face softly. "Always."

This time, he controlled the pace, pumping in and out of her. She lifted her hips as a deep-seated need spiked inside. The combination of feeling his passionate desire for her and her want for him wrapped them in a cocoon of ecstasy neither could get enough of.

Heather felt his release start first. White hot and just as explosive as hers, she wanted to know how intense it would get if she caressed his mark as he went over the edge. Her fingers gently brushed the area when she felt him shake as a growl escaped him. She felt his world splinter away as he ground his hips against hers. His movements touched her in just the right way, which had her following him over the edge.

"That will never get old." Storm brushed a few wet strands of hair from her face. His fingers brushed against her mark, causing her to suck in her breath and her muscles to tighten against him. "So our marks seem to intensify our intimacy. Good to know."

She brushed her fingers against his, causing the same reaction. "You know two can play at this game."

"And that would keep us here all night." He gave her a bright smile. "I can't think of a better way to spend the evening."

———

Storm walked into the medical center to find Heather pedaling away on a stationary bike. A small, dark circle on her left temple picked up all her readings as Kuarto put her through a series of tests.

"And how is my mate this morning?"

"She is very healthy, except for the fact I can't regulate

some of her basic chemical levels." Kuarto looked at Storm. "It isn't affecting the children. They are in perfect health."

"Good." He watched as she answered a round of questions a nurse asked her. "The dark circles under her eyes haven't disappeared, but she does look better."

"Her body knows what it needs better than we do, so I've been letting it dictate what she should be eating and drinking. Has she had any cravings?"

"No." Other than sex and he was happy to take care of that. "In fact, she's eating less right now."

"Nothing out of the ordinary? Like skipping dinner to have sweets? Only eating certain types of food?"

"No." Storm shook his head. "She has stuck to the diet you gave her and seems happy."

"Although I wouldn't mind a sweet every once in a while." She waved at them when they looked at her.

"There's nothing wrong with her hearing."

"It's hard to miss when you're in such a quiet room," responded Heather. The nurse turned off the bike for her and she pedaled a little longer so she could cool down before she joined Storm and Kuarto. "Nice to know that other than my odd deficiency everything is humming along." She rubbed her stomach for a moment. "What is the chance of me being able to get out of the embassy for a little while? Maybe go for a walk in the park nearby."

"What is wrong with our gardens?" asked Storm. "They are just as pretty and a lot more protective."

She sighed, but didn't argue. "I'm going to shower, then change."

As she walked away, Kuarto commented, "I don't think you understand what she was asking there. Heather wants to get out. Get away from the ever-watchful security system. Have a little time to herself."

"You mean feel free for a little while."

"Yes, and she'd never do anything against your will." Kuarto crossed his arms over his chest. "I know the Vespian way is for the man to make all the decisions and the mate to accept it without question and she follows that rule very well, but it's also the male's job to keep their mate happy, even when it might go against everything they believe is good for their mate."

"You've been reading again."

"There isn't a whole lot to do in this place."

"How about keep my sister happy?"

"Have you heard her complain at all?" He glared at Storm. "Her new position keeps her busy most of the time. There aren't that many sick people, so I have a lot of time on my hands and the Vespian way of life is fascinating."

"Now that you're required to abide by it." Storm realized he hit a nerve.

Kuarto shrugged. "Actually, I don't. Off-worlders who marry into the society don't have to follow any rule that goes against how they were brought up. I can show you the passage if you like."

"I am familiar with the passage. It also says that if you live on Vespia, you can still be tried and found guilty, Vespian or not."

"Of course. I did like that little tidbit." He grinned. "But we were talking about Heather, not Vespian tradition. She deserves a break."

"And how is my mate's needs or desires any of your business?" He hated when people thought they knew what he or his mate needed more than he did.

"When she is my sister, and don't be such an ass about it. No one will think less of you if you take her out of the embassy. They all know she does exactly what you ask of her. That picture proved that."

Storm wasn't happy with the way Kuarto spoke to him, but that always happened. Maybe they were a little too much alike. The man was right though. Heather did deserve a break.

He walked back to their rooms, wondering what he should do about it. His biggest fear was that something would happen to her.

What could possibly happen when I have you watching over me? He felt her thoughts caress his mind.

It's not nice to eavesdrop in on someone's thoughts.

Then don't send such strong thoughts my way. It's hard to ignore.

Storm walked into their rooms to find her brushing out her hair. "You going to leave it down for me?"

"Of course." She ran her fingers through it a couple of times to fluff it out then gave him a smile. "Did you wish to walk in the gardens with me?"

"Mother wishes me to work with the staff. Part of my training to be leader."

She nodded. "Looks like I'll be walking on my own then."

He could feel her strong desire to escape, yet she wasn't about to question his decision. "Perhaps I could call Kuarto."

"It's okay, Storm. I don't mind walking through the gardens by myself. There's no need to find me a babysitter."

"I won't let you go out without someone guarding you. I don't trust anyone outside this building."

"I'm only going into the gardens...wait. Are you letting me leave the embassy?"

"Not by yourself."

"Then I can wait for you." She touched his arm. "It's not as much fun without you."

"It could be a couple of hours."

"I'm sure I can find something to do for a couple of hours."

———

It took Storm three hours before he was excused from his mother's side. Sometimes he became bored with the security he had to deal with. This time, it was one of the staff not following protocol. He would have much rather been with Heather than enforcing their laws, but it was his job and he did it well.

He found her in their rooms, waiting patiently. The large leather book the computer had given her rested in her lap as she read from it.

"Learn anything new?" He went down on one knee beside the chair she sat in.

"Only that my mind hasn't begun to do half the things this says it can do." She closed the book. "The instructions are there for me to follow. I'll begin those exercises tonight."

"Then I can assume you're ready to go?"

"Only if you are." She wanted to go. He could feel it, but she wasn't going to beg or plead. If he wanted to take her, she would go. If he didn't, she would stay. Storm never realized how much she had accepted his way of life until her brother pointed it out to him.

And he was always giving her a hard time for questioning him when she felt he was wrong.

"Let's go." He offered her his hand.

"If you are sure."

"Come on." He escorted her down the hallway toward the main doors. "Understand that we're not going alone."

"As long as you are with me, I don't care."

Outside the doors stood twelve guards waiting for them. Most were the members of her squad. At least she was protected by those she trusted most.

The day was beautiful. A nice bright sunny day.

"It seems strange not to see two suns," commented Fridon.

"I felt the same way in the beginning." Heather grinned as they walked along the street. "But you get used to it."

"But this is your world."

"I know, but I never grew up here. I lived on a space station most of my life. The first time I stepped foot on this planet was quite an adjustment. Earth is a beautiful planet, just like Vespia." She tilted her face up to feel the warmth of the sun. The air had a slight nip in it but her gown protected her from the coolness.

The group moved in unison. Heather and Storm in the middle.

Heather could only imagine what spectators were thinking when she found her hand in a steely grip. As the hand tried to pull her out of her protective web, she grabbed two fingers and pulled back, not stopping until she heard the snap of several bones.

"Do you have him?"

Their guards shifted enough to allow Heather to see her assailant. He now knelt in front of her, pain etched across his face. She hadn't let go of his hand.

"I think you do, my heart." Storm was ready to tear the man's throat out, but his mate had him under control.

"Who sent you?" Her grip hadn't lessened, so when the man didn't answer, she pressed his hand backward. "If you don't answer me, I will break your wrist."

"I don't know."

"Right." She increased the pressure until she heard another snap. "I know better. I want to know who sent you and why. I also want to know how you knew we were going to be out here since this was a spur of the moment thing."

"I was sent the credits via computer. Never met the man."

"But you do know it was a man. Whose name was on the account?" When he didn't answer right away, she pushed his arm so the next thing to snap would be his elbow. "If you don't answer my questions I can turn you over to the Vespian guard here who have deliciously harmful ways of getting information out of you."

"They can't harm me. I'm an Earth citizen."

"They can if you are on Vespian soil." She turned to two of the guards. "Take him back to the embassy. I'm sure head of security would love a crack at this one."

The two she spoke to dragged the man off.

"I am sorry he ruined your outing, my heart." Storm pulled her into his warm embrace. "We are close to the park now, maybe it will take your mind off of what happened."

"I only wanted to get out for a little while. Get away from all of this, but I can't can I? No matter where I am he knows. How, Storm? How does he know what we're thinking?" She looked at her mate. "That damn sentry in my head. He's been tapping into it the whole time."

"But I haven't felt it activate." Storm had a link to the device in her mind.

"Maybe that's because it's always active but since all it is doing is watching what we do, you didn't realize what was going on." Heather's eyes grew wide at the implication. "That means he knows everything. How many times we're intimate, the book, any plans we have to stop him. Storm, we have to get that thing out of my head."

"Your brother is the only one who knows how."

———

Just as they approached the embassy, Gavin stepped up. "I know you have told her no, but Susan asked me to beg you to reconsider."

"Gavin," Heather pinched her nose. "I have more pressing matters right now than Susan's job. Someone just tried to kidnap me again."

"What?"

Storm urged them all into the safety of the building. *I don't like his timing, my heart.*

I agree, but it could just be a coincidence. Heather gestured for Gavin to take a seat in the main hall. "I thought you weren't going to associate with her anymore."

"I didn't want to, but she cornered me and followed me here. She's across the street right now."

Storm walked to a window and turned down the opaqueness of the panes so he could look out. There on the other side of the large walkway was Susan, waiting for an answer.

"Go tell her no. I will never change my mind."

"I already told her that and she didn't believe me. She won't believe anyone but you." Gavin gave her an apologetic smile. "It will only take five seconds and she promises to leave you alone."

Heather muttered under her breath as she stomped her way to the door. She was so sick of this woman and her conniving ways. Heather planned on giving her a piece of her mind. She had the door opened and was outside before anyone could react. Two steps were all it took before she was grabbed from behind and drugged. Her last thoughts were what a mistake she had made.

SEVEN

Storm felt her fear seconds before he lost contact with her thoughts. He couldn't get to the door fast enough. Whipping it open, Heather was nowhere in sight. Neither was Susan. In fact, the area was vacant when minutes before it had been crowded. It was all a setup. He turned to glare at Gavin. "Did she put you up to this?"

"What?" The color drained out of his face as he stood. "Susan said—"

"Put him with the other one. I'll deal with both in a moment." He didn't give Gavin a chance to finish his thought. He rubbed his face as he fought to control his fear. Fridon was the first person he made eye contact with so he gestured him over. "Get the surveillance and see how she was taken so fast. See if she was transported and find out where. I want my mate back."

———

Heather opened her eyes, feeling very disorientated. Her head swam and her mind felt all fuzzy. She reached out to

Storm, but couldn't connect with him. Fear knifed through her.

"Good to see you awake, my dear."

Oh God. Heather knew that voice anywhere. She closed her eyes at the implication. There was no way he was going to see how afraid she was. Once she felt she had control, she opened them again and looked at him. "Ialog. You know this wasn't a smart idea."

"Maybe not, but he has to find you first, and I have taken all the right precautions this time." He nodded at her. "Check your forehead. You'll find my handiwork."

Her fingers brushed across a smooth piece of metal resting in the center of her forehead. It wasn't very big but she found it did do the job. She couldn't hear Storm in her thoughts at all. Suddenly, she felt very alone.

"That will keep your thoughts to yourself." He moved about the room, checking readings at different monitors. Heather watched, taking in her surroundings at the same time. "Can't have you telling Storm or your brother your whereabouts."

"He's going to figure it out." So he knew about her brother. She wasn't going to rise to the bait. Heather felt the cool metal of the bed she had been placed on, but there were no restraints holding her down this time. That surprised her. He must have her someplace where she couldn't escape. Did he have her on a ship?

"Don't think so. Not this time." He walked up to where she lay. "I am going to allow you some freedoms while you're here, as long as you behave." He offered her a hand up.

Heather looked at the hand, ignoring it as she sat up on her own. "Send me home."

"You are home." He didn't seem upset that she didn't want him touching her. "And Storm will not miss you."

She sure didn't like the sound of that. Frustration filled

her. When she looked down, she noticed her hands were glowing again.

———

Heather sat in the main dining room at a well-dressed table, waiting to be served dinner. She wasn't hungry, but Ialog insisted. He had someone he wanted Heather to meet. An extra place was set so whoever was joining them would be eating with them.

Great.

She didn't want to see anyone either. Her pesky glow was still with her. She found it interesting that no one had made a comment about it yet.

The guest probably wouldn't be willing to help her either. Ialog wouldn't allow anyone to see her if he thought they could be willing to get word to Storm. So whoever was coming was someone she didn't like.

The door opened.

Her eyes narrowed. Like Susan for instance. The woman who just walked in the door.

She was all smiles when she saw Heather. "Not so tough now, are you?"

"You want to see what I'm capable of?" Heather stood, ready to beat Susan to a pulp. It would only take one strike to bring her to her knees. One more would knock her out, but Heather wanted to cause pain. A lot of pain.

"Now ladies, we must be civilized." Ialog smiled as he approached the table. He flashed a small box in Heather's direction.

The moment he did that, she found she couldn't move. Not one muscle.

"That little device on your forehead not only stops your thoughts from transmitting, but it can also stop you from moving."

"That is why you aren't worried about me leaving." She glared at him. "You can stop me if you have to."

He shrugged and gestured for them to take their seats. "I planned a special meal for us this evening. A bit of a celebration."

"I'm not celebrating, Ialog." White-hot anger filled her as he released her movements enough for her to sit. A part of her wanted to leap across the table and strangle him, but she knew he'd hit a button before she could reach him and immobilize her.

"So, Susan, are you happy now?" Heather gave her a sweet smile, sarcasm dripped from her words. "Knowing you have finally found a way to land your ass in jail?"

"Oh, Heather, you are so funny." She picked up her napkin and placed it on her lap. "But I will never be caught and you will never go home."

"You sound confident." Heather mimicked Susan's move.

"Oh, I am." Someone placed a plate in front of her and she attacked it.

Heather ignored her food. She knew there was a reason Ialog wanted her to see Susan. Not knowing the reason killed any appetite she might have had, if she could trust anything he gave her. So she waited. She knew it wouldn't take too long. Susan had never been known for her patience.

The meal ended and Susan stood.

"Sorry to eat and run, but I have someplace to go." She smiled at Heather once again. "I'll tell Storm you said hello."

She really wanted to punch the woman. Storm would never give her the time of day.

"You are sure you want to do this?" asked Ialog as he stood as well.

"You're not going back on your promise, are you?" Susan's voice became a little shrill. "Not after I did everything you asked. I got her for you, didn't I?"

"A promise is a promise. I will do as you ask, but you

might find it's not what you want after a while." He placed a small circular device behind her right ear. "This will do what you want."

Susan grinned. Heather was thinking of about a dozen ways she could wipe that smile off her face.

When it activated, Heather felt her heart drop. She was staring at her own features. Storm would have to be on his toes to see through that immediately, but she wasn't going to let Susan know how this affected her. "You want to be me so badly you plan on impersonating me?"

"I should have been the one chosen. Ialog promised me then."

Heather felt cold. He had said he pushed the council to look for her, but she didn't realize he was actually trying to orchestrate who Storm ended up with. That was why there was nothing in Susan's file. Ialog had planned on switching them out, but something went wrong.

"Got to ask what happened. You had planned on inter-cepting me before I met Storm and send Susan to him, but that didn't occur."

"No." He looked at her with a smile. Was he proud she had figured it out so fast? "I wasn't aware you weren't on Earth working. I thought I would be able to follow the trail of orders and intercept you before you fulfilled your mission."

"When you lost that trail because it went off world. You realized I wasn't on Earth and you had no idea where I could be, did you." She crossed her arms over her chest. "It makes perfect sense. That's why you forced the elders to look for me."

He nodded.

"In doing that you set forth a series of events that pushed me toward my destiny instead of changing it."

"Storm was never supposed to be your destiny."

"From the moment you created me, my destiny has always been Storm. You know that. You just refuse to believe it. That was why you couldn't find me. That was why you weren't able to keep me from doing my mission to protect him." She pointed to Susan. "But you're the reason she was on the list when she didn't have any of the things the elders were looking for. You had planned on sending her to Storm as a distraction while you intercepted me."

"She liked the idea of being the wife of an ambassador and was helpful when I needed it."

"And now?"

"I will send her where I should have months ago." He stepped up to Susan and adjusted the image a little more, plus tweaked her voice modulation to match Heathers. "Now I have held up my end of the bargain."

Susan smiled. "Yes you have."

Heather watched her go without another word. From what she saw, Ialog didn't do anything to help her deceive Storm. It wouldn't take him long to figure it out. Once Susan was out of the room, she had to ask. "Did you tell her I was pregnant?"

"She never asked any details about your life."

"So you're sending her into the embassy with nothing more than my looks? She'll be caught almost immediately."

"I got what I wanted out of the deal, Heather. That is all I care about." He sat back down at the table to resume his dinner. "She asked me for the disguise, which I gave. Susan never asked me for something to help her keep the position she coveted so badly."

For the first time, Heather actually felt bad for her.

———

Storm heard the perimeter alarm go off while he interrogated the man who attacked Heather. She had done a good job to his hand. As punishment for what he had done, Storm hadn't let Kuarto take a look at it yet. To him, the man deserved to suffer a little more.

He took off to the main doors to see what tripped the system. The guards on duty already had the intruder surrounded. Storm slowed when he saw Heather standing there. Why would his mate trip the alarm system when she had the coded device below her collarbone that allowed her to come and go freely? He watched the fear in her eyes fade away to happiness at the sight of him.

"Storm, thank God. Please get these people to let me in the door." She pleaded with him. Heather would have been too angry to plead. She would have been threatening their lives about now for not letting her in.

Something wasn't right. He could smell a difference in her. The faint scent he called her essence had changed. His mind worked on figuring out what his senses already seemed to know. He pressed a button on his collar and called for Kuarto, then faced her. He would go along with this until he figured out whether or not this woman was his mate. "Heather? Where have you been?"

"Someone grabbed me, but I was able to get away." She looked at him with wide violet eyes.

He frowned. Heather broke several bones on the last man who tried to take her. She would have done the same here. Storm walked around her, studying her. Where was their mindlink? He reached out a few times and found nothing. That made him more suspicious. "Really? What happened to Susan?"

"I don't know." She watched him warily. "I really didn't get a chance to see much when they grabbed me. I have never been so frightened."

The woman in front of him couldn't be Heather. Fear was a word she chose to ignore. He stepped close just to see what she would do. If this had been his mate, he was pretty sure she'd be wrapped around him, happy to be home without a scratch. Instead, the woman actually recoiled when he invaded her space for a moment. She seemed to realize she had made some sort of mistake because she blurted out. "Storm, hold me."

A cold smile worked its way onto his face. This wasn't his mate. He was sure of it, and there was one way to prove it. He placed his hand on her abdomen. His children always reacted to his touch, but this time nothing happened. There was no life there. "Take her."

"What?" She took a step back.

"You are not my mate." He started circling her. "Would you like to know how I know? Let me explain. One, Heather has a chip in her that allows her access to this embassy that you don't seem to have. That was why you set off an alarm my mate wouldn't have. Secondly, Heather and I have a mental connection that isn't here right now. And third, and this is a big one. You ready?" He stopped in front of her and leaned in, making sure she was looking him in the eyes. "You're not pregnant."

Kuarto entered the room at his last words. He stopped short when he saw Heather.

"It's not her."

"Another android?" Kuarto pulled out his scanner and ran it over her.

"No, Something more devious. Someone impersonating my mate." Storm stepped out of the way so the scanner wouldn't get any interference from him.

Kuarto looked at his readings. "Interesting. It looks like Heather, some sort of hologram I'd imagine, but my scanner says it's Susan."

"I was afraid of that. She was the one who had my mate stolen." He turned to the guards. "Take her to security for questioning."

"Wait." Susan lost a lot of her color when she realized

how fast they figured out who she was. "You can't keep me against my will."

"Honey, you impersonated a Vespian official and you are on Vespian soil so you can be tried by our laws." Storm gave her a predatory smile. "The penalty for doing this is death, by the way."

"Death?" she squealed as she was dragged off.

"You can't kill her, Storm," said Kuarto.

"She is responsible for the kidnapping of my mate. I can do whatever I deem necessary." Storm followed the guards and the now screaming Susan.

Kuarto followed. "Storm."

"My mate can talk me out of things, but you can't." He turned to look at his mate's brother. "Remember your place, doctor."

"Oh, you don't have to worry about that. There are too many here to constantly remind me." He placed a hand on his arm. "You can do what you want to the woman. That is up to you, but she knows where Heather is. Coming here, trying to pass herself off as your mate proves that. Where did she get the technology to pull this off? Earth doesn't have anything like this. We need that information more than you need revenge."

"You just can't help yourself, can you?" Storm looked at the hand on his shoulder before looking up at Kuarto. Anger shone in his eyes.

"Sorry, haven't been a Vespian as long as the rest of you." Kuarto wasn't frightened by him. In fact, he looked like he'd go toe to toe with Storm if necessary.

Storm couldn't help but laugh. "You are so much like your sister at times."

"Can I assume that is a good thing?"

"Yes." He walked into the security center. "I've had the men put Susan next to Gavin. Let's see how innocent he really is."

"If they are in on this together, then they're not going to say anything to each other."

"I know, but if he is innocent perhaps he'll get answers she might not give to us."

"You going to eavesdrop?" asked Kuarto.

Storm smiled as he hit the mike so they could listen in.

"Heather?" Gavin looked confused. "Why are you in here?"

"Because they don't believe I'm Heather. What did I do wrong, Gavin?" She stomped her foot and crossed her arms over her chest.

"Susan?" He stared at her in shock. "Oh, good Lord, what have you done?"

Storm wondered how he knew who it was so quick.

"How did you know it was me?" She glared at him.

"That stupid temper tantrum of yours." He mimicked her movements earlier. "You always do that when you don't get your way."

She made a rude noise and turned her back to him. "He was supposed to be mine, not hers. I'm just trying to take back what should have been mine."

"You're not making any sense." He scratched his head. "Are you talking about Heather and Storm? Those two belong together. If you had paid any attention to the interview you would have seen that." He looked over at her. "How'd you pull this off, anyway? Is that permanent?"

"The image?" She gestured to her look. "No. I have a device behind my ear."

"Then don't you think you should change back into your true look? I've done my research and you don't want these Vespians angry. They're not very nice when pissed off."

Storm turned to look at Kuarto. "He does know us well." He nodded to two of the guards standing by and they went to the cell and separated them. "We'll let them wait for a while. Let's see if their fear will loosen their tongues."

Heather sat at a formal dining table once again. She had figured out they were on a planet, but she didn't know which one yet. Ialog sat at the other end.

"You're not eating, my dear." He gestured to the food on her plate.

"I'm not hungry." She pushed the food away from her. He could say she was his guest all he wanted, she was trapped and she knew it.

"You're also not wearing the clothes I set out for you."

"With all the cameras you have watching my every move?" she gestured to the cameras trained on her at the moment. "I'm not undressing so you can play voyeur."

"Don't be crass, Heather." He set down his fork. "I would never watch you as you changed."

"You might not, but what is there to stop your guards?" She looked at the men he had stationed around the room. Too many for her to try to overtake, besides she'd have to get that stupid transmitter from him first. "I'm not taking the chance."

"I expect you to be dressed properly for the next meal." He watched her.

"I am dressed properly." She looked at her hands. The glow hadn't left her since she arrived. Good, let him see how frustrated she was. Sooner or later he'd comment on it. "This is proper attire for the mate of the future leader of Vespia."

"You are ancient and should dress accordingly," he shouted as he slammed his hand on the table. It took him a few minutes to regain his composure. "I will make sure you have a little privacy if you promise to put the gown on I left for you." He hesitated for a moment. "And take those damn rings off."

"This gown is self-cleaning. As long as you have any cameras trained on me, I won't be showering or bathing.

With this dress, I know my body will stay clean." A smile played on her lips as she messed with her rings, not acknowledging his second request. So he could be flustered. All she had to do was talk about Storm, and he lost his temper.

"The other gown is the same way. Where do you think the Vespians learned about that material?" He watched her as he became agitated again. "Dinner is over. If you refuse to change, I can send in someone to help you dress."

Heather stood, knowing he would follow through on his threat if she fought too hard. She nodded before she was escorted back to her room.

There wasn't much to the outfit. A floor length dress made out of a material that reminded her of gauze. Then some sort of formfitting vest. Not trusting him one bit, she slipped the gown on over her own dress, pulling the old one off as the new one fell to the floor. She folded her dress up and placed it on her bed. The little vest was a problem. For some reason, it tied in the back instead of the front and she couldn't get it on properly.

Her android look-alike walked into her room the moment she finished dressing. She reached for her clothes, but Heather stopped her.

"That garment doesn't leave this room." Heather took the dress out of her hands and placed back on her bed. "I'll need that when Storm comes and rescues me."

"But he has no idea where you are."

"Maybe not right now, but I have faith he'll figure it out." Heather presented her back. "You could help me with this thing, though."

Storm ran his fingers through his hair. He had no clue where Ialog could have taken his mate, which frustrated him. He knew Ialog had her and he had been smart enough to break their mindlink. It wouldn't stop him from getting her back, though. He would never give up looking.

Kuarto stared at him from across the room.

"What."

"Not sure, but there is something different about you." Kuarto tilted his head as he studied him. "Any new developments I should be aware of?"

"No, but I've been a little busy lately." Storm wished he could hear Heather's thoughts. It sure would make him feel better. Then it dawned on him he did have a way. "You know that sentry Heather has in her head? The one you hooked my mind up to?"

"What about it?"

"Do you think you could reverse engineer the linkage? Allow me to see what Heather sees? Maybe I can figure out where he has taken her if I can see her surroundings."

"I don't know, Storm. The mind is a very delicate thing, and I'm not sure what our tampering will do. What if he has built a safety feature to keep us from doing just that?"

"Yes or no, doctor." He hated when people didn't give him a direct answer.

"Maybe." Kuarto hesitated for a moment. "I'll need to do a little research first."

"Then get to it."

———

Heather sat on the bed in the room Ialog assigned her, playing with her rings. He hadn't taken them yet, but she knew he would. He hated what they represented.

She couldn't sleep. The little device strapped to her forehead had seen to that. Closing her eyes wasn't a problem, but she couldn't reach REM sleep with it there. She also couldn't communicate with her children the way she normally did, and they were reacting a little vigorously to that. Hoping it would work, she spoke to them softly as she rubbed her womb.

She did that most of the night, taking short rests when she needed it. It did seem to help them settle down.

Ialog noted the dark circles under her eyes and her always present faint glow when she was forced to join him for breakfast. "Is there something wrong with your room, Heather?"

"Other than calling my cell a room? No."

"Then why do you look like you haven't gotten any sleep?"

"Because I didn't." She tapped her head. "This blocks everything. My ability to reach REM, being able to talk to my children. Until this is removed, I don't think I will be able to sleep properly."

"Your children?"

"You know?" She pointed to her stomach. "It's the reason you kidnapped me the first time? Or so you say. I have been able to mentally communicate with them from almost the beginning, but now I suddenly can't and they are frightened. I can feel it."

"I can't take that off. Your mate would take advantage of that, but I can allow you to speak to the fetuses you carry. Explain things to them if that is what you wish to do."

She looked at him. Making concessions like this wasn't usual for him. He would want something in return, but she had already donned the dress he wanted so that should be enough. "I would like to calm them. Let them know everything is alright."

He gestured to the man behind him, who stepped up to Heather and made a few adjustments to the device. She sighed in relief when she could feel her connection to the twins once again. They felt the same joy at feeling her presence. She closed her eyes as she communicated with them.

Giving them a warning of the device that would keep them separate, she explained she would keep in touch by talking to them out loud and by rubbing her stomach so they would know she was thinking of them.

She opened her eyes once again and nodded at the man still standing in front of her. He reset everything back to the original settings before stepping back. She looked up into his face, feeling she had met him before. Gold eyes, jet black hair of a typical Vespian. How did he come to be working for this man?

Heather felt a shot of pain as it reactivated. She fought it, hoping she didn't show any reaction. The pain was worth being able to speak to her children, even if it was only for a few minutes.

———

"Anything?" asked Kuarto.

"No."

"Told you it would be tricky. It should have worked. Maybe it just needs a little time to make the proper connection." Kuarto scanned Storm's forehead once more. "Don't know what to tell you."

Storm frowned. "I need to know where she is, doctor. The longer she's gone the colder her trail will get."

"I know." He watched as Storm grabbed at his arm while trying to stand. "You okay?"

"Kuarto?" Storm's voice didn't sound right.

"Storm?"

"No." He shook his head as he tapped himself on the chest. "Heather. Tell him I'm—" Storm blinked several times. "What the hell just happened?"

"You tell me." Kuarto eased him back onto the medical bed he was trying to get off of. He raced to his monitors to pull up the last few minutes of readings his equipment measured. "You still have my scanner on, don't you?"

"Yes, why?"

"Because something just happened. Now, tell me what you saw." He pulled up the readings he wanted to see and isolated them.

"I was sitting here listening to you prattle on about why the link didn't work, then found myself in another room for a second then back here."

"Did you take in your surroundings?" Kuarto looked at Storm for a moment before he went back to the screen. The readings he needed showed a change in his thought patterns.

"I think I was in a dining room, sitting at a long table." Storm was quiet for a moment as more detail came to him. "There was a plate of food in front of me, untouched. The clothes I wore were soft, feminine in design." He tried to pull more detail to him but ended up shaking his head." It happened all so fast."

"I know. Heather didn't get a chance to say much." Kuarto smiled when he found what he was looking for. "The link did work, but not the way I thought it would."

"Heather was here?"

"Her mind was. In your body. She tried to tell me something, but as you said it happened too fast. All she said was 'tell Storm I'm…' I'm assuming she wanted to let you know that she was okay." He turned to look at Storm. "When it happens again you need to focus on what is around you. See if she leaves you any clues to finding her."

———

Heather wasn't sure what just happened, or how it happened. One instant she was sitting at the table with Ialog, the next she was staring at her brother, and then back again. She had switched bodies before with Anseri, but she didn't think it was possible while she wore the little contraption on her forehead. It was supposed to block all of her mental abilities. So how did it just happen?

She looked around to see if anyone noticed that someone else was in her body for a moment but no one seemed to care. Good. Now she had to see if she could recreate whatever happened.

If this could happen again, she wanted to be ready for it. Gather as much information for whoever she was switching with. This last time happened so fast she didn't know who she had jumped into. Only that her brother had been there so she knew it had to be one of the few she had touched minds with.

She wished she had her book. Heather had just started to scratch the surface of the information inside it when Ialog took her. The lessons it had on how to control and wield the power of her mind was in the next section she was going to read. If she had it, she just might be able to get around the stupid block.

"You're not eating."

Ialog brought her out of her thoughts. "Not hungry."

"You haven't eaten since you got here." He watched her as he spoke. "That's not good for your pregnancy."

"And I won't eat while I'm here." She pushed her plate away, then looked at him. "Send me home and my children will be fine."

"You are home, Heather." He put down his fork. "You belong with me."

"I belong with Storm, the father of my children." She refused to back down. He had tried before and failed. Heather would make sure he failed again.

"Please don't push me, Heather. You don't want to see me when I'm angry."

"Really? You haven't seen anger until you see Storm again. He will tear you limb from limb because of this."

Heather stood. "I wish to go back to my room and wait for him."

"No."

"Then you will see me angry." She wrapped her hands around the top of her chair, anger racing through her. Heather looked at her hands and noted she was glowing brighter. "I'm not going to give you the satisfaction by acting like some demure little woman waiting to be rescued, and I will be rescued. I'm going to fight you every inch of the way."

"Sit down." He slammed his hands against the table and pushed himself to his feet.

"No." She shook her head. "You will not be telling me what to do, Ialog. You don't have that right."

"I am the one who is in control right now, Heather." He leaned on the table. "I can make your life miserable."

"Any more miserable than it is right now? Separated from the thoughts of my children, my mate? Not being able to touch Storm whenever I want is heartbreaking. I need him." She didn't care about the device he had to immobilize her. Everything inside her wanted to be free of him.

"You don't need that stupid piece of flesh."

"How dare you!" She slammed the chair she had been gripping. Heather took several steps toward him before she could stop herself. "That stupid piece of flesh is as much your progeny as I am. You created him and his sister and you will not insult what is mine. Do you understand? I didn't create this situation you did."

"You were supposed to be mine," he said, his voice harsh.

"Why? And don't give me the 'I wanted a companion' story." She jammed her hands on her hips. "You could have created an android for that." She pointed to her look-alike. "In fact, you did. We both know you have the ability to make her age and you could program her to shut down when you die. She laughs, and thinks on her own so she'd seem alive."

"It isn't the same." He crossed his arms over his chest.

Heather knew he was in a state of denial, so decided to change tactics. "You made me a sexual being with the ability to procreate yet you have shown no sexual desire toward me." Heather rubbed her stomach to prove her point. "Why? What was your real agenda?"

"I also made you have superior intelligence. Why don't you tell me what your guesses are and I'll let you know how far off the mark you are."

"You wanted to recreate the ancients in your own image."

He smiled. "Your dinner is getting cold."

He didn't have to say a thing. The smile was all she needed to know she was right. No wonder why he was so angry about her mating with Storm. All he really wanted was a baby machine, and their relationship interfered with that. The thought made her cold. "I'm not eating, so either let me go back to my room or we can argue some more."

He sighed, but nodded to the guard near her chair so he would escort her back to her room.

———

Storm looked at the bed he and Heather shared and found he couldn't face it without her. He needed something to keep him occupied and he had three reasons waiting for him in security. Susan, Gavin and the man who attacked Heather sat in their cells, waiting. Maybe a little interrogation would help. He stared about the room for a moment, feeling he was forgetting something, before he headed out the doors. About two seconds later he came back in and picked up the two leather-bound books the computer gave them several months ago. Then he headed to security.

He wasn't sure why he grabbed them, but he felt better with them in his arms. It had been a week since Heather had been taken. The United Countries of Earth were demanding he release his three guests but he wasn't ready. He needed answers first and he was going to get them.

Walking into security, he ignored the startled guards and headed to his office. Within two minutes, a shadow filled the doorway.

"Sir? Are you doing an impromptu inspection?"

"No." He looked up at the nervous face of Fridon. "The UCE is pushing me to release our guests so I thought I'd question a couple of them once more before releasing them."

"Of course, sir." Fridon remained quiet for a moment. "Shall I move the attacker to the interrogation room first?"

"Yes." The man didn't really know anything. Storm was pretty sure about that but he wanted to give it one more try to see if he would inadvertently give a piece of information he might have accidentally learned.

It didn't take Fridon long to get the man moved. He sat in the small room, staring around wildly. Storm smiled. Now, at least he could take out his frustration before releasing the man.

EIGHT

Heather found it hard to sleep and ended up pacing in her quarters. She wished she could wander around the compound when she couldn't rest, but knew the place was her prison, not a guest room. Her door opened, which surprised her. There, in the doorway, stood her look-alike.

"I noticed you were having problems sleeping."

"Yes." It was weird to see herself like that.

"Perhaps you would like to go for a walk?"

"That would be wonderful." Heather wondered why the android was showing her any attention. There had to be a reason. "Why do you want to do this?"

"I am created in your image. I find that curious." She gestured for Heather to walk beside her.

"Me too." Heather fell into step. "Why do you think Ialog did this?"

The robot walked beside Heather. "I do not know. He never explained to me."

"Are you a learning computer?"

"Yes." They turned a corner.

"And what have you learned so far?" Heather wasn't

sure what to call her. No one ever used a name for her. She just knew when she was being addressed.

"That although Ialog created you, he can't control you the way he can control me. All he has to do is upload a new file to change my program, but no matter what he tries with you doesn't work. It upsets him."

"Very true. But being flesh and blood makes our creation different." Heather took her time as she walked. "Does that bother you?"

"No, should it?"

"I wasn't sure if you were programmed with emotion. I have seen you smile a couple times but not much else."

"I remember your comment to Ialog. He felt it would get in the way of my programming so just gave me a basic program. It is enough for me to blend in with others and not be detected, but I don't have the more intricate program that is available." Her look-alike watched her for a moment. "Your womb is growing."

"Yes." Heather smiled as she rubbed her stomach. Joy washed over her as she thought about the life growing inside her. "Yours should be doing the same thing soon."

"Not necessary."

"What do you mean by that? Did something happen to the egg?" Was that why Ialog had taken her? He lost the egg so went back to his original plan of keeping her?

"No." The android looked at her, confused at her fear. "It has already fully matured."

"The gestational time for my eggs is about eighteen months, Vespian time, how could it have it matured already?" Heather felt a chill run down her spine. What did he do?

"Ialog wanted her to mature as fast as possible so gave the egg an accelerant that would cause the child to be fully matured in one year."

"What?" Heather stopped walking. How could he do that to her daughter?

"You are angry." She tilted her head as she studied Heather.

"Of course I am! A child is supposed to develop naturally by being nurtured and cared for. They learn as they age so when they are mature, they are ready to go out into the universe. My child won't have any of that. I was worried enough, knowing she wouldn't be able to bond with her mother, but this is wrong."

"It is a very safe procedure."

"Maybe for the body, but what about the mind? The soul? A person has to mature mentally as well as physically. She won't be able to mature properly."

"Ialog has done everything to be sure she has the knowledge expected for a full-grown adult."

Heather could tell the android didn't understand why she was so upset about this.

"Would you like to see her?"

"Can I?" She didn't expect that.

"Yes. Ialog will allow this if it will calm you." She looked at Heather. "You have been glowing since you arrived, but when you're upset you brighten."

"I know." Heather wasn't sure if it would calm her, but she'd pretend whatever they want if it gave her a chance to see her daughter for the first time.

"It doesn't seem to be life-threatening."

"It is caused by the frustration of this situation."

"Then perhaps seeing your daughter will help get rid of that frustration."

————

Storm sat at his desk, rubbing his eyes. The attacker didn't know anything. He had never worked for the man who hired him before and didn't know how he got his name. Once Storm was satisfied with his answers, he turned him over to the Earth Police so they could decide what to do with him. Storm also gave them a long list of crimes he had confessed to. Hopefully, they could use the list to incarcerate the man for a long time.

It felt good to have something to occupy his time.

Kuarto came into the office with two guards. What did he want now? Storm just stared at them, almost daring them to cross him.

"When was the last time you slept?" Kuarto crossed his arms over his chest.

"I'm not tired, doctor." Storm didn't have time for this.

"Right. Answer the question."

"Why?" He gave Kuarto a bored look. "I'm not tired."

"Your readings say different." He leaned onto Storm's desk. "I have been sent by your mother with an ultimatum. I don't care if your muscles have muscles. You either go rest on your own or I am to sedate you and take you to the medlab."

"Sedate me? Like to see you try." Storm didn't move.

"If that is your choice." Kuarto moved fast. Faster than Storm thought he could and hit him with a hypo before he could stop him.

Kuarto was right. He was tired. If he had been at his normal peak performance, Kuarto never would have gotten the best of him. Storm slumped in his chair.

———

Heather had refused to eat another meal, which angered Ialog. She feared he would refuse to let her see her daughter because of her stubbornness, but the android came by her room as promised.

"I didn't think you would come," said Heather.

"You don't want to see your daughter?" She sounded confused.

"Oh, I do, but Ialog was angry with me for not eating." She stood. "I thought he would punish me by not letting me see her."

"He didn't change his agreement, so I am here to escort you." She gestured for Heather to walk with her. "Why aren't you eating?"

"I'm afraid he'll try to drug me again."

"He can not."

"What is to stop him?"

"He has no desire to hurt you. He only wants your companionship. The last time he had hoped to change your memories so you would stay with him, but now your mind is too strong for him to try to manipulate it again. He hopes to convince you this is where you belong. That is why he gets upset at your resistance."

"He has no real control of me, does he?"

"Not of your mind, which is growing every day, but he can control your environment." Her look-alike took her outside. It was the first time Heather had been allowed outside since she had arrived. "He wishes to convince you to stay with him."

Squinting at the bright sunlight, Heather smiled. At least she knew she was still on Earth. "That won't happen."

The android didn't react to her words. "Your daughter is over there."

Heather looked in the direction the android pointed. She saw a young girl, about eight, sitting by herself. "May I approach her?"

"Yes."

Heather nodded and walked to where the child was. Her hair was a golden color, not black like her father's or white blonde like hers, which surprised Heather. The child looked up at her when she approached. Beautiful violet eyes with a bright gold ring watched her.

"Hello," said Heather. Her heart went out to the beautiful child in front of her.

"Hello." The child tilted her head to one side. "You do look just like the android, don't you?"

"It's actually the other way around." Heather smiled. She wasn't afraid of her, just curious. "She was created to look like me."

"True." The child turned her gaze back to the odd puzzle she had been working on.

"What are you doing?" Heather sat down beside the girl. She studied the puzzle. It looked like a complex DNA sequence, but without the puzzle assembled she wasn't sure.

"Studying." The girl looked up at her for a moment before turning her attention back to the pieces she gazed at so intently. She picked up one piece. "Are you my mother?"

"Yes."

"Okay." She didn't say anything else, just started placing the pieces in rapid succession until she had completed the puzzle. In seconds it dematerialized and a second one filled its place.

Heather felt a tear slide down her cheek. What had they done to her? Instead of being full of laughter and joy she seemed emotionless. Like a robot told what to do. Heather had felt like that at times in her life and she hated this for her daughter. "Do you have a name?"

"Yes." She looked at Heather, reached out and touched the tear sliding down her cheek. "Why are you crying?"

"For you." Heather touched her small cheek gently. "I never wanted this for you. My goal was to get you back before you were born, not have your life accelerated far too fast."

"What is wrong with being accelerated?" She didn't seem upset, just curious.

"You don't get to be a child. You won't learn from your mistakes because you wouldn't have made that many."

"But I am getting those lessons downloaded into my mind as I sleep." She tapped the side of her neck. Her daughter didn't see a problem with what was happening with her, then again she didn't know any better. "It will be fine."

Heather was horrified, but knew her daughter didn't see anything wrong with the way she was being raised and taught. "So, what shall I call you?"

"I have been named Samistwitha, but most of the people here call me Sam." She studied the next puzzle given to her.

"Sam." Heather smiled. "I like it. And what do you do for fun, Sam?"

"Fun? Studying is fun. I find the things I have learned to be very interesting." She shrugged. "My training is very intense." She was quiet for a few moments. "Are you planning on taking me with you when you leave this place?"

"Yes. You're my daughter. I won't leave you again." Heather wondered if Ialog allowed her to see Sam because he hoped it would cause a bond between them and soften her resolve about leaving. Nothing would keep her from getting back home. Storm would come and rescue them.

———

Storm stared at the cameraman as Fridon questioned him for the fifth time. The man was exhausted from lack of sleep and being badgered so much, but his story hadn't changed. Storm stood and silently signaled for Fridon to leave the room.

"My mate is missing, Gavin, and I need your help to find her."

"I want to help, Storm, but I don't know anything. She could be anywhere."

"She is still on this planet."

"How can you be so sure?" asked Gavin. "He could have left orbit at any time."

"Because the UCE took my threat seriously when I told them I would have the Vespian ship in orbit shoot any ship that tried to leave the planet and they suspended anyone leaving any station until she is found."

"You can do that?"

"Being the ambassador has its perks. Now didn't you help record the interview with Ialog? Your file says you are Susan's exclusive photographer."

"I am or was, but when she did those interviews she went by herself." He frowned. "In fact, I offered to go with her and she just about took my head off. She didn't want to give me any information. It took a lot for her to tell me how long she planned to be gone and she wouldn't have given me that if we hadn't had another assignment that could be jeopardized if she wasn't back in time."

"So how long was she gone for?" He felt excitement fill him. This small detail could be what he needed to find his mate.

"About four hours. Taking into consideration that the interview normally takes two to three hours."

"Any idea how she traveled?"

"I believe she used a company transport."

"Then they would have a record of where she traveled." Storm stood. Finally, a clue as to where his heart was.

———

Heather spent as much time as she was allowed with her daughter. Sam was very bright and quick to understand anything they talked about. She found the girl a delight to be around. It didn't take long for their bond to develop. Sam thrived on the affection Heather gave her.

"It looks like it is time for me to go," Heather commented when she spotted the android coming her way.

"Because she has made her presence known to you?" Sam looked from the robot to Heather, her curiosity evident.

"Yes." Heather touched Sam on the chin and stood.

"Why do you touch me?"

"To show you affection." She had to smile. Her daughter wasn't afraid to ask when she didn't understand something.

"Ialog says he cares, but never touches me."

"I didn't think he did." Heather had wondered about that. He hated that she had become sexually active with Storm, yet had kept his distance from her the whole time she had been there. She found it odd. If he wanted her, why hadn't he shown her any physical affection? "But I have learned that touching someone you care for makes you feel better. I learned that from your father."

"The man Ialog speaks about with disdain. Why doesn't he like my father?"

"Because he feels your father took me away from him." Heather smiled again. "Can I show you another physical form of affection?"

"What?" Sam stood, interested in learning something new.

"A hug. People use it to say hello, to show they care when a friend is hurting. It allows a mother to show she cares for her child."

"Really? A hug can do all that?"

"Yes." Heather opened her arms for Sam. "May I hug you?"

"Alright."

Heather gathered her into her embrace, her eyes closed as she held her.

"This is very nice." Sam wrapped her arms around Heather's waist. "Can I have more of these?"

Heather tightened her embrace a little. "You can have one from me whenever you wish."

————

Susan sat in their interrogation room by herself. Storm watched her on a monitor, wondering why the woman seemed to be so fixated on him. She had been chattering away since they put her in there three hours ago. Didn't she realize she was alone?

Most of what she said didn't mean anything. Storm figured it was to fill the void. Some women were like that. Thank God Heather wasn't. The constant noise was annoying him.

"Heather's commander is on the line, sir," said Fridon who had just stepped into his office. "He wishes to speak to you." He looked at the screen. "Has she stopped for air yet?"

"I don't think so." He turned the volume down and made sure everything she said was being recorded before he opened the link to Heather's old commander. "You wish to speak to me?"

"I'm supposed to tell you we are sorry over the mishap with Heather." He sighed as he paused. "Look, the government realizes they made a mistake. And if they could do it all over again they would have never asked her to come back, but let her respond the way she wanted to, via comlink from Vespia."

"It would have saved all of us a lot of heartache." Storm didn't really care about that now. He just wanted his mate back.

"I personally pulled the data from Susan's company. I sent a security team to examine the transport she used. It wasn't one they used a lot because of its age. The data we gathered was sent to Fridon a few minutes ago, so you'll have what we learned." He pulled up a map of the North American continent. "She went to this area here the day the interview was done. I also did a little digging and found a large area of land was rented for a huge amount of money with no time limit. There was no name on the paperwork, but the transfer of monies came from an account off world. That I was able to trace."

"Ialog."

"Yes."

"Then I'm going to bring her home."

"My government will stop you if you try." Bear didn't look happy as he relayed the information to Storm. "They want to be the ones to rescue her."

"They have no idea who they are dealing with. She is my mate. It is my job." Storm reached for the button to break their conversation when Bear made one comment that had him pause.

"And he expects that, Storm. He's going to be ready for you. Wouldn't it make more sense to let my government do this? If they are successful, great. Heather will be back where she belongs, and my government will feel better about their blunder. If they aren't, you will know what his defenses are and you can plan accordingly."

"It doesn't matter either way."

"You need to let my people take care of this." Bear sounded embarrassed. "My government has surrounded the embassy. I tried to reason with them, but they want to do this their way. If you step out of the embassy without permission, you will be arrested."

"Bear."

"Check your monitors."

Storm growled as he turned on the exterior camera. Anger filled him when he saw the guards surrounding the building. "He will still expect me to rescue her."

"True, but he won't expect the first attack to be from

Earth. We will weaken him so it will be easier for you to go in and rescue her."

"There is no such thing as weakening him." Storm glared at the man.

"Please don't make this worse by challenging those men out there. Let us have the time we need to do this. I'll make you aware as soon as it is over."

"I should at least be there when your government tries."

"I tried that too. Hell, I want to be there because I feel like I caused all this by forcing her to come home. If something were to happen to her I'll never forgive myself." He sighed. "I want her home as much as you do. Going along with this will show that you respect our way. It shouldn't be more than a day. The moment I hear you'll know."

Storm didn't want to go along with this, but he knew he could embarrass both planets if he didn't. He also needed to go through the data Bear sent over. That was the only reason he'd wait until he heard from Bear.

———

Sleep still eluded her. Heather tried resting her eyes, but found it did her no good. Kuarto was going to be very mad at her when she got home. She rarely ate. Only what she considered safe which was fresh vegetables with nothing on them. Thank goodness Ialog noticed she would eat a salad or greens if left alone because he had been serving more of that for her to consume.

Her door opened.

"Do you wish to walk?"

Heather smiled. She had a most unlikely companion in the android that looked like her. They walked just about every night, unless Ialog had something for the robot to do. "That would be great."

"You are not sleeping."

"I know. I wish I could, but this blocker is keeping me from getting any rest." Heather followed the robot out into the night. Stars filled the sky. What a beautiful sight.

"Ialog doesn't believe you. He says you should still be able to sleep or rest, just not have dreams." The android led her to a worn path through the small wooded area. "I am hoping the fresh air here will help you relax enough to sleep."

Heather didn't think it would help, but didn't say anything. Let Al think what he wanted. He was the reason the look-alike came to her. He didn't know how to handle her volatile moods so used it as a mediator. At least the ever present glow she had hadn't gotten worse. Her look-alike constantly checked her to make sure it remained at a certain level.

"He also wants to know what it will take to get you to eat regularly."

"I doubt if he can do anything that will allow me that kind of trust in him." Heather took a deep breath of the fresh air. Being outside helped lighten her mood. "Every time I have been in his presence he has done something that I consider untrustworthy."

"Like what?"

"Well." Heather needed to choose her words carefully so the android would understand why she didn't trust him. If she was a learning system, then maybe Heather could sway her. "The first time he had me he tried to make me believe Storm and I had never met. When I didn't fall for that, he tried to steal my children and ended up with one of my eggs. The second time he tricked me into fertilizing my stolen egg, then, without my permission, he accelerated the aging process on that egg. And now he had me kidnapped and has placed this damaging piece of equipment on my forehead so I can't rest." Heather paused. "How can I feel safe with the food he places in front of me?"

"He wonders if this will help." She opened her hand to reveal a scanner close to the one Heather's brother used all the time. "You can program it yourself to check whatever you wish. Food, drinks, any shots he wishes you to take."

"No shots. I will not allow him to inject me with anything." She hadn't taken the scanner from the android yet as much as she wanted to. She wanted to be sure she wasn't promising him something she shouldn't first.

"But your system is being depleted, and he fears for your children." The android lifted the scanner toward her.

"I fear for them, too." Heather ignored it as she touched her womb. "But this is all his doing so he can only blame himself."

"He still wants you to use the scanner. It is brand new so you can't say he has tampered with it."

Heather took the scanner and slipped it into her pocket. "I'll program it when I get back to my room."

"There is one more thing."

Heather pinched the bridge of her nose, knowing she shouldn't have taken the scanner until the android forced it on her.

"He wants your rings. It would be better if you gave them to me, but I have been told not to leave you without them."

She looked down at the rings on her left hand, wanting to kick herself when she realized she had taken the scanner too soon. She wished she had waited a little longer as she pulled them off her hand. "He can't destroy them."

"That is not his plan," she said as she held out her hand for the rings.

All that did was make her wonder what he had planned for them.

Storm had let her sit in the room for a few more hours before he walked in and sat opposite Susan. He waited to see what she would do or say first. The litany of words she had been spouting since she arrived proved he wouldn't have to wait too long.

"I was wondering when you would show your face."

"Got tired of the constant chatter." He crossed his arms over his chest. "Do you ever shut up?"

She glared at him. "Most men find me charming."

"I'm not most men." He watched her for a moment. She seemed uncomfortable, but kept quiet. "I want to know what Al promised you."

She remained silent. Susan even turned her head away from him a little. Was she afraid she'd give something away?

"You will stay here until I get my answers." He placed one foot, then the other on top of each other on the table. The bang of each boot made her jump in her seat.

"You can't keep me like this."

"Ah, you don't seem to understand. I can. Everything you perpetrated was done on Vespian soil. Your government is well aware of your incarceration and why I am keeping you. I have their permission. I can prove it if you like." He leaned forward and turned on a small screen that faced him. Storm angled the screen so she could see it, too. On the screen was Heather's commander. "Explain to Susan why she is still here."

"I thought you did a good job a few moments ago. But if she doesn't like your accommodations I'm sure I can find some little hole to stick her in. Red tape can be a real pain when it comes to committing a crime on foreign soil."

"But I didn't do anything wrong!"

"Really?" Storm couldn't keep the sarcasm out of his voice. "Let's see. You impersonated a military officer, a government official, the ambassador's wife. That's three strikes with one very stupid move."

"We also have the details on where you went when you did your interview with Heather's kidnapper," said Heather's boss. "I have gotten a hold of all the footage from the interviews. He's a madman, yet you painted him to look like a saint, and that slant took three different interviews. Why did you work so hard to make him look good?"

"You would never understand." She turned her head from the screen, choosing to look at a wall instead of Storm, or the monitor.

"Really?" Storm slid his feet off the desk and leaned forward. "I know this. My mate is gone because of you. You had some sort of selfish agenda that didn't work out the way you wanted it so you decided to punish her because you didn't get your way."

"You were supposed to be mine." She glared at him.

"You sound like Al. He keeps saying that about Heather."

"What is it about her, anyway? She is nothing. An orphan. Yet she always was the one everyone talked about at the academy. They always called her their smartest and brightest. Even made her valedictorian over me. Me! And my family donated so much to the academy to allow stupid people like Heather to go there. It just wasn't fair."

Storm waited for his translator to explain what a valedictorian was. It didn't surprise him. He knew she was brilliant, but Ialog made her that way.

"Fair? You want to talk about fair? How is it fair that you decide what I want in my life? You don't even know me." Anger snapped in his eyes. He leaned back in his chair. "You only wanted me because of Heather."

"No. I wanted you because of the job. You think I want to be a newscaster for the rest of my life? I don't get to tell the real news. Only the gossip stuff. They said I wasn't good enough to cover the breaking news, so I got stuck doing interviews and stories no one really cares about."

"And you thought I'd be an easy out."

"How hard could the job be? Get a bunch of people to sign a treaty then sit back and enjoy the rest of my life. I've done my research. Vespia doesn't have any poverty and you live in a palace."

"Everyone on Vespia works. Including Heather." The idea of keeping her home all the time did have his libido liking it a lot. There could be many mid-afternoon rendezvous for them if she didn't work. Although their sex life wasn't hampered by their jobs at all. "In fact, she holds down two jobs. If you were on Vespia, you would have to work just like everyone else."

"But you're the ambassador."

"Only when I'm here. I'm also head of security on Vespia. How can I expect the people to work if I refuse to?" He couldn't believe she thought Heather sat at home all day long and did nothing. "You'd never fit into Vespian society." He stood. "I still expect you to answer my question. I'll give you time to think about it. See if a little more time will help you give me the answers I want."

———

Heather still avoided heavily sauced foods. They just didn't appeal to her, but the scanner did make her feel more secure about eating the meals put in front of her. Each day that went by made her a little more despondent. Where was Storm? Why hadn't he come crashing through those doors yet?

Ialog watched her as she used the device before slipping it into her pocket. Picking up her fork, she speared a piece of meat and popped it into her mouth. It was hard to eat with him staring at her. She chewed what she had and swallowed before confronting him. "What do you want, Ialog?"

"Why do you ask?"

"Because you're staring at me."

"Sorry. I'm just happy to see you eating again." He sat his

fork down. "I'm glad the scanner has come in handy. Now all I have to do is get you to feel comfortable enough to smile."

"My smiles are only for one person." She didn't look at him, knowing her words would upset him. She continued to eat.

"What about your child?"

"What about her?" That got her attention. She looked up to study his face.

"You have smiles for her."

"Of course." She watched him warily, not liking the comment he made. "She is my flesh and blood."

"Would you like her to join us for our meals?"

"Whatever you wish." Inside, she did want to spend as much time as she could with her daughter, but she wasn't about to give that information to Ialog.

He nodded to one of his guards who opened the doors he stood near. Sam stood in the doorway, hesitant and frightened. Heather gestured for her to come in.

"You know, it would help if you showed her she's not breaking any rules." Heather wanted to throw her plate at Ialog. Didn't he understand a small gesture of affection went a long way? "Look at how frightened she is."

"You may enter, Sam."

Heather was surprised he used the nickname most called her. She smiled at the girl as she crossed to the table and took the empty seat opposite Heather. One of the servants filled her plate before stepping back.

Sam picked up her fork and held it, not quite sure if she should eat. She would look at her mother, then to Ialog before looking at her plate. Heather took her fork and speared a piece of broccoli. Lifting it to her lips, she bit into it, hoping Sam would see it was okay. She felt her heart flutter a little when Sam mimicked her moves. The child was already trusting her to show her what was right and wrong.

Time for the next step.

"What did you learn today, Sam?" asked Heather.

Sam just stared at her for a moment. "I had to work on my science project."

"I never see you with instructors, but you always seem to be studying. Who teaches you?"

She turned her head and pointed to a row of small metal buttons just below her ear. "This is my instructor. Because of it, I am able to absorb information faster."

"What did Ialog decide was important for you to learn?"

"I'm fully versed in ancient, the history, the science, the language." Sam took her napkin and placed it across her lap.

"What about the legends?" Heather stabbed another piece of meat with her fork.

"Legends?" She looked at Ialog for a moment before turning her attention back to Heather. "I wasn't aware of any legends."

"There are wonderful stories about the ancients all over the walls at the main hall on Vespia." Heather looked at Ialog to see how he was reacting to what she said. "I find them fascinating and I plan on showing them to you."

"Then you can read ancient."

"Yes. I also speak it. You?" Heather spoke in the language.

"Yes. Although I'm not as versed as I should be," she returned. "Ialog says it's because I'm not speaking the language enough."

"Then we will converse in ancient when we're together. I have very little chance of speaking it as well because most of those who are close to me don't speak the language." Heather sat back and pushed her plate away.

"You haven't finished your meal," said Ialog.

"It's not sitting well with me." She suddenly felt ill. What a great time for her pregnancy to make her sick. "May I be excused?" She didn't wait for an answer before she jumped up out of her chair and ran for the nearest door. She just made it outside when she lost everything she had eaten. Her stomach rolled a little, warning her she could have another bout.

She rested her back against the wall as she slid down into a sitting position. Her eyes closed. Heather hoped she could calm her stomach before it heaved again.

"Mother?"

Heather opened her eyes. "You've never called me that before."

"Is it okay?" She looked frightened.

"Of course." She gestured for Sam to sit beside her. "I'm very happy you feel comfortable enough to call me your mother since I haven't been here for you."

"Why did you run out the way you did?" Sam touched her hand hesitantly. "I was worried."

"Sorry." Heather took her hand and pressed it against her stomach. One of the infants took that moment to kick her. She smiled. "You felt that?"

The little girl looked at her in awe. "Is that the fetuses inside you?"

"I think of them as children, not fetuses. They are your brother and sister." She rubbed her hand against the growing bump. "If you hadn't been accelerated you would have been their triplet."

"Would I have been in there with them?"

"If we had gotten you early enough maybe, but it is a moot point now." Heather touched her face. "You were created like I was, and I didn't want that for you. But it was my decision to give you to Ialog so I feel responsible."

"I'm not sure I understand."

"Ialog had your father, aunt, and uncle. My choice was simple. Either allow you to be created or let all of them die."

"You made the right choice, then."

"I hope so." Heather pulled the girl into her embrace. "But you haven't known love and that upsets me."

"Why?"

"Because I grew up with no family." Heather pressed a kiss against her forehead. "I know what it is like to not feel simple affection day to day. No one should be raised that way. Your father proved that to me."

"Then he gives you the affection you didn't get as a child?"

"Yes. In so many little ways." She leaned her head against the wall she rested against. "A touch of his hand, a kiss against my forehead. Simple things that you don't always pay attention to unless they are suddenly absent."

"You miss him."

"More than you know." She fought back the tears that threatened to spill.

———

Storm sat at his desk, thinking about breaking his promise to Bear. He wanted to contact him to find out the status, but he had already pestered the man three times. He needed to be patient. Fridon stepped into his office. Storm didn't like the fear in his eyes. "Something wrong?"

"This just arrived." Fridon placed a small box in front of him.

Storm recognized the ancient writing. "When did it arrive?"

"About a half an hour ago. I made sure it was safe before I brought it to you."

He pressed the button to open the box. There, nestled in the center, were Heather's rings. He sat back. Why would Heather give up her rings? He knew they meant a lot to her. Ialog sent them to anger him, but he knew Heather was also trying to send him a message. So what was the message?

"Admiral Barrister has also contacted us. He wishes to speak to you outside."

There must be news from their attempt. The fact that Heather wasn't here told him things didn't go well, but at least he could now do something. Sitting around waiting was annoying. The warmth of the sun felt good when he stepped outside.

One of the guards spoke softly to himself before he addressed Storm.

"Admiral Barrister is waiting for you there." He pointed to a path nearby for Storm to follow.

Storm wondered why Bear didn't come into the embassy. Did he have to say something he didn't want on record? "I take it things didn't go well?" he said when he caught up with Bear.

"No." He hesitated. "We were no match for his defenses."

Storm knew they wouldn't be successful, but so did Bear. He and Heather had gone up against the man twice now, and a frontal assault was a waste of time. The only way to beat him was to think like him. "What happened?"

"I think it would be better to show you." Bear pulled out a pad and handed it to Storm who watched as Earth security advanced. One by one they disappeared. "I don't know what he used or how he was able to install anything since he wasn't allowed to alter any of our sensors, but they are gone. No residue, nothing. I have sent this along with our attack plan to Fridon so you can go through it. I hope you can figure it out because I fear you'll lose your best if you don't."

"I have been up against this man twice now." Storm handed the pad back. "He is a genius, but he hasn't been able to keep Heather and me apart. I will get my mate back."

"If there is anything I can do to help you."

"I'll let you know, Bear." Storm continued to walk through the park. He didn't normally run, but the desire was strong in him now. It would help him think. He took off at a quick pace, going over the data he already had from the ship orbiting the planet and what Bear had sent him before. The territory Ialog had rented was huge and well-guarded. The grid around the wooded area was probably the easiest place to enter, but that was where Earth security tried to gain access to, and it didn't work. Somehow, he had to figure out how to sneak up on him. He needed to study the files more before he could solidify his plan.

So many questions plagued him. What evaporated the security force sent to bring Heather home? And why did Heather allow Ialog to take her rings? There had to be something more important to her there, and she sacrificed the rings because of it. But what? Why didn't Ialog just leave Earth once he had Heather? Why did he stay on the planet? If only he had their mindlink. Heather would be able to answer so many of his questions.

He found the path he had chosen easy to follow. The sounds of the woods filled his ears. The call of a bird, the scampering of a small creature when he got close to them. His vision sharpened so he could see a long distance in front of him. This was probably the calmest he had been in days. He raced along, his paws pounding against the ground.

"Paws?" Storm looked down again, but saw only his hands. No paws. He also noticed he was naked. When did he take off his clothes? "This just can't be good."

NINE

Heather walked along with her daughter and the android, her own little entourage. Sam had suggested they walk in the woods, following a well-worn path.

"Why did you want to walk here?" asked Heather.

"Because as much as I wanted to, I haven't been permitted. Although it is within my safety range Ialog said it was too dangerous with the wild animals that inhabit the area." Sam smiled up at her. "But since I have an adult and security I thought we would be allowed this time."

"What sort of wild animals?" Heather didn't want anything to happen to her daughter and if it turned out to be too dangerous, then she would make them all turn around and go back where it would be safer.

"Deer, maybe a bear or two, a couple of wolves." She grabbed Heather's hand. "I promise not to stray away, but I would love to see a wolf in person. We'll make sure we stay where the cameras are so if there is any trouble nothing will happen to us."

"Is that what you mean by safety range?"

"No." Her look-alike spoke up. "There is a device built

into Sam's insert. If she were to wander too far, she would be knocked unconscious."

"Because Ialog doesn't want her running away?"

"Yes. He also doesn't want someone kidnapping her."

"They could revive her once they got her to safety."

"If she were taken beyond the range of the security system a poison would be released by her insert. She would be dead in seconds."

Heather stopped moving. Trying to rescue her daughter could kill her? "Why would he build such a failsafe? What if he were to need to move her quickly?"

"There is a function on his remote to override the poison in such a case."

"I see." She wanted to scream but knew any reaction would be recorded and shown to Ialog. Time to change the subject back to something safer. "So there are some areas that are not under surveillance?"

"Yes. The people who own this land were very specific about where he could put cameras." Sam looked about as they continued to move. "Including a very pretty area near a pond where he couldn't put cameras."

"Show me." So Ialog didn't own the land, but rented it. Good information to share with her mate when she got the chance.

———

Storm strode into his mother's room. "I think we need to talk."

She stepped up to him and pulled a twig from his hair. "It has happened, hasn't it?"

"What, Mother?" He glared at her. "What is going on?"

"Why don't you tell me what happened first?" Anseri sat back down at the table and gestured for him to do the same.

"I hate it when you get like this." He remained standing

and ran his fingers through his hair. "Why won't you just come out and tell me?"

"You won't believe me." She gestured to another chair again.

"I saw paws."

"I wondered." She nodded.

"Mother." Anger filled him. He heard himself growl at his mother. It didn't seem to faze her.

"Storm, the glowing eyes, enhanced smell, all the little things you have experienced say you have the shape-shifting ability that runs in the family. I wasn't sure how much you would have of it. For some, it is just the glowing eyes. Others are able to completely shift."

"And you?" He couldn't believe she never told him about this.

"Your father had this talent. It came from his side of the family. He had feared my reaction, so I never saw to what extent he had the ability." She pressed her hands against the table. "I only recognized these few because your father couldn't disguise them from me."

"So I'm running blind with this." He ran his fingers through his hair again.

"I am sorry." She pressed a hand to his cheek. "But Kuarto has dealt with many different races. Perhaps he has dealt with shape-shifters as well and can help you."

"I'm supposed to trust him with something like this?"

"You trusted him with Heather's secret and your sister's heart."

———

Heather turned in a circle. The small meadow was perfect for a few moments to herself. If Ialog would allow such a thing. "This has no cameras or security devices?"

"No," responded the android. "Ialog doesn't have

permission to place sensors in this area. It goes against the contract he signed when he acquired the territory."

Thank goodness androids couldn't lie. "Who would know?"

"The Earth government would. The technology buried throughout the area is designed to pick up anything illegal added. This is a national public reserve designed for citizens to rent at their discretion, but they cannot change anything."

"Then the building was already here?"

"Yes." She tilted her head at Heather. "Why?"

"Just curious." That could work to their advantage. It meant the blueprints of the building were in Earth's archives. Anyone could access the information. But how was she going to get the information to Storm? Heather sat on the soft grass and closed her eyes.

"What are you doing?" asked Sam as she did the same thing.

"I want to see if I can meditate here. Haven't been able to do it in my room." Heather opened one eye and looked at her daughter.

Sam closed her eyes as well.

Heather couldn't help but smile as she closed her eyes again and settled her thoughts. She centered herself so she could focus her mind on the device on her forehead. Her main goal was to try to find a way out of it. Somehow, she should be able to get around the blockage. Her mind was strong enough.

Heather sat there for a while, working against the block on her mind. She couldn't see where she had made a dent, but her mind was exhausted, so she knew it was time to stop. Opening her eyes, she found her look-alike staring at her.

The moment Heather started moving the android did too. It must have been in a sleep mode until she was ready to go. "I wish to ask for this space to be mine. An hour or two every day so I can meditate and have a little time to myself."

So far, Ialog had given her anything she asked for. Even though she had to give something in return, she hoped that would continue.

"I will make Ialog aware."

———

Storm hated waiting. Kuarto was working on something that he felt was more important than Storm's problem. That was how he viewed what was happening to him. Of all the times for this to come to fruition, the timing couldn't have been any worse. He needed to bring Heather home, not worry about whether or not he could control this new ability long enough to get his family back together.

"Are you done yet, doctor?" Frustration filled him.

"Just a few more moments, Storm." He hadn't looked up once since Storm walked into the room.

Storm's irritation came out in a deep, throaty sound.

"Are you growling at me?" Kuarto finally looked up from his work and stared.

Storm didn't like the way he was staring at him. Was something wrong? He looked down at his hands and found paws again. This time, he tried to not react, but he watched in awe as the change came over him again.

"Whoa." Kuarto grabbed him by the arms and dragged him into a small room. "You're naked."

Storm tried to talk but found his vocal cords didn't want to work. Kuarto didn't seem to mind though he continued to prattle on while Storm fought to regain his voice.

"What...clothes?" He sounded so raspy and his tongue felt too thick for his mouth. Storm thought about being dressed and clothes appeared on his body, thanks to the unit from the underground computer.

"It's not unusual to have trouble speaking right after

shifting back. Although physically you're now human your readings are still showing some of the wolf."

Storm nodded as he smacked his lips a few times, waiting for everything to go back to normal. "They...disappear... each time."

"Each time? So this has happened before?"

Storm nodded. He looked down to make sure everything was as it should be.

"What is happening to you?"

"I don't know." That came out normal.

"You need to have a full body scan. Let's go."

Storm dug in his heels. "Thought you were reading my vitals with this stupid necklace."

"And it's been sending me very interesting data, but never showed any shape-shifter DNA. At least nothing I recognized. Your unit has wanted to do a deep scan since your DNA started to change and I bet you haven't allowed it. Now is the time."

"My private life—"

"I know, is your business. But as your doctor, I'm supposed to be privy to your private life." He continued to pull Storm with him. "Hell, we shared your intimate relationship with my sister until she learned to block it. This is something you have to learn to control and doing it yourself might cause more trouble. I have worked with many races and know how difficult the first few months can be when something like this manifests."

"Doctor."

"You need me, Storm, whether you believe it or not." He stopped walking, then turned to face his mate's brother. Kuarto crossed his arms over his chest. "So you going to lead the way to your room or shall we do everything right here in the medlab so your secret is known by all?"

"You are more discrete than that." Storm rubbed his hand over his face. He didn't want to deal with this, but knew the doctor would push until he got what he wanted. Straightening his shoulders, Storm headed to his room. "What makes you think the computer has that type of technology with it?"

"You forget all the things that computer has been able to do for you?" He pointedly looked at his clothes. "You sure do use them enough."

"Fine." They approached the doors to Storm and Heather's room, then entered.

"Computer, how much of your technology did you bring with you?" asked Storm.

"I'm not sure I understand your question."

"Storm needs a deep, full-body scan. Are you capable of doing that here?"

"Of course." A soft turquoise light encased Storm for a few seconds before it disappeared. Next, a three-dimensional image of him appeared.

Kuarto stepped up to the image, checking the readings that caught his attention. "I need all the data on this section of his DNA." He read the data and smiled. Touching one section of the information, he asked, "Is this voluntary or involuntary?"

"Voluntary," replied the computer.

"Good." He touched another section of the three-dimensional image to pull up a few more bits of information he wanted to look at. "Is the shifting focused on one creature, or any creature?"

"Although the shifter can imitate any shape they normally focus on one. Muscle memory makes it more realistic so the more they shift into one form the better they get at it. Each creature they mimic will take practice."

"What keeps happening to my clothes?" interjected Storm.

"When you go back to your natural form your body is doing it instinctively right now so it doesn't think about clothes. As you master the technique, you will be able to add things like clothing to your shift."

"Makes sense." Storm wondered if he could use this to his advantage. "Computer, can you pull up the file on the failed attempt to rescue Heather?"

"Failed?" Kuarto continued working with Storm's information. "Oh, wow. When you shift, your DNA reads as an animal not human."

"Is that good or bad?"

"It's very rare, but it means you'd be accepted because your scent would match whatever you're trying to mimic."

The image popped up on the main screen. They watched as one by one the security force disappeared from the screen.

"Did you see that?" Storm couldn't hide the excitement in his voice. "Computer, can you back that up about thirty seconds? I also need you to focus on this section here." He touched the screen where he wanted the computer to zoom in on.

The small brush was partially blocked by a human leg. Behind it, though, was a squirrel inching its way toward the compound. It would take a few steps and freeze, before it would move again. The human leg moved with it, then suddenly vanished where the squirrel continued until it moved out of range.

Kuarto looked at Storm and smiled. "Can you pull up a three-dimensional image of the wolf that is indigenous to the northwest coast of Earth's United States?"

A beautiful gray wolf appeared in front of them.

Kuarto turned to Storm. "Can you try to shift into this animal?"

"I'll try."

"Do you remember how you shifted before? What you were thinking?"

"I was trying to figure out a way to rescue Heather the first time I noticed I had paws instead of feet." He shook his head. "And this last time I was aggravated with you ignoring me."

"So you didn't focus on anything but the emotion you were feeling at the moment?" Kuarto walked toward the door. "I need my pad. I won't be gone long, but see if you can imitate this image and try to hold it as long as you can."

————

Heather sat on the soft grass with her eyes closed. Ialog had gone along with her request so she could finally have some privacy, for which she was very grateful. She wasn't sure what he would ask for in return. The subject hadn't come up yet.

Here she could be herself for a little while. Her first goal was to try to escape, but she found her movements became lethargic when she tried to go beyond the boundary of the pond. She pushed herself as far as she could go before her body stopped moving. Ialog made sure she couldn't run. So she decided to work on the block on her mind. There had to be a weak spot in the device. Some section she could work on so she could reach her mate again. She just had to find it.

Her mind worked against the block. In her mind, she imagined herself standing in front of a large rectangle hanging on a wall. It looked like a big blank canvas hanging there. First she studied it, looking for a slight discoloration or speck of color. Something that stood out from the smooth surface.

It took her a while. She had almost given up when she noticed the slight blue tone in one corner. That was where she needed to work.

————

Kuarto walked back into Storm's room, tapping onto his pad as he entered. His attention on the pad instead of where he was going had him practically knocking Storm over before he could stop himself. "Sorry." He stopped and stared. "Oh, wow."

The large gray wolf growled at him.

"Can't talk?"

The wolf shook his head.

"Good. At least you can't talk back to me." He reached out and heard another growl. "I have to test this ability of yours. We need to be sure it's one hundred percent believable."

Storm made a deep, breathy sound before sitting back on his haunches and waited for Kuarto to prove his point. Knowing Kuarto was going to touch him made Storm look away when he reached out to put his hands on him again. He felt the gentle brush of his hand against his head.

That wasn't so bad. Then Kuarto dug his fingers into his fur and pulled.

Storm shifted back to human to yell at his mate's brother but found his vocal cords wouldn't quite work.

"That's what I wondered. You can't break your concentration no matter what." Kuarto put his pad down. "What if someone were to step on your tail accidentally? You going to shift that instant and bark at them?"

"Voice."

"That will probably get easier as you learn to do this. Can you move okay?"

Storm took several steps so he stood inches from Kuarto, grabbed his collar, and lifted him.

"That doesn't seem to be affected." He waited for Storm to put him back down.

He wished he could talk because he had a few choice words for his mate's brother.

"If what we saw on that screen works and you can break

through Ialog's parameters, what are you going to do?" Kuarto pushed a few keys on his pad as he went back to their conversation. Storm's silence made him look up. "No one else can get through."

"Recon." His vocal cords allowed him to say that without too much trouble. "Need to…find a way."

"You'll need to hold this image for a long time then, and my scans show you're not rested enough to do that." Kuarto leaned a hip against the table. "You are so worried about your mate you aren't taking care of yourself, and I hate to say she has been doing the same thing. Although I'm not getting any of her daily readings, when her sensor updated I found I still get the downloads and according to the latest readings she hasn't been sleeping or eating right."

"Why didn't…you tell me." Storm didn't like it when Kuarto kept information from him.

"I got the update about three hours ago, but didn't see it until a few moments ago." He hit a few more keys as he spoke. "The system updates every two weeks, but I didn't expect my system to pick up any information because of her distance from us. Finding that file surprised me."

"Is she okay?" Worry filled him.

"She's fine, but she needs to rest and eat." Kuarto walked to his image and touched a few more places, and waited for the data to load to his handheld. "Just like someone else I know. Oh, did you bring my truck like I asked?"

"Yes." Storm didn't understand why he requested someone go back to Vespia to pick up the silly contraption. They had plenty of transports to utilize. "Although I don't… know why."

"I wanted it to steal my mate away so we could have some time to ourselves, but now I have a better idea." He moved around Storm's image, downloading data as he saw what he needed.

"What?" Storm didn't like the tone in his voice.

"To sneak you in." He stepped over to the main computer and sat his pad down.

"In that?" Glad he finally got his voice back, he turned toward Kuarto. He refused to climb into that ancient contraption.

"He's probably looking for modern transports, not something like my truck." Kuarto grinned when he turned at looked at the three-dimensional image of the wolf. "We should be able to get close enough without being detected."

"Not in that thing." Storm rubbed his hands on his face. He had a feeling he wasn't going to win this conversation.

"You really don't have a choice if you want to get your mate back."

Storm stared at the image. Kuarto was right. He needed to get in and find out what was going on. Find a way to turn off the defenses that evaporated the people from Earth's security. But could he hold the shift for a long time? "How long do you think it will fool him?"

"As long as you stay in animal form I would think forever. It depends on how much of a strain it puts on you." Kuarto looked at his naked form. "You just need to test it before we let you go there."

Storm shifted back into wolf form. He would hold this for as long as it took if it meant he would be able to be with his mate.

"I'm amazed at how easy that seems to be for you. You don't seem to have any pain when you shift."

"That is built into his DNA," the computer commented. "He won't become fatigued by the shift, either. The only thing Storm has to worry about is his focus. That will break the shift."

"How much do you know about his ability?"

"I have thousands of years of research as different people dealt with this shifting ability, but I believe all the information he needs is in his book."

"Book?" He looked at Storm.

Storm padded over to the table near the door and rested his head next to the leather-bound books. He had been taking them with him to his office, but just couldn't seem to open them without Heather at his side.

"May I?" asked Kuarto. He waited for Storm to nod before he picked one up and leafed through it. "Is this ancient?" He put down the larger of the two and opened the second one. A smile spread across his lips. "This one I can read, with your permission, of course."

Storm nodded again.

He worked his way through the book. Knowing what to look for had him skimming most of it. Once he hit the information he felt was important, he sat and read. Kuarto lost track of time as he scoured the book.

The doors opened and Storm's sister walked in. "There you are."

"I'm sorry. I lost track of time." He lifted the book in his hand. "You mad?"

"No." She touched his face. "But with everything that has happened, I was worried." She paused when she saw the wolf. "Why is there a wolf in my brother's quarters?"

"What do you think?" asked Kuarto. She had a knack for seeing the truth.

"I think he is beautiful, but my brother won't be pleased to have a wild animal in his room. By the way, where is my brother?"

"He's around." He pulled his mate into his embrace.

"I need to talk to him." Toki closed her eyes and rested her head against his shoulder. It was a comfort position for them, very close to the hand over the heart that Heather and Storm did. "I had a vision about Heather."

"What sort of vision?"

"It was very strange." She brushed a piece of hair behind

her ears. "I saw everything in black and white. It was like I was an animal of some sort."

"You mean like a wolf?" He looked at the animal sitting just a few feet from them.

"Yes." She walked over to the wolf who watched her approach. "This thing is quite docile."

"Most of the time."

The wolf bared its teeth at Kuarto.

"He doesn't seem to be too happy with you." Toki touched the wolf softly on the head. Her body stiffened for a second before she fell to the floor unconscious.

Kuarto was at her side in seconds. He scooped her up off the floor and gently laid her on the couch. His scanner hummed for a few seconds while he waved it over her. "She should be back with us in a moment."

Her eyes fluttered open.

"Everything okay?"

"Yes." She smiled as she touched his face again. "Didn't mean to frighten you."

"Those visions just take over at times and I worry about you when no one is around." He cupped her cheek. "Can you just surround yourself with pillows so I know you're safe?"

She laughed. "Timing is everything and I have never hurt myself."

"So far."

She got to her feet and walked over to the wolf. "You were in the center of my vision." Toki brushed her fingers against the thick coat of the beautiful animal. Once she was sure that she wouldn't be sucked into another vision, she dug her fingers deep into the fur. "I saw you as her companion, protector."

"You sure it was this wolf?" Kuarto came up beside her and crouched down. He placed his hand on Storm's head.

"Yes. Look at his eyes. There aren't too many eyes like that. Golden, with an amber ring."

Kuarto smiled. She knew.

––––––

Storm sat in his office waiting for Fridon. He needed to get him working on the blueprints before he went to Heather. The young man stepped into his office, looking nervous. No one liked it when Storm singled them out. Many feared he was angry with them.

"You wish to see me?" He stood the way Heather did when she knew she was in trouble.

"Have you completed all your assignments?" It brought a slight smile to his lips. The two of them had spent a lot of time together since Fridon had been injured and it looked like he was picking up some of her habits. He schooled his features. Storm enjoyed keeping his men in suspense from time to time and it had been a while since he had messed with Fridon.

"Almost, sir, but I'm going to have it done before deadline."

"Good." Storm stood and walked around his desk. "Come with me." He headed out of security and down several corridors until he stood in front of a secured door away from everything. He had moved the computer in here so the man wouldn't have access to his private quarters. Storm hoped to have Heather home within the day and didn't want the man underfoot while he spent time with his mate. Pressing the code to open the door, he stepped in.

Fridon crossed the threshold and found he couldn't move. "Sir?"

"Right." He made sure the doors had closed before he spoke to the computer. "He has permission to be here, by Heather. It should be in your system already. This is Fridon."

"Thank you, Storm. Heather has given this man permission to learn my systems." The computer released him so he could enter the room. "How are you doing, Fridon?"

He looked at Storm in total awe. "Computer?"

"Yes. I am a computer. I believe you first heard about me on the mission to rescue Storm, Kuarto and Toki."

"You're the one Heather told me was a prototype?"

"Yes."

"Fridon, we want you to study the system. Learn what you can about it. This will be part of your new assignment and it is a permanent one." The man never looked so happy. "Heather will give you all the details of your assignment when she gets back. I hope to have her home quickly. In the meantime, I have loaded everything that the admiral sent us into this system. It will help you get what we need to bring her home. I need to know about the security system. Probably ancient in design. Need to find a way to either turn it off or bypass it."

"Yes, sir." He looked at the computer. "Thank you, sir."

"Thank Heather. She is the one who recommended you."

———

Kuarto drove his truck as close as he could to the compound Ialog had rented. They had to be getting close to where the security cameras started, and he didn't want to be seen with Storm. Al would know the wolf was tied to them if he did spot them.

"I can't believe you talked my mother into going back and getting this thing." He had fought the idea when Kuarto first asked, but when his mother asked him, he made sure it was retrieved.

"It helps when your mate has a vision about it being with us while we're here on Earth." Kuarto pulled the vehicle over and turned the engine off. He turned to face Storm. "I don't want to get any closer. Do you think you can find your way?"

Storm closed his eyes and sniffed. Her scent floated on the air. He smiled. "Yes."

"Don't forget the cameras. Don't shift until you have to. Even if you see Heather."

"I would never do anything to jeopardize my mate." Storm glared at Kuarto. "And you know that."

"I do, but you have been too quiet since we started talking about you going in as a wolf, and that worries me." He tapped the side of his head. "I know your libido."

"I know my job, doctor. My goal is to get in, find the controls to his defenses, and turn them off. I want her home."

"I know you do." He slapped Storm's shoulder. "I'll be back here in a few hours to check-in. But Toki's visions are extremely accurate. We need to pick a location so I know where to look for notes from you and leave your supplies."

"I'll find anything you leave me."

"Fine, but how am I to find any notes you might leave if we don't have a drop-off point? My sense of smell isn't as strong as yours."

Storm picked out a tree with a hollow base. It was off the road a little so no one should be able to stumble across the spot easily, but Kuarto could get to it without too much trouble. Kuarto kept talking, giving him last minute instructions and Storm wanted to growl. He needed to get to his mate. Make sure she was okay.

The moment Kuarto finished, he shifted and took off. Sniffing the air, he found her scent quickly and followed his nose. The animal reserve was protected by a computerized sentry. Ialog must have tapped into that with his security.

Storm stopped moving for a second and reinforced his image. It had to fool the system for this to work.

He took a few steps into the reserve and waited for the sentry to figure out he was human but the system remained inert. Picking up Heather's scent again, he lopped along, working his way in and out of the wooded area because of the shifting wind.

He came across a clearing and stopped. He had to be close. Her scent was too strong. The area looked clear, though. The sun shone brightly. A slight movement caught his eye and he focused on the small pond to his left. Heather floated in the water, eyes closed and face pointed up toward the sun.

She must have sensed his presence because she shifted in the water so only her head was exposed and looked around. He spotted the small strip of metal on her forehead. Was that what kept her from leaving? Or did she know about the sentry?

Storm wasn't sure what to do. In this shape, he could frighten her. He sat and just watched, enjoying the view as she climbed out of the water. The little droplets glowed as they slid down her wet body. How he wanted to take her in his arms, touch her heart and bury himself deep inside.

Her breasts looked larger, the hard pink nipples softening in the heat of the sun. Her stomach showed more, too. The twins were growing a lot faster than he thought they would have in the few short weeks since her disappearance. Overall, she was breathtaking.

He thought of the first time he had seen her at the embassy. How she had walked away from the spectacle he had been forced to create. But there was something about him that made her turn around and look at him before she reentered the building. Their eyes locked across the area and everything disappeared but the two of them. He knew he had to have her from that moment.

Storm lost focus as his desire for her overpowered him. He knew he couldn't drop the wolf image, not for an instant. Using everything he had, he pushed the memories back and stopped the shift that had started. Inwardly, he grinned. He could control this.

Heather snatched up her dress and hugged it to her form. Did he do something to give himself away?

"Who's there?" Her voice sounded like music to his ears.

He wanted to identify himself so badly. Wipe away the fear etched on her face.

"Ialog wishes you to return." It was her voice. From his angle, he could see the android standing beyond a small row of trees.

Heather sighed as she slipped back into her dress. She must have thought the robot was the one who startled her.

"You know he doesn't like it when you wear that dress."

"It is a lot easier to get out of when I wish to bathe." She finished sealing her dress. "That thing he wants me to wear all the time takes two people to get it off and since I'm the only one I allow here I would have to bathe with that stupid dress on. Sorry, but I don't want to do that."

"I could always follow you into your heaven and help you out of it."

"No. That is my private little area and I want to keep it that way. I'm not wearing it in his presence, so unless he wishes to create another outfit that I could remove on my own, I will wear this gown to the pond."

"I will speak to him."

"I'd appreciate it." Storm could tell by her face she didn't want to give up this dress, yet she didn't argue with the android. He wondered why.

Storm watched them leave. He followed at a safe distance, wanting to be near her as long as he could. Once they entered the building, he headed back to the spot where he and Kuarto would leave messages for each other. In the small pack, he found clothes, food and water for him. Storm took advantage of the food and water.

He wondered how often Heather came outside and did

she always have the android with her. He crossed back into the reserve, wanting to watch the compound plus catch a glimpse of her whenever he could.

———

Heather found sleep elusive once again. Her late night partner walked beside her. She wished she could sleep instead of having a computer ask her questions, but at least she wasn't trapped in her room waiting for time to tick by.

"Your lack of sleep is taking its toll on you." The android followed her outside, where they did their nightly stroll now. "I can see your energy levels are not where they should be. Your glow hasn't disappeared. You have some sort of deficiency that seems to be causing trouble with your system now. If you don't find a way to rest soon Ialog fears you will harm your children."

"Then why won't he let me go home? I don't belong here and he knows it." She had feared the same thing. Her children weren't as active as they should be inside her, and that worried her. Her head hurt and her body felt wrong.

"He disagrees and wishes you would accept your situation."

"I am Storm's mate. I carry his children." Heather touched her unborn children as she looked around. She felt like she was being watched. The sensation was strangely comforting. It wasn't Ialog. She always seemed to know when he was around and watching her. It always gave her the creeps. So who was watching her? Could Storm be out there? "Ialog has tried to come between that too many times. He fears for my safety, yet keeps me against my will. Do you know why I glow? Because I'm frustrated. He doesn't care about my happiness or he would return me to my mate."

"He feels you never should have been with Storm in the first place. If the leaders of the Vespian society hadn't interfered with your development, you never would have met your mate."

"But it didn't happen that way, did it?" She looked out into the woods and caught a flash of something. "I don't belong to Ialog. Storm is who I belong to. Until Ialog accepts that Storm will never stop and he has to before my mate gets so fed-up he kills him."

"That won't happen."

"What do you mean?" Heather didn't want to spend the rest of her life fearing Ialog. He needed to understand and leave her alone.

"Ialog can't be killed."

"Excuse me?" She saw it for a moment. Eyes glowing in the dark. They reminded her of Storm's. Desire for him filled her.

"Mortal wounds don't harm him. He can only die of old age."

That got her attention. If that was true, they'd never get rid of him.

TEN

Storm listened and watched as Heather walked along with that stupid android. Then she looked in his direction and all he could focus on was her. She saw him, he was positive of it. The moment their eyes met, her desire skyrocketed. He could smell it, see it surround her as she moved.

His vision was so different in wolf form. He could see in color just like he did in human form, but he could see more. He found he could tell which animal was tired by the colors surrounding their bodies. He could see the illness in others and see what would heal them.

The moment Heather's desire rose he saw it on so many levels. He felt it deep inside and found his focus wavering. He ducked back, fighting his own desire responding to hers. His body shook with need and he fought the shift back to human. He should just run and try to regain his composure or stay and fight for his focus. His desire to be near her won out and he stayed and battled to keep the shape of the wolf.

This was going to be the true test of his strength, because being near her was only going to heighten his need for her.

The next day, Heather waited for her time in the clearing. She always enjoyed the time alone. It gave her the freedom to work on the device on her mind as well as allow her to feel the sadness of her separation from Storm.

She sat on the soft grass with her eyes closed. The canvas was in front of her again. This time, though, the corner she had been working on was now black and bent. She was making headway. The block still kept her from connecting with Storm but she hoped with a little more work she would be able to touch his mind as she had always done. It had allowed her to sort of reconnect with her children. She couldn't communicate with them like before but they could now sense each other. It had a calming effect on both parties.

As she sat there, pushing against the block, she felt the presence again. Something was watching her. Focusing her mind to continue to work on the device, she opened one eye. About twenty feet in front of her was the most beautiful wolf she had ever seen. They just looked at each other. Heather was afraid to move because it could frighten the animal off.

It must have felt comfortable with her because it sat back on its haunches when she didn't react to its presence.

The eyes drew her. She was positive this was the same animal that she saw last night. The one who made her think of her mate. She missed Storm so much. The pain she felt from their separation sliced her deep in the heart.

The wolf whimpered and rested his nose on the ground. Heather couldn't help but smile. It was as if he shared her pain. "You sure don't seem very frightened of me."

The wolf lifted his head and gazed at her.

Heather laughed. She meditated a little while longer before she stood. "Hope you don't mind but it is time for me to bathe."

The animal sat up at her words.

She removed her dress and dove into the water. The cool sensation felt good against her skin. Heather could feel the slight rise in her body temperature and feared she was getting sick. The android had noticed it. So did her daughter. Something was out of whack with her, but she continued to refuse Ialog's desire to give her something that could cure it. She knew she could be complicating things, but she couldn't go back on her promise to herself to not let that man inject her with anything, even if it meant she could be harming herself and her children.

The soap her look-alike left for her lathered in her hand. She rubbed it in her hair before she stood so she could rub the soap on her body. A slight sound from the direction of the wolf made her look at it.

"I promise this isn't hurting the environment. It will actually help keep the water clean." He sure reacted when she broke out the soap.

It made a sorting sound before resting its head on its paws.

That seemed to mollify it. She continued with her bath, wishing she was in the shower on Vespia where she and Storm had been intimate so many times. She could feel his hands on her as he buried himself deep inside.

"Oh, God." She squashed the image as fast as she could. Heightening her arousal would just make her cranky. Heather had tried masturbating but found it only frustrated her more. She did a surface dive to go deep enough to freeze her libido. Anything to stop her mind from making matters worse.

When she finally resurfaced, she found the wolf at the edge of the water staring into its depths. He was so close she could touch him. Hesitantly, she lifted her hand and gently placed it on his furry neck. "It's okay. Just needed to clear my head."

The wolf snorted, but stayed where he was, allowing her

to dig her fingers deep into his coat. He wasn't afraid of her at all. "You sure are docile for a wild animal." Heather scratched him behind the ears. "I'm going to need you to step back or you'll get soaked as I climb out of this pond."

The wolf tilted his head to one side but didn't move.

Heather shrugged. He'd move eventually. All it would probably take was a splash of water to get him to take off. She braced her hands on the edge of the pond and pulled herself up. Swinging her hips so she could sit on the edge, she brought her legs up. She stood and looked down at the wolf. He hadn't moved a muscle.

"Wow. Thought you would have run the moment I started to move." Heather patted him on the head before crossing to her dress. It slipped on easily, absorbing the water as it slid against her skin. "I'm going to have to leave soon."

The wolf looked at her.

"My doppelganger is going to come after me soon. I only get to come out here for about an hour." She touched his head again. "I hope you are here again tomorrow."

———

Storm watched as Heather walked away. It took every ounce of his strength to remain in his wolf form when his mate climbed out of the pond naked. Water droplets from her breasts fell on his nose, which he licked off with his tongue. His paws itched to touch her, make her moan for him.

This was going to be a lot harder than he realized.

———

Heather entered her little haven feeling under the weather. Whatever was wrong was really starting to take its toll. The android made a comment about the dark circles under her eyes and the dip in her energy levels again. They had been sliding for the last few days.

She could feel that something was wrong deep inside. Normally, Kuarto would give her a shot and clear up the problem, but she wasn't at home anymore. How was she going to fix this? She sat on the grass with a heavy heart. Somehow, she had to protect her children.

She lay back on the grass and stared up at the sky. Not knowing what to do depressed her.

A soft sound caught her attention and made her prop herself up on her elbows. Sitting very close to her was the wolf she had seen yesterday, with a branch filled with berries in its mouth. He dropped it into her lap.

"For me?" She ran her fingers over the berries on one of the branches. Heather pulled out a scanner from her pocket and she noticed the wolf backed up. "Oh, this won't hurt you. I'm just going to check these berries real quick. Need to be sure they are not poisonous."

He only nosed them while they sat in her lap, like he didn't care what the scanner said as long as she ate the berries.

Should she trust the wolf without checking the berries? He sure seemed insistent. She ended up popping one into her mouth at his bark. The sweet juices slid over her tongue and down her throat. Just that little bit made her feel better. She ate a half a dozen more and felt the amazing healing power fill her.

She took the scanner and ran it over the berries, amazed at how quickly they worked. Heather pulled herself up to her knees and wrapped her arms around the wolf's neck. "Thank you. You have saved all of us." She buried her face into the soft fur and allowed the tears to fall.

Everything she had been holding back came out of her. The fear she would never go home, missing her mate with all her heart. The not knowing. All of it had taken its toll and this was the first time she felt safe enough to let it all out.

The android found her clutching the wolf and crying. "Heather?"

She lifted her face. "Is it time already?"

"Yes."

Heather stood and wiped her eyes.

"You are looking much healthier. How did you do that?"

"These berries." She handed her the branch. "My friend here brought them to me."

She analyzed the berries quickly, storing the data in her files. "Are you ready?"

Heather nodded and crouched down beside the wolf. "Thank you again." She stood and took a few steps only to find the wolf following her. "I don't think Ialog will allow you in the building."

"He has no policy with pets."

"A wolf isn't exactly a pet." Heather touched his head gently.

"Many are domesticated now." The android looked at Storm. "He seems very docile."

"Ialog won't let me keep him with me, will he?"

"As you say. The only thing you can do is ask."

———

Storm couldn't believe his luck. He had been trying to figure out how to get into the building and hadn't been successful. This would give him a chance to be with his mate and see how he could get to the defenses. He'd behave as docile as possible if it allowed him in.

———

"We don't even know if he is going to follow us." Heather started walking and to her surprise the wolf kept pace with them. She felt the butterflies take flight at the thought of having this animal with her all the time. It was something she really wanted, so what would Ialog demand from her in return?

As they approached the compound, he came out to greet them. "What do we have here?"

"Heather wishes it to be her companion."

So much for easing into her wants. Heather sighed. "He has befriended me."

"That is a wild animal." He eyed the animal wearily.

"A very docile one," countered Heather. She dug her hands into his fur. "I think he might have been domesticated, then released back into the wilderness."

He studied her for a moment. She hoped he didn't try to read anything into her comment. "You look much better, Heather."

"Thank you. He brought me berries that seemed to work." She patted the wolf on the head. Her heart pounded in her chest. He hadn't dismissed the idea. Would he allow her to keep him?

"And how long has this wolf been your little friend?"

It sounded so demeaning when he said it that way. It made her defensive. "Why?"

"Just curious." He studied the wolf. "If I allow you to keep this animal what will I gain?"

Here it came. "What do you want, Ialog?"

"Perhaps you will allow me to give you the injections you need for your children."

"That berry has everything in it that Heather needs." The android handed the branch Heather had given her earlier over to Ialog. "I will do a full analysis on it once you give me clearance, but my initial analysis shows it has great healing power."

Ialog nodded his approval and handed back the branch. Heather's look-alike took the berries and headed into the building.

Heather arched a brow at Ialog. He now had to find something else that he wished her to give in on. There were so many things she fought him on she wondered what he would choose.

"You seemed to have bonded with the animal pretty quickly."

"Wouldn't you if it had only seen you a few times and was able to figure out what was wrong with you and give you the cure? I trust him."

"I really dislike that gown."

"I only wear it because it is easier to get in and out of when I go to the pond. I have worked hard to not wear it around you."

"True. If I were to give you another dress for that purpose?"

"I will give this dress up." So he wanted to remove another tie to her old life. Heather looked at the wolf. She would do almost anything to keep him with her, but she wasn't about to tell Ialog that. "May I at least keep the dress?"

"No."

"I will hide it where you'll never have to see it again, so you know I won't be able to wear it." She knew that was what he wanted. He feared if she kept it the dress would still haunt him. Heather refused to accept that she was his guest and the gown was evidence. If he could remove every scrap of her old life, he would live under the illusion she had accepted her fate. She knew better, but if it would allow the wolf to stay with her she'd let him have his illusion.

He had been watching the wolf this whole time, but her words had him looking at her. "And you will never wear it again?"

"No." Not until she was free again and with her family.

"You must also wear your hair the way I prefer." He was willing to give her this if she gave a little more.

"Fine." She could wear her hair up if it meant having a true ally in the building.

"Good. I will see you at dinner." He looked at the wolf. "Leave him in your room."

Heather nodded and headed into the cool interior. She took the wolf into her room and proceeded to change. "I'm going to need to come up with a name for you."

She pulled the gauze gown over her head and let it slide down her frame, then released the seals on her old dress and waited for it to pool at her feet. Next, she picked up the little vest and did her best to secure it properly. She couldn't reach the back closers and couldn't get the lace to close properly if she used the eyelets to secure it. What she wouldn't do for an extra pair of hands.

Once she did the best she could, she folded her gown and sat it on the bed. The next time she was allowed to go to the pond she would bury it in a safe place.

"Come. I'd like you to meet someone." Heather headed out the door with the wolf on her heals. She was stopped by the android.

"Ialog has asked me to get your Vespian dress."

"Why? He said I could keep it as long as I don't wear it again."

"He wished me to deliver your new gown for your dips in the pond." She placed the new gown on the bed. "He also wants me to seal your old gown in something you wouldn't be able to get into easily. It will also help protect it when you bury it."

Heather sighed again. "It's on my bed. My scanner is still in the pocket. Please leave it on the nightstand." Heather felt she could trust the robot to not mess with her items. The few she had now. "Is Sam available?"

"She is out in the gardens today. Do you wish an escort?"

"Is that your way of saying I can't go there by myself?"

"Let me get your gown first." Her look-alike stepped into Heather's room for a moment before exiting with her gown in hand. "You need help with the vest again?"

Heather nodded and presented her back. Once the vest fitted properly, they fell into step, the clicking of the wolf's claws a new addition to the sounds they made as they walked toward the doors.

The bright sunshine had Heather shielding her eyes. She squinted for a moment as her eyes adjusted. They turned to the left and headed to the gardens.

Heather spotted her daughter quickly. "Sam."

The young girl turned to face them. "Hello, Mother."

———

Mother? Storm looked at the girl, just at the beginning stages of budding into a young woman. Why was she calling Heather mother

He stood between them. Not sure what type of lies Ialog had fed his mate.

Heather laughed. "Don't fear her, she is my daughter."

He studied the girl. She did resemble Heather. Her hair was golden instead of white blond, but she did have the violet eyes. Like most Vespians, she had the bright ring around the edge of the cornea, but hers was golden. Where the gold normally resided was violet. Her eyes were backward from his. He inhaled her scent and it was very close to Heather's.

Daughter? This was the child in the egg? The more he watched her, the more family resemblances he spotted, but how had she aged so quickly? The children inside Heather still had almost a year before they could be born.

"This is Sam." She turned to her daughter. "I'd like you to meet my new friend. I need help coming up with a name for him. Do you think you're up for the task?"

"Really?" Excitement laced her voice. She studied him so intently. She wanted to touch him, he could smell her desire, but she kept her hands behind her instead. "I have never seen a wolf up close like this before."

"Perhaps we could sit?" Heather gestured to the ground before she sat on the soft grass. "See if he'll go to you?"

Sam nodded. She sat next to Heather, a big grin on her face. "So what's next?"

"We wait." Heather touched her hand. "Give him a chance to get used to you."

Storm sat close to them, sniffing them both. The scent between them was almost identical. This was his daughter. He stood on all four paws, looking from Heather to Sam. His mate looked frightened, like she was afraid he wouldn't approach their daughter. He couldn't help himself. He padded over to his mate and gave her a big lick.

The laughter that came after was like music to his ears.

He then moved to their daughter. He sat in front of her and studied her, tilting his head one way then the other. She offered her hand to him, which he nudged up so it rested on his head. She looked at Heather and grinned. Hesitantly, she brushed her fingers against his fur.

"He is beautiful."

"I know." Heather climbed up on her knees and wrapped her arms around him. "So, what should we name him?"

"He's so regal. The alpha male. How about Hero?"

"Hero." Heather patted him on the head. "I like it."

———

Heather tried to leave Hero behind at dinner time, but he wouldn't allow it. When she walked out of the room the first time, he whined as loud as he could. She couldn't leave him when he sounded so wounded. Then she tried several tricks to get him to stay behind, but she couldn't walk away when he fought her.

"Ialog asked me to leave you behind." She had a worried look on her face. "I don't want to jeopardize your chance to stay with me."

"Heather, you are late for dinner."

"I know." She turned to face her look-alike. "He won't stay behind."

The android stood there for a few moments. "Ialog gives permission to bring him, but if he shows any sign of aggression he will rescind his promise that he can stay with you."

"I understand." She looked down at Hero as he trotted beside her. "And I hope you do if you want to continue to have this great roof over your head."

———

Storm gave her a little woof. This would give him a chance to look around. So far, he had only seen the corridor she took from her room to the outdoors. As they followed the android, he used his nose and ears. The doors they passed were closed, but he could hear movement behind a few. They weren't what he was looking for.

Heather brushed against him, making him forget about his reason for being there. He didn't care where they were as long as he was close to her. His desire for her grew, especially when she stripped in front of him the way she had earlier that day. He was sure his heart pounded in his chest as he caught glimpses of her body as one dress came off and the other went on. The way she dressed surprised him, but he knew she probably did it because of all the cameras. Knowing anyone could be watching brought out the shyness he knew lurked just underneath all her bravado.

They entered a formal dining room, which surprised him, but it was familiar. This was where he had sat when he switched places with Heather. Three places were set. Heather took her seat and he lay at her feet. He heard the footsteps of another and one whiff let him know it was their daughter. That only left one person to enter. He sat up and rested his head on Heather's lap. The desire to protect her was so strong, but he knew he couldn't jeopardize anything right now.

She rested her hand on his head as the meal was placed in front of her. Heather pulled her scanner out of her pocket and discreetly scanned her meal before she started to eat.

Having his nose so close to her core had him fighting his desire for her once again. He could smell her need, her frustration. It would be so easy to slip his head under her skirts and use his tongue to taste her once again. Her stripping in front of him earlier made him painfully hard. Knowing all that beautiful flesh was so close had him wanting to throw caution to the wind. It had been too long. His want for her overpowered him. Luckily, he had kept a tight rein on his control.

Heather and Sam talked as they ate, but he didn't listen. He could only think of her essence surrounding him and how badly he wanted to slip within her folds and feel her muscles tighten around him once again.

He felt his hold on this shape start to waiver. Maybe this wasn't such a good idea.

———

Heather found it hard to eat with a wolf at her crotch. She didn't know why, but since he had come into her life, she found it harder to keep her libido in check. How she missed Storm. His touch could bring her to such heights.

"Heather?"

"Yes?" Ialog's voice dragged her out of her thoughts.

"You're not eating again."

"Sorry, lost in thoughts." She picked up her fork and took a few bites. "I would like to ask a question."

He looked at her, waiting.

"Shall I expect Hero to fend for himself or will you provide for him?" The wolf lifted his head from her lap. Was he recognizing his name already?

"I would assume he would look for food when he is hungry. So you are now asking me to feed him as well?"

"No." She speared another item from her plate. "Just wasn't sure if you would let him come and go without question." Heather popped it into her mouth and chewed as she waited for a comment from Ialog.

"He is an animal, Heather. I have no reason to fear him."

"You have no reason to fear me either, yet I can't come and go as I please."

"That is because I know you will run to your mate and never come back."

"That is because I belong with Storm. Not you."

"I created you for me, not him."

"Which is why Sam is now here." She looked at her daughter. It hurt to reveal this information in front of her, but she had no choice. "You know I belong to Storm. That you can't come between us."

"This isn't proper dinner conversation."

She had to agree, although she wanted him to understand keeping her this way was wrong, having Sam there to hear it all wasn't right either. Once the meal was over, she walked back to her room, the only sound was the clicking of Hero's claws against the tiled floor.

She sat on her bed, her feet pulled up against her. There had to be a way to get Ialog to see the truth and let her go home. Hero jumped up on the bed beside her. Her hands buried themselves into his fur. Heather pressed her face into his neck, wishing with all her heart she would see Storm soon. Tears flowed as she held the wolf tight.

———

Storm could see her heart breaking just by looking in her eyes. How he wished he could wipe the pain from her, but all he could do was allow her to cling to him as she tried to regain her composure. It took her a few minutes before she straightened herself and brushed her fingers through his fur.

"I guess I should warn you that I can't sleep." She touched the weird device on her forehead. "This keeps me from getting any rest. I do try, but normally fail."

No wonder she had shown those signs of illness. Kuarto had mentioned she wasn't getting enough sleep but he didn't tell him she wasn't getting any sleep.

She lay on the bed, staring up at the ceiling. Restlessness set in and she shifted to her side before laying on her back again. He wondered why she even tried.

Resting his nose on the edge of the bed, he waited for her to find a comfortable position before he inched closer. Once she adjusted to him being closer, placing her hand on his head and petting him quietly, he shifted again so he could lay his head on her abdomen. Then he inched his head up until his nose rested between her breasts.

Her heart-beat lulled him into deep relaxation. How he had missed something so simple as listening to the beat of her heart. He had the joy of feeling the double beat of his children's hearts against his neck. He hadn't planned on moving anytime soon. Slowly, he noticed her breathing deepened and her body relaxed. She had slipped into a dreamless slumber all because of his presence.

———

Heather opened her eyes, surprised to see the sun streaming into her window. Hero was draped over her, his nose nestled between her breasts. It was intimate yet comforting. It had allowed her to rest for the first time since she had been taken. She ran her fingers through Hero's hair, waiting until he opened his eyes, before trying to sit up. He looked at her with such trust she had to smile.

"You are very good for me." She sat up and stretched. Her body felt rested. Heather swung her feet off the bed and stood. When she opened the door, she was surprised to find her android standing outside. "Have you been standing there all night?"

"Yes." She stepped aside so Heather could leave her room. "When I arrived for our normal walk I found you resting. Knowing how difficult any sleep has been for you to reach, I waited to see if you would feel like walking when you woke. You slept through the night."

"Unusual, but I feel very rested." She fell into step with her look-alike, Hero at her heels. "Do we have enough time before breakfast, then? Ialog doesn't like it when I'm late, but I would love to walk a little. It is about the only exercise I get."

"He has stepped away today so you may break your fast whenever you feel. He does wish you to stick to your basic schedule, but I think he would approve of you walking a little before you eat."

Heather looked at the robot. There were times when she wondered if the ancient computer they found on Vespia had taken over her programming. The way she defended Heather with the wolf yesterday was a perfect example. "I would like that. I'm sure Hero needs to go out too."

They stepped outside into the warm sunshine. Heather looked down at Hero. "I'm sure you need to find food and relieve yourself."

He continued to walk beside her. She tried to shoo him off a couple of times, but he just looked at her like she had lost her mind.

"I'm sure he will go when he is ready," commented the android.

"I guess so." Heather found both of their reactions strange. The wolf should have taken off the moment he stepped outside but didn't, and her look-alike acted like this was normal behavior. "I wasn't aware Ialog had to go anywhere."

"He doesn't answer to you."

She looked at her look-alike. If a human had said it, she would have taken it as an insult. But the machine was just stating facts. "True, but he has always been straight-forward with me. I'm just a little surprised. That is all."

"He didn't think you would be so curious about his mission. He will be back by the end of the day."

Heather nodded. "Since you're allowing me to step away from my basic schedule by this walk is there a chance we can make a few changes in another part of my schedule?"

"I'm not sure I understand." The android looked at Heather.

"Since Ialog is gone I was hoping for a little more time at the pond." Heather took a deep breath of the morning fresh air. "The hour I'm allotted seems so short when I'm there."

"Ialog worries while you are there. He can't keep you under surveillance during that time, so won't know if you are hurt."

Heather knew better. He feared she'd find a way to contact Storm. "I can defend myself. If he wishes to test me, he may do so."

"He knows your capabilities and that you can defend yourself, but it doesn't stop him from worrying."

"May I have more time today or not?" Heather found

talking to the android tiring at times. All she wanted was a yes or no.

"Yes, but I will be near."

"You are always near. Just make sure you keep the distance I requested." Heather smiled. Maybe she could get a little more work done on that block since she didn't get a chance to work on it at all yesterday.

———

Heather sat cross-legged on the grass. With her eyes closed, she focused on the image in her mind. That one corner was almost gone. She was close to breaking through.

The weight of Hero's head as he laid it on her lap jarred her for a moment, coming close to pulling her out of her task. When he remained still after that, she was able to focus once again on the corner of the canvas she had in front of her. Heather kept working at it, pulling and pushing, hoping to break part of it off so she could reach her mate and family. Just when she was about to give up for the day, a small section came off in her hand.

Her mind shifted and stretched, dragging her out of her own body again and into someone else's. Where the hell was she?

She looked down. Male, definitely. He was also naked, with an erection. "Talk about bad timing."

"What did you say, Kuarto?"

"Great. I landed in my brother."

Toki stepped into the room wearing a soft robe. Her hair was wet from a recent bath. "Are you okay?"

"Yes." Heather smiled. "But I think I should warn you. I'm not myself."

"And who do you think you are?" Her hands went to the sash that held the robe closed.

"Heather."

She tightened the ties after she had started to loosen them.

"Don't worry, this won't last very long. Never does." Heather looked around. "Where is Storm?"

"Kuarto told me he went after you. That is all I know."

Heather felt the world go fuzzy once again, and she was back in her own body.

———

Kuarto looked around at the wooded area he suddenly found himself in. "What the hell?" Looking down, he frowned when he spotted breasts, a swelling womb and a wolf on his lap. "Where the hell am I?"

He tried to get to his feet but found the body he was in difficult to move. He ended up staying where he was. "I'm Heather, aren't I?"

The wolf nodded.

"At least I know you found her. Can I assume you haven't left her side? I haven't seen a note and after the first time I left you provisions you haven't touched any of the food I have left for you. Thought you wanted to rescue her."

Storm tilted his head.

"You're right, if it was me I wouldn't have left my mate either. Ohh, I hope Toki understands. We were about to...you know." He knew Storm still had a slight problem with their relationship, so he didn't want to push it. "Have you been able to get into the compound and look for the security system?"

Storm sighed.

"Too many questions, huh? Okay, have you gotten into the compound?"

He nodded.

"What about the security system? Have you been looking for it?"

He growled deep in his throat.

"Okay. I get it. It's kind of hard to just wander the compound as a wolf. You have to stay with Heather to keep this charade up." He paused for a minute. "How are you handling being around her all the time?"

Storm dropped his head to the ground and put a paw over his nose.

"That bad? You know you—" he found himself back in his own body. "Toki?" He touched his chest as he saw his mate. "I'm back."

"What the hell was that?" She looked very mad. "One minute you're begging me to join you in bed and the next minute Heather is talking to me."

"I'm sorry." He walked to her side. "She transferred minds with me. I'm sure she didn't do it on purpose." He wrapped his arms around her.

"I hope not, but why didn't she switch with Storm's mind instead?"

That was the question. Was it because he was the wolf at her side?

———

Heather sat there for a moment. She had just switched minds with Kuarto. Could she do that whenever she wanted now? Was it something she could control?

"Hero, did you notice anything different? Could you tell I wasn't here for a little while?" She doubted it, since his head was still on her lap when she came back.

———

Storm kept his head on her lap, wondering how he should handle this. If she had a direct line to Kuarto now, she might read his mind and find out where he was. If she didn't, then revealing himself might make matters worse. The moment Kuarto stopped talking, he knew they were switching back, so moved quickly to get back to the position she had left him in.

She didn't seem too worried about it because she gave him a quick pat before standing. "I didn't get my bath yesterday, so I need to make sure I do today."

He watched as she removed her new gown, revealing all that glorious skin. Storm wanted to kiss every inch of it. He couldn't help but rub himself up against her naked form just before she jumped into the water.

She floated in the water, little droplets looking like jewels against her skin. Heather paddled to the edge to gather her cleaning supplies and proceeded to wash. What he wouldn't give to be able to offer her a hand, rub the bubbly substance all over her, then slowly rinse her off.

He'd take his time bringing her to ecstasy. Showing her how much she meant to him in every little touch or kiss. His desire for her was becoming painful, knowing he couldn't do anything about it. Storm had to quiet his libido. Leaping into the cold water, he felt it seep into his system, his resolve strengthened.

"Hero? You felt you needed a bath as well?" Heather floated beside him, her hair slicked back against her head.

He snorted. What he needed was her body. Having it this close and not being able to touch it drove him wild.

She dipped under the water once more before climbing out. Picking up her dress, she slipped it on and closed the seals. Once done, she turned to face him. "You can stay in as long as you like, but my allotted time has passed and I'm not sure how much extra time I've been given."

She moved to a nice sunny spot and lay on the soft grass.

With her legs stretched out, she closed her eyes and enjoyed the sunshine.

Storm watched her from the edge of the water. Ialog treated her like a bird in a cage. He wanted her to feel comfortable and had given her several things a prisoner would never earn yet she was still trapped. The pain she felt from her separation was obvious to him. The only time he ever saw a smile was here where she felt safe. Even when she was with their daughter, it wasn't the beautiful one he remembered. It was strained.

———

"You seem disappointed that I came back so early." Ialog sat opposite her at the formal dinner table.

"I did enjoy my time alone today." She gripped the arms of her chair. Every time she faced him she pushed. "Let me go home."

"You are my guest." He nodded at the server nearby, who brought them their meal.

"I don't want to be your guest. I want to go home." Heather looked at the plate in front of her. Food didn't appeal. She was far too homesick to want to eat.

"You really should eat, Heather. It can't be good for the children." He shook a fork at her.

Storm would probably say the same thing.

She folded her hands and placed them in her lap. "Not hungry."

"Heather, I have given you the scanner so you can check everything I give you. I would think you'd want to make sure your unborn children get the nourishment they need."

"Would you be hungry if you were being held against your will?" She gripped the table. "If you missed your family so much you didn't feel whole?"

"I would make sure I kept my strength up. You don't

have it bad here, Heather. I have treated you with great respect."

"But you won't let me go home. Why?" She felt strange. Her mind seemed to stretch. Crap. She was switching bodies again. Who was she taking over this time? And would they be able to fool Ialog long enough for her to return to her frame?

ELEVEN

She felt her mind speed along a path, bringing her into whoever's body rather quickly. They must be close for her to land so fast. She blinked and looked around. Heather frowned. She was still in the same room. Her viewpoint was a little lower, but Ialog was still sitting at the head of the table. What was going on?

Very strange. If she was now sitting on the floor, then who was sitting in the chair? She looked up at herself. There was stark fear in her eyes. Why?

Wait. If she could see herself, then she could only be in one body. Hero's. Heather looked at her paws. Yep, she was definitely the wolf. How?

The list of who this could be was very short, and she knew she could remove two right away. She had just seen them a few hours earlier. That left only one person.

Storm.

———

He realized they had switched and knew he was in trouble. Before, he had been upset when he realized she could move her mind into another body and hadn't done it with him. Now he wished she had picked anyone but him.

Heather probably already knew who the wolf was. She was too smart not to figure it out. If he knew how to make her body respond to his commands, he'd be heading out the door. Instead, all he could do was sit there and watch as she stared at him.

———

Heather stared at the floor for a moment. It made perfect sense. The changes he had been going through pointed to shape-shifter. She never felt comfortable trapped here until the wolf showed up. He made her feel so much more secure. Safe. The same way her mate made her feel.

She looked back up at her own face. But he never expected her to find out this way. Heather had ten thousand questions. They had to talk. How was she going to accomplish that? The only place she knew was clear of surveillance equipment was her little haven, but she had already been there today. Ialog was very specific about where and when she could move around the place. Would he allow her to go back?

Just as quickly, she found herself back in her own body. Storm tried to slink off, but she grabbed him by the fur and didn't let go. He wasn't going to leave her sight until she had a chance to speak to him. She pretended to eat to keep Ialog happy. Once the plate had been removed, she sat back and sighed.

"What, Heather?"

"Nothing." She maneuvered Storm's head back onto her lap so she could pet him. Everything had to look natural. "I had hoped I could spend a little more time at the pond, but that was before you got back."

"You were able to spend more time there than normal

BARBARA DONLON BRADLEY

earlier today. Wasn't that enough?" He sat back in his seat, watching her.

"You're right." Heather stood. Looking down at her mate, she spoke softly. "Come."

"What is it about that place that makes you want to be there so much?"

"It is the only place I feel I can be myself. I also need a few more of those berries, but it can wait until tomorrow." Heather didn't want to wait, but would if she had to. She took a few steps away from the table, making sure Storm came with her. He wasn't going to get a chance to leave her.

"You take and take, yet give so little," Ialog complained.

"You took everything from me. Why should I give anything?" She glared at him as she rubbed her stomach. Her way of showing him her children were about the only thing he hadn't taken from her and she wouldn't put it past him to try to do that too. "You have all the power. I can only do what you allow me to do."

"Fine." He narrowed his eyes at her.

She sensed he was wondering what she really wanted. Heather looked at him, keeping eye contact.

"I will only give you a half an hour," he said with a slight hesitation.

She knew he suspected something, but her comment a few moments ago must have mollified him enough to allow her this. She gave him a slight nod before she headed out the door. Keeping her pace as relaxed as she could, she walked to her room to switch clothes. She knew she couldn't deviate from her normal routine or Ialog would become too suspicious. Once she had been helped out of the vest she switched her dress and headed straight to her little haven.

Checking behind her, she made sure Storm kept up. By the way, the wolf hung his head he knew she wasn't happy with the way she found out the truth. The moment she knew it was safe to talk she turned to face him.

"You have been with me for how long and didn't think to tell me?" He sat at her feet, keeping his head down. Heather wanted answers. "Shift."

He whined at her but remained as a wolf.

"Damn it, Storm." She felt her frustration starting to build. "Talk to me."

He sat there, looking at her for a few more moments before he shifted in front of her. Watching him change was nothing like she thought it would be. No weird half man half wolf combination. One moment he was a wolf, the next her mate stood in front of her, sadness etched on his face.

A sob escaped her. Without saying a word, she ran to him and wrapped her arms around him. Tears fell when she felt his arms wrap around her, too. How she missed something so simple as a hug. His hands touched her, touched her face, making her pull back to look at him again.

"Why are you so sad?" She touched his face as well, half fearing this was only a fantasy and he would be gone the moment she tried to touch him.

"You...not...right."

"This isn't how you planned on letting me know? I hope not." She held him close. "I'm just so glad you're here now."

His hand roamed over her body, touching all the right places to arouse her. She wanted to be with him so bad she had started working on the seals of her dress, then realized Ialog would know. As badly as she needed him she knew they had to stay away from each other. She took a step back.

"...heart...need..." He was having trouble speaking, and she assumed it was a side effect of the shift. His hands moved to her dress, pulling the long skirt up. Motor skills weren't working that well either. He fought with the cloth more than anything.

Heather knew she had to stop him. Make him see this could harm them. She grabbed his hands to halt them from their task. He shook her hands off as he continued to inch the hem of her skirt higher. "Storm. No."

She tried to back away. Her android scanned her constantly and she feared it would show up if they were intimate. No matter how badly she needed him. "Storm, we can't."

He seemed to ignore her words as he wrapped one arm around her waist and held her still as he continued to fight with her dress. His touch sent her desire spiraling out of control but she had to stop him. He wasn't thinking straight.

"Storm, listen to me." She tried to break his hold on her but found his grip sure.

"Must...can't..." Pain filled his eyes as he tried to explain, but words failed him. He held her as he brought them both to the ground. Storm continued to fight with the cloth until he finally got the dress out of his way. In one quick thrust, he buried himself deep inside her.

She shook at the welcoming invasion. Her body stretched to accommodate him. She felt need unfurl inside her. It had been too long. She wanted this as badly as he did, but knew the repercussions could be horrible when they were found out. Her fear for what Ialog could do to her mate had tears sliding down her cheeks. But she couldn't, wouldn't, stop him now. It was already too late. All it would take was one drop of semen for Ialog to know the truth, and she knew that could have already happened. Besides, they needed each other too badly.

"Dress...please...off."

Emotions boiled inside her as desire warred with logic. She knew he was too far gone to be stopped, but she would be lying to herself if she said she didn't want this. She gave in to her needs and allowed the joy of being with her mate once again to fill her the way it always did. Heather worked at the seams that held the dress together so they could be flesh to flesh. A sigh escaped her when she felt his skin rubbing against hers. Tears formed in her eyes again as joy raced through her blood. To have him with her, inside her once more was more than she could handle. Those tears spilled down her cheek.

His lips found her mark, sucking it into his mouth as he pounded into her. His tongue played against the tender skin, arousing her, making her whole body shake at the power of the threatening climax. He filled her again and again. Each time he filled her everything tightened. She could feel her muscles clamp down on him. The friction between them increased. She arched up against him. "So close."

The vibration started in her chest first. Storm felt it too, because he moved his mouth from her throat to her lips just in time to swallow the scream she released when her orgasm overtook her.

————

He made her scream. Normally he would be elated, but he had also made her fear him and that was the one thing he never wanted to do. His vocal cords had finally settled into place so he could speak again. He wasn't sure why it took so long this time but it must have been because he had held the wolf form for so long.

"My heart, I never meant to frighten you." He brushed hair from her face. Saddened by what he did to her.

She smiled and touched his face tenderly. "Storm, you will never frighten me. You are my heart, too. I just wanted to warn you, to stop you before it was too late because he's going to know. He has that android scan me all the time. Ialog says it's to make sure the children are okay, but he's probably looking for signs of your presence. He has to know we can't stay away from each other."

"I don't care. Being with you without being able to touch you was killing me. I came here to find his security system, but being near you sidetracked me a little." He grinned as he looked down at her. "Do you know where he keeps it?"

"No. He only allows me to go in certain areas. If I try to veer off, my look alike steers me back."

"Then you'll have to tell me where you can't go. It has to be there." He slid his fingers along her jawline.

"Turning off the defenses won't let me leave."

"Why not?" He frowned. "Is it because of Sam?"

"There is this remote Ialog has that controls this." She pointed to the metal on her forehead. "He can control my motor reflexes with it, stop me from leaving. Sam has the same type of thing, but hers can kill her if she goes too far out of range. All I know is it is tied to her insert."

"Could it be tied to the remote?"

"I don't know." She shook her head. "When I ask too many questions it raises flags."

"We'll figure out a way to get that remote from him. Maybe having that will free you both."

"He never leaves it out, but always has it with him." She shifted under him and sucked in her breath. "I've been threatened with it several times, so I know he always has it close."

"My heart, I'll get it from him, even if I have to kill him."

"That's just it, you can't." She touched his face again. She still feared he'd disappear in front of her, so she found she had to keep touching him to prove to herself he was really with her. "My look-alike explained to me that he won't die from a mortal wound."

He growled and he felt her muscles tighten around him. "You are very sensitive."

"It has been too long." She stretched and slid her legs along his.

"I thought you were worried about Ialog finding out?" Her movements made him need her all over again. He started to nibble on her throat. Lathing her mark between kisses.

"That was before, but now all I can think about is you inside me and the joy we feel when we reach our orgasms." She lifted her hips a little and smiled when she felt him pulse inside her.

"Now that is the mate I know and care for." He pulled out and slid back in, making Heather arch against him as he stroked just the right spot.

"Oh, you are in trouble. Be prepared." She looked at him. "My body has begged for release so much I just might explode."

"You didn't masturbate at all?"

"I tried, but it just wasn't the same. You have spoiled me, my heart."

"I find that hard to believe." He knew her sexual appetite was as strong as his. That was one of the things that made them a good match.

"Really?" She shifted in his arms, practically purring when he went in a little deeper. "Did you?"

He blinked at her question. "No."

"Use a pleasurer?"

"Of course not." He knew she would say it was alright, but both were quite territorial when it came to each other's body. If he had, it would have hurt her.

"Then why is it so hard to believe that I couldn't?"

"Because I have created a monster when it comes to sex." He started moving within her, setting a tempo that could make her moan her delight.

"But I'm your favorite monster." She sucked in her breath and wrapped her legs higher on his waist. "No more talking. That android will be back soon, and I want to be sure we're both satisfied. At least for a little while."

Storm wrapped his arms around her to keep her secure as he shifted into a seated position with his legs beneath him.

He knew their minds wouldn't meld, but their bodies knew what to do to bring them to the heights they wanted to reach.

Heather leaned her head against him, a sigh of contentment escaping her.

His fingers slipped into her folds, finding the spot that always made her shatter in his arms. As he helped her set the tempo again his hand stayed between them, squeezing and massaging her until he sensed she was about to moan.

They couldn't be heard. The risk was too great, so he covered her lips with his, drawing her tongue into the dance they always shared, pulling her moan into his mouth.

Her arms wrapped around him as she rode him, holding him as close as she could. She broke the kiss as her head dropped back.

He continued to rub that one spot within her folds, which caused her body to shake as she drew closer to her orgasm. Heather quickened the pace, her sheath squeezing him in an exquisitely tight hold. Storm felt his orgasm gathering steam, too.

Naturally, his mind reached for hers but found disappointment when there was no connection. It was something so automatic for them. Her body started to quake in his arms. Storm placed his hands on her hips and kept up the pace. The intensity of this release was just as strong as the last one for her, and he knew all she could do was feel right now.

Heather sucked in her breath as she hit her orgasm. He felt her vibrate, muscles contracting against him. The way they rippled, tightened, then squeezed sent him over the edge as well. Even without the mindmeld they hit their release as one.

He held her after that, enjoying the way their bodies were intertwined. He hated breaking the moment they just had, but it was time to go back. "We need to talk about the earlier rescue attempt."

"Rescue attempt? What rescue attempt?" She leaned back to look at him.

"You didn't hear anything? There wasn't a heavy shift of guards?"

She shook her head. "No. Nothing."

"Earth security tried a rescue attempt that wiped out every single person. Ialog has a defense that can evaporate a person with no sign of a weapon. What we noticed when we watched the attempt was that the humans were eradicated, but the animals weren't."

"How many?" Her eyes held unshed tears.

"Enough." He didn't think she needed the extra burden of knowing how many died trying to save her.

"Then how did you get in here?" Her eyes widened. "It let your wolf through?"

He nodded. "Kuarto found out when I shift, my human DNA is masked. It tricked the system."

"But he rented this place. According to what my look alike told me, he couldn't alter anything. The government has the area wired and they would know about any changes."

"Bear made a comment about that. I'll have to get that info to Fridon so he can see what he can find out. He is working on your rescue while I'm here." He nuzzled her neck, finding it hard to keep his hands to himself. "And Bear promised to help us. We'll get the answers. What else have you learned?"

"You keep this up and I won't be able to focus." She relaxed in his embrace as his lips turned her body into jelly. "I know there is a lot more to the complex than what I've seen."

"Have you asked the robot to let you into the other areas?" He lifted his face so he could look in her eyes.

"No. Ialog is strict in where I go and what I see."

"Keep trying. Perhaps I can help in that aspect."

"Don't do anything out of character. He might seem all calm and sweet, but he is very dangerous and very suspicious." She touched his face once again before she realized time was flying by. Heather was the first to move. "I'm going into the pond."

"Your worry over me isn't necessary."

"Storm, the man hates you as much as you hate him. Put yourself in his shoes. What would you do if you found out your enemy had been able to sneak into your camp, was trying to learn your weaknesses, and had sex with what you coveted?"

"I'd probably kill him."

"Thank you. Hence the pond. Let's see if I can wash away enough of the evidence to keep us safe so you can get the information you need." She jumped in and submerged herself. "I don't want him to suspect anything."

Storm decided to join her.

"You are defeating the purpose." She swam to the side and grabbed her cleaning supplies.

"I thought I could help." His innocent look wasn't lost on her. Heather laughed. It felt good to hear her laughter again.

"I would be very happy with your help, another time. Right now, I think you need to let me do this."

"But I can reach some of those places that might be hard for you."

She knew he would just take advantage of being able to touch her body once again, but the wonderful cocoon they had developed shattered at the sound of the android.

"Heather."

"Yes." She turned to where the android stood just beyond their sight.

"It is time."

"Already?" Heather washed herself quickly before she climbed out of the water and walked to her dress. The fear she felt flashed in her eyes as she watched Storm, as a wolf, climb out of the pond as well. He had shifted when he heard the android. Now he stood next to her, looking up at her as if this was the most natural thing they did.

He was right. No one would suspect a thing if she didn't show her fear. She took a deep breath and plastered a smile on her face to mask her worry. Turning, she approached the spot where the robot waited. "That went by very quickly."

He padded along beside her.

"You look very relaxed. I am glad you were able to finally masturbate."

Heather could only give her a plastic smile.

———

She sat at the table the next morning for breakfast. Hunger had a grip over her, but it wasn't for food. Knowing her mate sat at her feet had her wanting something she shouldn't. They could get caught too easily.

The fact that no one said anything yet made her nervous. She had washed herself best she could to try to get rid of any evidence, but she knew better than to assume they were safe. Had she been scanned without her knowledge?

"You seem awfully quiet this morning." Ialog pulled a few pieces of fruit onto his plate. "Understand you have been able to rest better."

"Hero helps me relax." She patted him on the head. He leaned into her and rested his head on her lap. "And I thought you didn't want to argue at every meal."

"I don't." He watched her for a moment. "I have another dress for you to wear."

"Why?" A new dress? What was he up to? "Are you making changes to my schedule today?"

"Why?"

"Because you have been known to change it from time to time, especially when you do something like give me another dress. You said this one would keep me clean, so why would you give me a new one? Is there something going on?" She set her fork down. Did he know? Was he planning on examining her dress for evidence?

"Your schedule shall remain the same." He watched her for a moment or two before he waved his hand to have his plate cleared. "I'm expecting company for lunch. You think you can control your animal long enough for us to enjoy a meal without him?"

"I don't know. He does have a mind of his own." She stood. "But I will do my best to get him to stay in my cell. May I be dismissed?"

He nodded.

Her android walked her out of the hall and took her back to her room. She held the new gown in her hand. "He only questioned you because of the changes you wanted yesterday."

"Ialog keeps saying he wants me to feel comfortable here, yet he questions every little thing I do. Never lets me go where I wish. I never know what to think." She sat on her bed. Fear for being found out had her worrying about everything. "I am nothing more than some trophy for him to flaunt." She ran her fingers through Hero's fur. "Who is the guest?"

"Your brother." Her look-alike handed her the dress.

"Brother?" She frowned. Heather never told Ialog about a brother. She remembered he had mentioned her brother before, but she had never responded to his comment.

"Yes. Kuarto."

"Kuarto?" Heather busied herself by lifting the gown to see what made it so special. "Why him?"

"Because Ialog thought if he let him come and examine you, you might believe he only has your best interests at heart."

"I never mentioned I had a brother. How did he find out?" She knew better than to try to deny this.

"He knew you had shared a womb with someone else all along, so knew you had a twin somewhere in the universe. He wasn't aware it was the doctor until he ran his first test on Kuarto while he was a guest at his other compound. His DNA pattern revealed his relation to you."

That made sense. He did seem to know a lot about her. "And the fact that my brother is a doctor and can report back that I am healthy didn't have any influence."

"Ialog wishes you to show your brother that you are happy here."

"But I'm not. I want to go home." Heather set the gown beside her on the bed.

"That will not happen."

"Does he have a direct line to you?" Her words were so close to what Ialog would say she already suspected the answer. "Does he know what we talk about while we're talking?"

"Yes." She tilted her head at Heather. Something she picked up from being around her so much. "Why?"

"That lack of privacy thing. How can I trust him or you if I feel like I'm being spied on?"

She watched Heather for a moment. "You wish to speak to me candidly?"

"There have been times when I did. To know Ialog eaves-dropped bothers me." Heather never told her anything she didn't want Ialog to know because she knew the android couldn't grasp the concept of what it meant to keep informa-tion from him. "I knew you informed him of our conversa-tions, but never suspected he listened in."

"And that bothers you."

"Yes." Heather patted the bed, inviting Hero to join her. She buried her face into his fur for a moment. "What has Kuarto been told?"

"That you are healthy and safe."

"Why not let Storm come instead?" She petted Hero on the head.

"Out of the question. Your mate would try to take advantage of being physically near you. Ialog can't allow that. He hopes if your brother proves you are doing fine under his care, Storm might back off."

"My mate will never stop until he gets me back." Heather looked up at the android. "No matter how pretty you make this look he won't stop until I'm home."

"Your brother will be here in two hours. Your daughter will be joining you when you speak to him." She picked up the dress. "I will help you change."

———

Heather was happy to see Kuarto. He smiled, his relief to see her healthy evident.

"You look wonderful." He pulled her into his embrace. "No dark circles under the eyes. How did you manage that?"

"My little buddy here." Heather returned the hug before she brushed her fingers through Storm's fur. "He found the berries for me."

"Berries?"

"Yes. He seemed to know what I needed and brought me these simple berries. The android has scanned and studied them. I'm sure she has all the data you need to study to see how they helped. I'm just glad they worked for me."

"Well, I'm glad he found you." He patted the wolf on the head, but she could see he was leery of him. "Ialog has said I can see your files when our visit is over, so I'll check into the information about the berries then."

"How is Storm?" She watched as her brother looked at the wolf before answering her question. In that instant, she knew Kuarto was aware of Storm's shape-shifting ability.

"Worried about you and your children." He looked at her. "He wants you home."

"I want to be home. I miss him terribly." She looked at Storm before she looked back at her brother and shrugged. "But as Ialog has said I am healthy and safe, so are the children."

"Is that the theme of this meeting?" He offered her his arm. "We're all okay?"

"That was what I was told to tell you." She linked arms with him. "Do you mind if we walk a little? It's one of the few things I do get to do here without too much of a hassle."

They walked outside, Storm at their heels. The bright sunlight making her blink before her eyes adjusted. She looked behind them to check for the android. Heather was surprised her shadow didn't follow her.

"Why do you keep looking behind you?"

"Sorry. This is the first time my lookalike hasn't followed me everywhere. It's a little strange." She took her time walking, discreetly pointing when she could, making sure he could see all the cameras and listening devices along the way. "How is Toki?"

"Worried about you, too." He patted her arm. "I was surprised Al let me come and see you."

"He believes I will accept my circumstances if I'm allowed to see family members." She sighed. "He doesn't understand that my heart is Storm and I want to be at his side."

"You don't think he's going to let you go?"

"There are a couple of small problems. One is this piece of metal. It's like the one Toki had on her neck. He can literally stop me if I try to leave." Heather looked at her brother. "Then there is Sam."

"Sam?"

"You'll see." She gave her brother her brightest smile. "Ialog had a few surprises for me when I arrived."

"Did you tell him I was your brother?" Kuarto looked at her.

"He figured out this one on his own. The details he knows about my life is kind of scary." She brushed her fingers through the wolf's fur.

"Are you holding up okay?" He touched her shoulder. The doctor in him had him looking for tale-tell signs of abuse. "Getting enough to eat? Sleep?"

"Okay, I guess." She patted Hero's head. "Ialog gave me a scanner so I can check the food they put in front of me, so I'm eating better. And Hero here has helped me relax and sleep." She touched the small slip of metal on her forehead. "This won't let me reach REM, so I wasn't sleeping until he showed up."

"It seems odd that Ialog would let you have a pet."

"I know." She brushed her fingers through Storm's fur again. "It's like he's confident I won't be leaving any time soon, so wants me comfortable. He keeps trying to defend my incarceration. But I refuse to alter the way I feel about being here."

"Yes." Kuarto hesitated as he tried to choose his words. "Storm is working with your government to bring you home."

"That explains what is taking so long. Tell Storm not to use the rent a cops my government can use." She saw Kuarto frown for a moment. Heather hoped he would figure out the keywords she gave him to bring back to Fridon and Bear.

"I was worried when I got your last set of readings." He pulled out his scanner. "I want to update your files. Your transmitter is sending data from time to time, but not enough to keep me happy."

"I get scanned all the time by my doppelganger. I'm sure if you ask her nicely she'll share." Heather wrapped an arm around his waist. "Besides, I have something more important for you to scan."

"I want my own data, thank you very much." He slowed her down. Heather sighed, but stopped long enough for him to use his little device. He checked the readings real quick before he stuck it back in his pocket. "So what is it you want me to see?"

Heather saw Sam waiting next to her android. "Storm's and my daughter."

"Excuse me?" Kuarto's steps slowed.

"The egg you fertilized? Remember that?" At his nod, she continued. "Ialog had the incubation time sped up. She's aging quicker too. At the rate she's growing, she'll be an adult in a very short time."

They approached Sam, who stood next to the robot, unmoving. Heather gestured for her to step away from her look-alike and join her and her brother.

"Sam, this is my brother." She wrapped an arm around the young woman. "Your uncle."

"I have an uncle?" She showed a little more enthusiasm when she realized who he was. She studied him as much as he studied her. He broke out his scanner and ran it around her.

"How old was she when you first arrived?" He looked at Heather.

"She looked about eight then, but has been maturing so fast I haven't been able to calculate her age properly." Heather touched her daughter's hair and the child leaned into her like it was the most natural thing to do.

Kuarto scanned her, studying her face while he did it. "You look just like your mother."

"Thank you." She watched him with wide-eyed curiosity. "What does that do?"

"It allows me to see your insides." He looked at the readings. "Make sure everything is working okay."

"It gives you the information like my insert gives me."

"You have an insert?"

"Yes. It allows me to download information I need."

"Then this is close." He looked at Heather, who ran her hand over her block. Kuarto made a few adjustments and ran it again. "It looks to see if there are any problems inside you."

"Did you find anything?"

"You are very healthy." He smiled at her. "And about fourteen now. You should shoot up in your height very soon."

"I have already started." She looked up at her mother.

Heather brushed a stray hair behind Sam's ear. "Go on back to your studies and I'll come by and see you later. Okay?"

Sam smiled, hugged her, then headed back to the android.

"I have something for you." He held out his hand and revealed her rings.

She touched them reverently, wishing she could take them. "Keep them safe for me."

"You don't want them?"

"I do, but I'm afraid that if I wear them anywhere near Ialog he'll take them from me again and destroy them. I can't take that chance. They mean too much to me."

Kuarto slipped them back into his pocket. "They're safe until you come home."

"Thank you." She walked a little further before she spoke again. "So how are my readings?"

"Overall great." He looked at his scanner. "I'm not seeing any signs of the issues you had a couple of weeks ago. And my last update from your scanner showed you hadn't been eating, so I was worried you were close to losing the children."

"To be honest I was too. I couldn't trust anything Ialog fed me. Not after the way he drugged me the last time he held me captive."

"Then he gave you the scanner?"

"Yes. It was brand new so I had to program it myself." She held it out to him so he could look at it.

Kuarto took it from her, rolling it in his hand as he studied it. "So it is working for you?"

"So far."

He held it up and ran a scan. "Seems to be almost as good as mine."

Heather grinned as he handed it back to her. "Then I'll take that as a good thing." She looked down at the wolf. "And Hero here. He came to me at just the right moment. Like a knight in shining armor. If he hadn't been there and given me these particular berries, I'm afraid I would have lost our children." She felt the pain she had felt then all over again.

"Storm would have never forgiven me if I had lost them because of my pride," her voice came out small, frightened.

"What are you talking about?"

"I should have done anything to protect my children." She looked at Kuarto, unshed tears made her eyes overly bright. "He said that to me over and over again, but I never listened. Even when I put their life at risk. I didn't trust Ialog to have my best interest at heart. Didn't know what he could have done to me and to them through food and drink. Not knowing made me put them in harm's way."

"Heather." Kuarto lifted her chin so she would look him in the eyes. "Storm would have understood."

"I know. He would have said all the right things if some-thing had happened, but I know deep inside he would have wondered if there was more I could have done. I would have wondered the same thing. I would have never forgiven myself and no matter what he would say to me I would have felt like I failed him." Heather hugged herself. "That's why the name Hero fits him. He saved me when I couldn't save myself."

"You can't blame yourself for these circumstances." Kuarto wrapped her in his arms. "Your mate would never question any decision you had to make while you were or should I say are kidnapped."

"But Ialog hasn't harmed me." She didn't want to be touched so moved away to break his contact with her. "I jeopardized my children needlessly."

"You have not harmed your children." He paused as the rest of her words sunk in. "He hasn't tried anything?"

"No. As crazy as this sounds he has been the perfect gentleman." She looked at her brother, one tear finally sliding down her cheek. "I really only see him at meals where I annoy the life out of him by begging to be sent back home and then I go back to my room."

"Interesting."

"As hard as he tried to make me believe Storm wasn't my mate the last time I'm not quite sure why he hasn't tried again." Hero bumped her leg and whined. She petted him. "I know you don't like hearing this, but I've been asking myself the same question over and over again. Why? Why kidnap me if he hadn't planned on making me his, one way or another. It just doesn't make sense."

"Could he have gotten in too deep and not know how to get out?"

"Anything is possible." Heather continued to walk with Kuarto. "If I could read his mind I'd be able to answer all of these questions."

"I wanted to ask you about that strip across your forehead."

"Ah, my blocker. A whole lot of fun. Can't sleep with it. At least not reach REM so I'm not resting properly. Ialog placed it here to keep me from using any part of my mind and to keep me here."

"Does he know what you can do?"

"Probably more than I do." She shrugged her shoulders.

"I have barely scratched the surface of what I can do and he has to know that."

Silence fell between them. Heather looked at her brother. "Can I ask a favor?"

"Of course." Kuarto smiled at her.

"Toki told me of an ancient prayer that she thought would help me. In fact, Uncle mentioned it once or twice too. I'd like a copy of it."

"Okay. Do you remember the name of it?"

"Sorry." She gave him a look she hoped he recognized. The prayer she wanted was the one uncle used to bind Ialog.

"I'll ask them both and see if they can remember which it is." He gave her a confused look. Kuarto would do his best but wasn't sure if he would be successful.

"Thanks." She knew their time was coming to an end. Her shadow had been trailing then for the last few minutes. "Make sure everyone knows I'm okay. I miss them and want to be home very badly, but I'm being treated well."

"What do you want me to tell Storm?"

"My heart knows." She ruffled Hero's fur. "Isn't that right?"

"I'll come back if Ialog allows me to." He looked at her and then the wolf.

Heather smiled. It was the only way she could think of to let him know she knew where Storm was without Ialog figuring it out. "I hope you get to come back. It's nice to have a familiar face around. Even if it is only for a few moments."

She hugged her brother once more before she said her goodbyes and walked back into the building.

She headed to the doors to spend her hour near the pond when she heard her name. Turning, she looked at Ialog. "Yes?"

"Did you enjoy your visit?"

She looked down at Hero. Not sure why he asked. "Yes. Thank you."

He seemed happy with her thanks because he allowed her to continue outside to her oasis. Whenever he spoke to her, she became nervous. What was he up to? What did he really want? He always had a reason for everything he did.

She stopped once she was within the area where she knew there were no security devices. Turning to face Storm she waited for him to shift. The moment he did she peeled off her dress and stepped up to him. There was no need for talking. They knew what they wanted.

TWELVE

Storm captured her lips with his as he picked her up. Her long legs wrapped around him, guiding him to where she wanted him most. After centering himself on her core, he thrust himself deep inside her then held her as her body settled around him. Her wet, hot sheath hugged his shaft. The magnificent sensation drove him to his knees. He heard her purr as the jarring movement made him slip in a little bit further.

Heather held on to him tightly as their bodies took a moment to adjust to their joining. Storm's mouth moved from her lips to her throat, seeking out her sensitive mark. All he had to do was breathe on it now and he felt the muscles surrounding him react. Her heightened sensitivity sent a little thrill through him.

She started to move up and down, drawing a moan from him as her muscles slid against him. "My...heart." He still was having a little problem speaking. It was going to take a little more time before his vocal cords settled down once again.

"God, Storm, I'm going to explode."

"Not...too...soon."

Heather closed her eyes and tilted her head back. She picked up the pace, building an exquisite friction between them. He helped guide her, but she had control over how their mutual release would happen. She squeezed him tight as a ripple raced through her. "Oh."

He lathed the side of her throat, causing those muscles to constrict and release him once again. She was close. Storm could smell it. Excitement raced through her blood. She clutched at him, trying to reach the climax that was eluding her for the moment. He held her hips and pushed against her with a little grinding action and she splintered into a thousand pieces in his arms.

Every time they were together it was glorious. Even now, with these stolen moments, it was no different. She did things to him that made him so happy she was a part of his life. His orgasm had been just as powerful as hers, but he didn't even care if he had one as long as she was there to share such a wonderful intimacy with him.

He held her close, brushing her hair away from her face. "You are...so beautiful."

"You make me that way." She touched his face gently.

"Why would...you think that I...would be upset if...you had lost the children while...you were here?" Every time she berated herself he had wanted to stop her as she spoke to Kuarto, but all he could do was listen.

He saw the shadow fill her eyes. "Because you would find a way to get around it if you were in this situation."

"Heather, you are...the most important thing to me." His vocal cords were with him once again. "Would I mourn the loss of our children?" He had to pause. "Of course I would, but you are my life." His fingers caressed her face. "I can't live without you."

She wouldn't look at him.

"My heart." He hugged her, not sure what he could say that would convince her he would never blame her if she had lost their children.

"I came so close, Storm. When you showed up that first day, I knew I was really close to losing them. If you hadn't come to my rescue, then I would have." She rested her head on his shoulder. "And because of this stupid block, I can't see if there is any kind of damage done to their delicate brains. I have been able to chip away at it so I know they gained from the berries, but I don't know how much the berries healed. I hope I haven't harmed them."

"So we need to see if there is a way to break through that device." He wanted to take that pain away. If he had been doing his job, she never would have been taken.

Heather nodded. Tears spilling from her eyes and running down his chest.

"What about the book?" He brushed more tears from her cheek.

"The ones the ancients left for me?" She looked up at him. "I don't know. There was a lot of information I haven't touched in there. There could be something to help me break this device's hold."

"Then I'll get them for us and give you the chance to find out."

———

Storm sat next to the tree where he was to leave messages for Kuarto, waiting for his system to settle properly so he could record the note to have Kuarto bring their books to them. He heard a sound behind him and rose to defend himself. Kuarto came around the corner just as he regained his vocal cords.

"Sorry. Didn't mean to startle you, but had hoped you

would show up." Kuarto held his hands up to show he meant no harm. "How long has Heather known?"

"What are you talking about?"

"Please." He held up his scanner. "This doesn't miss a thing."

"Then she is in danger." Storm had to get back to make sure she was protected.

"Why?"

"If that thing can detect she's had sex recently, then Ialog would know as well. Even if he is acting like he doesn't."

"Not necessarily. It depends on what he has his system programmed to scan for."

"I can't take any chances. Is everyone in place?"

"Of course. They are awaiting orders." Kuarto nodded. "You found the sentry computer?"

"No. Ialog doesn't allow Heather to go too many places inside the compound. I was hoping to talk her into asking for a tour, acting like she is settling in."

"Fridon thinks he knows where it is." Kuarto broke out the blueprints they had gotten from Bear. "This is the dining area where I met Heather. Where is her room?"

"Down this corridor here." Storm showed him the spot.

"Right past the dining hall and leads to the outside." He touched the area Storm spoke about, then moved his finger to another area. "Fridon believes it is here."

"And he has everything ready for the moment I get that shield to drop?"

"Yes. We already have troops in place waiting for your signal. What should we look for?"

"Unless I can join you I'll have to give the signal in my other form."

"So listen for a howl. Got it."

"Good. Heather wants her leather book. The one I started carrying around with me after she was kidnapped. Bring both in case we need them." Storm shifted and took off. He never should have left her side.

———

"Where is your shadow?" asked Ialog.

Heather gestured over her shoulder. Her look-alike stood a few feet down the corridor, waiting for her to move.

"I don't mean my android. I'm talking about the wolf."

"Oh. He takes off from time to time." His question made her nervous. Being trapped inside without Storm there worried her. "I'm assuming he has gone to find food or meet up with his pack for a few moments. He always comes back."

"So he has done this before."

"Sure, but he normally does it while I'm near the pond." She smiled at Ialog. "I think he senses I need time to myself and gives it to me."

He watched her. Heather had no idea why he wanted to question her, so she stared back, keeping her fear locked up deep inside. He looked like he was about to say something when he heard the barking of her pet.

She continued to stare at him. Those cold blue eyes staring back. Fear that Ialog wouldn't let Storm back in pierced her, but she kept it at bay while she waited for him to do something. "You going to let him back in, or do I have to go outside to be with him?"

He broke eye contact long enough to nod at a guard who allowed Storm to enter. The wolf trotted to her side and sat at her feet.

"Anything else?"

"No." He looked from Heather to Hero. Running his fingers through his blond hair he said, "You are free to go."

Heather turned and walked toward her room. Once in her room, she gave Storm a hug. "Glad to have you back.

Ialog didn't realize you took off every day to do whatever it is you do when you leave. He wasn't pleased."

Hero bumped her arm.

"I know, maybe he'll start feeding you so you won't have to go off the way you do." She wrapped her arms around his neck. "I'm just glad you're back."

He rested his head on her shoulder.

Nervous, Heather spent the next few hours with her daughter, then kept herself as busy as possible, walking or meditating, until it was time for dinner. Ialog watched her with his never wavering gaze, but remained silent. She wasn't sure what to think about that. Instead of questioning him she ate her meal quietly. Her head was starting to ache a little, so she asked to be excused. Hero followed her back to her room and jumped up on the bed. "I see. You think I need a nap?"

Hero barked at her.

"Okay, fine. I'll try to rest for a little while." She lay on the bed and he rested his head on her ribcage, so his nose lay between her breasts. The ache she felt intensified. Shooting pains raced through her brain next and she knew she was in trouble.

———

Storm sensed something wrong while they were at dinner. Heather started to smell wrong. Then he noticed a change to her aura. Not knowing what to do had him whining. Once she lapsed into unconsciousness, he started barking. He barked and barked before her door finally opened, revealing the android. It didn't matter who stood there as long as they helped his mate.

She stepped into the room and noticed Heather's unconscious body. She lifted one eyelid before picking her up in her arms and carrying her down the hall. Storm followed, his nails clicking against the hard floor.

They entered the medical area. He looked to the right. That was the corridor the system should be on. He wanted to go down it, but couldn't leave his mate. The android dropped Heather onto the only bed in the place and hooked her up to the monitors around it. It didn't take long before Ialog walked in.

"Is there a problem?" He spotted Storm in the room. "And what is he doing here?"

"He has sat there the whole time, so I didn't see his presence as a problem." She continued to work on Heather's body. "She is unconscious."

"What is causing this?" He stepped up to look at her readings.

"Unknown." She watched data fill the screen at a lightning pace, pressing the screen from time to time. Storm couldn't keep up with the speed. "It seems that your inhibitor is causing this."

"Has her mind started expanding faster?" He moved to another monitor to check those readings as well. "That is the only thing that could cause this."

"Her mind has been expanding at the same speed as before and the inhibitor has kept up with that." The android pulled up the information on Heather's mind to show there had been no change. "This is caused by something else. What about the visions she has been known to have? That is something this device wouldn't be able to control."

"She doesn't have that many for it to be a factor."

"True, but her mind does warn her when her life is threatened. There is no way to predict when a vision will happen." The android continued the train of thought even though he had dismissed it. "If her mind is trying to warn her about something and the device is blocking that, then her mind could draw her in deep to circumvent the device. That safety feature would have to find a way to get her the information if the normal way is blocked."

"And you think that is what is happening?" Ialog studied the data, touching a few spots when something caught his attention.

Storm wondered if that was what was going on with his mate. Not being able to touch her mind had him fearing the worst.

"Yes. If she goes in deep enough, when she comes back out, she could destroy the inhibitor."

"She cannot be allowed to escape."

"I can place another device to allow you to control her motor skills, but she will learn how to overpower that as well. Her mind will be able to stop it from controlling her."

"Do it. I'll create something to replace the inhibitor." Ialog looked at Storm. "In the meantime, please get rid of that wolf."

"Of course." She walked over to him and scooped him up. The hold she grabbed him in wouldn't allow any escape. The moment they stepped out of the building she released him. "I know you are concerned about Heather, but so is Ialog. He doesn't want any harm to come to her, either."

Storm wasn't sure what to do. If he fought to get back inside, he could get hurt and be no good to his mate. He whined as he paced in front of Heather's look-alike.

"I promise to get you the moment she gains consciousness again."

He watched in frustration as she walked back in, allowing the door to close behind her. Being a wolf had its drawbacks. Storm decided to check to see if Kuarto had brought the books he had asked for, so he ran to the spot they had chosen just outside the compound. There, in their little hiding place, were the two books as well as a note.

Storm,

Here's the books and the prayer Heather asked for.
Kuarto

Everything was placed in a small satchel for him to carry easily in his animal form. Once he found a safe place to bury it, he headed back to the door where he had been evicted and waited.

It wasn't long before the android came out to where he sat. "You may come in. Heather is awake and has been asking for you."

He jumped as she opened the door. The moment he cleared the opening, he took off, loping down the hallway until he bounced off the door to the room she was in. He skidded to a stop next to the bed. The moment he bounded into the room she sat up.

"Hero!" She patted the bed so he would jump up and join her. He hesitated for a moment before jumping up beside her. A sigh escaped her when she wrapped her arms around his neck. "So glad to see you."

"Do you wish to walk, Heather?" Her doppelganger asked.

"That would be nice." Heather swung her legs off the bed and stood. "Perhaps you could explain to me what happened."

"I can tell you what I know." The android gestured for her to walk in front of her. Once they were back outside, they walked side by side, with Storm trotting beside his mate. "Hero started barking and scratching at the door. His odd behavior brought me to your room. I found you on your bed, unconscious, so I picked you up and carried you to the lab."

Heather nodded.

"Did you have another vision?"

"Yes." She didn't keep this to herself, which surprised Storm. "One that really frightens me."

"What was your vision?"

BARBARA DONLON BRADLEY

Heather laughed. "I wish it was that easy. It's all very fuzzy right now. It will take me some time to work through it."

"Perhaps I can help you with that."

Heather hesitated for a moment. "The images are jumping around too much. Can I have a little time? I need to sort them out a little more before I figure out their sequence."

"Of course."

"I have noticed the block has been removed." She touched her forehead and felt nothing but skin. Storm had noticed it was missing too and had wondered about it. "Why?"

"Because you destroyed it. When you were found unconscious, there were only a few things that could have caused that. When your visions wanted to reach you and couldn't, they pulled you deep inside. When you came back out of the vision, the power of your mind came with you and caused you to short-circuit the device. It's a prototype, so there was no repairing it."

With the inhibitor gone their minds could be one once again. Storm reached for her mind. Joy shot through him when they connected. Now he could let her know what he needed to get her home.

"How does Ialog plan on controlling me now?"

"He can't control your mind and he knows it." The android touched the back of Heather's neck. "But Ialog still wishes to keep you as his guest. This will give him that ability."

"Is this like the one Toki had on her neck?"

"Yes."

"Interesting." Heather knew better than to argue now. She looked down at Storm. Her smile spoke volumes. "And how long do you think this will keep me here?"

"Long enough for him to create a new one."

"He is afraid of what I can do or he never would have put that thing on my forehead in the first place."

"Yes."

"And he'll do whatever it takes to keep me here?"

"Yes."

"That is what worries me."

———

It felt like forever before they could go to Heather's little haven. She stood a few feet away while Storm sat and shifted back to human. When she went unconscious, his heart dropped to his toes. Not knowing what caused it had frightened him.

Their minds touched, but he had problems communicating with her as a wolf.

Heather removed her dress, then approached him. He wrapped his arms around her and held her close. She pressed her face against his chest. Storm wished his voice would come back to him a little quicker than it did, but as usual he had to wait for his voice to settle. He knew her vision had upset her and he needed to know what she saw. Not being able to ask frustrated him.

A sigh escaped her as she relaxed against him. Her soft breath brushed against his mark, heightening his need for her. When he should be comforting her because of her frightening vision, all he could think of was her heat surrounding him. "...heart..."

She looked up at him with bright eyes. Unshed tears clung to her lashes. "He figured out who you were and he pulled a gun on you. Sam was there. She jumped in front of the blast. I couldn't let her die."

"You..."

"It didn't hurt." She nodded as she touched her chest.

"But the fear in your eyes said it wasn't good. You have to promise me you won't shift in front of him, no matter what."

"Heather." His voice was coming back.

"Promise me."

He needed to speak. "I…must…protect."

"The best way to protect me is to do as I ask. No shifting." She watched as he struggled for words. "My heart, it is the only way. My vision was very clear. If you show him who you are, he'll get angry and act rash. I could lose everyone if that happens."

"If…he…threatens."

"Storm, he'd never harm me. I'm too important to him." She brushed her fingers against his jaw. "It's you I worry about. You have destroyed his plans for me and he will try to separate us at all costs to get them back in motion."

He pulled her body against his. "Stuck…with…me."

"You make it sound like a punishment."

Storm lowered his head toward hers, capturing her lips with his. Heather worked her way to the ground, bringing him with her, while he continued to ravage her mouth. There were times when he couldn't get enough of her. "You taste… so good."

"You feel so good," she said, her voice soft. Heather's eyes closed when he filled her. A cat-like smile spread across her face.

He buried himself as deep as he could, knowing it normally brought a gasp out of her. This time was no different.

"I swear you are larger. Perhaps it is a side effect of your shape-shifting." She shifted her hips so he rubbed her in the right place each time he filled her.

"Are you complaining?" That he was able to say without trouble.

"Oh, no, more like getting spoiled." She sighed as her body shook from the sweet invasion. "I can't get enough."

"When we get out of here." He had to pause for a moment to get his voice to work properly. "I promise to keep you in bed for days."

"Going to try to wear me out?" Her head lifted back when he stroked her just the right way.

"Yes. We won't be able to walk from all the sex." He ground his hips against hers, knowing it always heightened her release.

She practically purred at his words. Her mind brushed up against his. Joy shot through him as their minds merged for the first time in a while.

I have missed this. He shifted the rhythm and found a better one. His mate tightened against him, making every movement more exciting. Storm picked up the tempo and felt Heather draw close to her orgasm. Her release blossomed near her core, spreading out until it had her body vibrating as it overcame her. It didn't take him too long before he joined her.

He pressed kisses against her cheek, then her eyes before capturing her lips with his again. The stolen moments were all they had and he cherished every one of them.

"Your book is here." He hated to break the moment, but their time there was fleeting and he knew she needed the knowledge in the book.

"Really?" She wanted to go get it, but he still had her pinned beneath him.

The tree they lay under had a small hole near the base. Storm pulled the satchel out and dropped it on her chest.

"Thank you." She pulled at the cords until she could remove her book easily. He knew it was difficult for her to read on her back, but she didn't ask him to move. A single sheet of paper fluttered out of her book. Heather hugged it to her. "Thank you, Toki."

"What is that?"

"The prayer I asked for." She studied the page until she had it memorized.

"Could you explain that to me? Why would you want some prayer?"

"Because, my heart, this is the prayer that bound Ialog."

"The one my uncle used?"

She nodded. "I'm hoping this will keep us all safe."

THIRTEEN

Heather played with her food. Dinner bored her. Every night they sat at this huge table, barely speaking. Ialog watched her as he always did, and she pretended she could tolerate being in the same room as him. Tonight, she didn't feel like going along with the charade. Perhaps it was because she no longer had the block on her mind.

Heather wanted to see what she could do with it, not sit there in the awkward silence they always shared. She wasn't sure where the bravado was coming from, but she needed a change.

She petted Hero's head as she contemplated what she wanted to do. The last few days she had spent some of their time alone reading her book, learning how to use her mind. The mind jump was one of the first things in there. It was something simple and easy for her to learn to control, which was why she had been doing it inadvertently since she had jumped into the mind of Storm's mother. Holding it was the trick now. She had practiced a few times while she and Storm were in her little haven, but he was very good at distracting her, so she couldn't keep her focus. As much as she loved the way he distracted her, she needed to do it where he couldn't stop her.

Could she do it now? She knew Ialog was constantly watching. Could she do it without being caught?

Storm must have sensed something because he looked up at her. Touching his muzzle, she locked eyes with him and mouthed the words to allow them to switch. As she got better at it, she wouldn't need to use the words. They were more to help her focus so she could use her mind properly.

Storm fought her for a moment or two before he relaxed. In her book, it showed her how to force the exchange if she had to, but Storm, who didn't like being switched, seemed to know she needed to do this. He hated being in her body if they weren't being intimate, but understood her need to master this.

He had a bit of an issue trying to maneuver her body once they had switched, and holding a fork was hard. He couldn't get her fingers to do what he wanted. Heather rested her head on his lap, enjoying the simple act of him petting her. He sighed as he gave up on the utensil. Heather understood. She found it difficult in the beginning too. Adjusting to someone else's body took time and sometimes that wasn't available. Her power to hold onto the person was where she was the weakest. Heather found this adapting a challenge and she loved challenges. Switching with Storm while he was in wolf form made it easier for her to learn how to work the body. Once she mastered his animal form, she hoped it would be easier for her to step into other people and be able to manipulate their systems quicker.

Ialog didn't seem to notice Storm's silence and lack of eating. He kept watching them, but didn't speak. Perhaps he was enjoying the fact that she wasn't arguing with him for once. Once the meal was done, he excused them to return to her room.

Storm sat on her bed and glared at her. Just by his look

she knew he wanted to know how long she planned on hijacking his body. If she could laugh, she would. The test was to see how long she could keep her mind in his body. She was getting better at it, and this was the longest she had controlled his so far. Heather also knew if she kept it too long he'd fight harder when she wanted to practice again. Relaxing, her mind slid back into her body, allowing Storm to have his back.

Don't do that again.

But you're my only guinea pig. How am I supposed to learn if I can't use you? While in Ialog's custody, she didn't stay connected with Storm all the time. She had no clue what the android was recording and what would show up so didn't want to take any chances.

He snuffed at her as he rested his head on her lap. She buried her fingers into his fur. *I would like to see how far I can go before my mind snaps back into my body, too.*

So the next chance you get, you want to take off? Leave me trapped in your body without you near in case something goes wrong?

She buried her face in his fur. *Do you mind?*

He didn't answer her. Heather knew it would be dangerous to leave him, but she needed to test this new ability she had. Her chance came almost immediately. The android came to see if she wanted to go for a walk. Storm opened his mind for her and she jumped into his form. Once she was sure he could function properly, she took off.

Running felt wonderful. Something she hadn't been able to do in a while. Claws dug into the ground as she dashed along. A thrill ran through her as she felt the air slicing through her fur. No wonder Storm liked this form so much.

She found the tree he told her was the meeting place for him and Kuarto. She could smell their presence in the air. Heather found that fascinating as she skidded to a stop. Now the fun part would begin. How was she going to be able to convey what she wanted when she couldn't talk to her brother as a wolf?

It didn't take Kuarto long to get there. He held his scanner and another small satchel. "You going to shift?"

Storm was the shifter, not her. She shook her head.

"Why not?" Kuarto watched her. "You can't. Let me see what is going here. Maybe I can fix whatever is stopping you." He frowned when he read the readings. "Your brainwaves are all wrong." It took a second or two before the brainwaves matched with another set. He looked at her in shock. "Heather?"

She barked at him.

"Unbelievable." He looked at his scanner once more before putting it in his pocket. "How did you get around the device you had on your forehead?"

Heather looked at him and yawned.

"Right. You can't answer. I need to ask yes and no questions, don't I?"

She barked again.

"I wouldn't bark too often. Ialog could have sensors out here."

Heather nodded. Her main reason for seeing Kuarto was to tell him of her vision. She knew Storm would never bring it up to him, and she wanted Kuarto's help in avoiding what she saw. So how was she going to tell him? Not having opposable thumbs made writing out of the question. Or did it?

The ground beneath her paws was soft. Looking around, Heather spotted a small stick. She picked it up with her mouth and started to painstakingly write one word.

"Vision?" Kuarto stared at her for a moment. "You had a vision?"

She nodded.

"One of those where you're supposed to die?"

She whined.

"And you want me to ask Storm about it."

Heather jumped when he figured it out. That was fast.

"Then you're going to let him take over his body again."

She nodded again. Relaxing herself, her mind searched for her body. After brushing her mind up against Storm's, she took her body back, guiding him to his.

"You seem awfully quiet," said to her look-alike.

"Do I?" She was sure Storm had his hands full just trying to keep her body moving. Heather looked down and brushed her hands against her womb. "I guess I've been keeping it internally. I haven't been able to speak to my children in a while, so we've been communing with each other."

"And how are they doing?" She scanned Heather. The android looked at her reading, then looked up at Heather. "You've had intercourse."

———

Kuarto watched as Storm entered his body. "Welcome back."

Storm shifted the moment he had control. It took him a few more minutes before he tried talking. "Don't like the... mind switch."

"Yeah, well, you're not going to be happy to know Heather was able to communicate one word to me. Vision. She was making sure you'd tell me about it. While you're at it can you explain to me how she had a vision? That device was designed to block anything like that."

Storm frowned. He should have known she'd get Kuarto enough information to make him ask too many questions. He waited until his vocal cords were working before answering. "She fell unconscious on me. Not knowing what was wrong with her had me a little crazy." He paused to take a deep breath. "There are some limitations as a wolf. I'm getting my vocal cords back faster, but it's like I'm out of breath."

Kuarto nodded. He scanned him to make sure everything was okay then waited for Storm to continue.

"I was able to make that android come and they took her to the medical center. The android said Heather's mind was trying to give her the information to protect herself and the device was in the way, so her brain shut down to get the vision to her. She ended up damaging the block when she regained consciousness. Ialog had to remove it then."

"Then why didn't you two escape?"

"He put another device on her. One that controls her motor reflexes. She hasn't been able to break its hold yet."

"What did she see?" Kuarto waited for his answer.

"She saw me shift, revealing my presence and being shot by Ialog." Storm had felt her anguish over the whole thing. It bothered him just talking about it. "Our daughter, Samantha, stepped in the way of the blast to protect me and of course Heather stepped in the way to protect her. She took the brunt of it. The vision ended after that."

"Does she know when?"

"No, but we need to act now, before my mate can be put into jeopardy like that."

———

Heather became agitated when her look-alike brought her a new dress to wear. Storm didn't understand why.

Because this is what I wore in my vision.

It doesn't mean it's going to happen today. You can't let this get to you or we won't be able to change what you saw.

He was right, but it didn't stop her from worrying. If she knew how, she'd lock Storm in his animal form so he couldn't shift if he wanted to. The android now knew somehow Storm had been with her. It wouldn't take Ialog long to figure out how she had been intimate with her mate.

Dinner was served in the usual style. Ialog watched her like a hawk. "I understand you have had sex recently."

Heather had a grip on Storm to keep him still. "And how would I have accomplished that?"

"I'm sure there are ways since it has happened." He pulled out a blaster and pointed at her. "Where is he, Heather? Is it your trusted companion?"

She didn't look at Storm. She knew better. One look would prove his question, and she refused to do that. "If Storm was here, he would have rescued me by now."

"Not if he hasn't figured out how to turn off my security system. I know he has this place surrounded, it has been like that for a few days now. How could you? Even under my roof you couldn't stay away from him. I didn't create you to be that way."

"What are you talking about?" She kept a death grip on Storm, trying to keep her vision from coming true. "Part of my DNA is Vespian, and they are one of the most sexually active groups I have ever seen. My mate is the perfect example."

"That gene was told to be dormant." He stood and came around to her side of the table.

"And it was, until I met Storm. He's the one who awakened my sexual appetite." Heather looked at Sam. "That is what you did to my daughter, isn't it? Manipulated her DNA, so she appears almost unemotional."

"I only dampened a few emotions that would get in the way of her training." Ialog gestured for her to step clear of her pet. "He has to go. Either make him leave or I'll shoot him."

Heather knelt in front of Storm. "Go, Hero. Go outside and play."

He sat at her feet, not budging.

Please, Storm. He'll kill you if you don't go. Leave, bring back reinforcements. Rescue me. Heather stomped her foot, which made the wolf jump. He hesitated for a few more seconds before he took off.

Storm's sensitive ears heard the click of the blaster lever release. He turned in time to see the beam coming straight for him. Then, just like Heather's vision, their daughter stepped into the line of fire. Storm couldn't move as his mate blocked the shot from hitting Sam. What did surprise him was when the android took the blast instead of Heather. The robot shoved her out of the way, sending her flying into a wall.

He heard someone shout 'No' but was too busy watching his mate crumple to the floor. The desire to make sure she was okay overpowered his desire to kill Ialog. He would deal with him in a moment. Storm was at her side in seconds. He had shifted so he could touch her face.

"I'm fine, my heart, but you have got to go. Before he takes another shot at you."

She was right. Storm looked at Ialog who had raised the weapon for a second time. If he didn't move, Heather's vision could come true. He had hoped to sneak in and turn the system off, but now he would have to barge in and do it then send the signal.

———

Heather pushed herself to her feet. Her shoulder screamed in pain. She was pretty sure she had dislocated it again. "Why?"

"He isn't worthy of you."

"Isn't that my decision to make?" She walked to where the android lay. Big ugly hole through the center of her. Just like her vision. No wonder why she didn't feel it. The blast wasn't meant for her but her look-alike.

"You are blinded by the passion he draws out of you." Ialog still held the weapon and now had it pointed at her.

Heather went to her daughter to make sure she was okay. The young woman stood and nodded.

Time to end this. The prayer filled her mind first, which allowed it to build in volume and power. Slowly, the words started to flow from her lips. The rhythm made the words sound beautiful as they filled the air. As her voice got louder, so she could be heard, she felt the strength of the words fill her. There was a faint color following the cadence.

"What are you doing?" Ialog stared at her in shock.

Heather felt the energy surround her, giving her a strength she had never felt before. Her mind continued the prayer as she answered him.

"What I should have done a while ago. Stop you from hurting my family anymore." She then continued speaking the words that would bind him. The colors brightened as the words flowed out of her.

Those colors surrounded him, grabbing hold and tightening as she continued.

His arms locked to his side. He tried to take a few steps toward her, but found moving too difficult. "You have to stop."

Heather ignored him as she spoke the prayer. Ialog fell to the floor. She walked to his side, not stopping until his eyes glazed over and there was no movement from him. The colors solidified into a cocoon around him.

Once she was sure he wouldn't be going anywhere for a while, she went to her daughter. She touched her face. "I didn't mean to ignore what you did, protecting your father by jumping in front of him, but I knew you were okay because of my vision." Heather pointed to Ialog. "I know he has been your father figure, but I had to stop him."

"He never showed me the love you did." Sam looked down at the incased figure of Ialog. "I feel sorry for him, but am not upset you did this."

Heather hugged her. "I wish I could take all this back.

Have you in here with your brother and sister." She touched her womb.

"In all the things I have studied I have learned that things happen for a reason." She returned Heather's hug. "My destiny was to go through this."

"How's my look-alike?" Heather glanced over at the android.

"You never could give her a name, could you?" They walked over to where the android lay.

"No. She looked a little too much like me. Do you think she has been destroyed?"

"I am still functional." The android made a slight motion, showing she was still with them. The big ugly burn mark that covered her chest had Heather wondering. "He said no harm could come to you. Why would he shoot you if he meant that?"

"Why didn't the ancient computer take you over like it said it would?" Heather shook her head. If it had she never would have been shot at. Then again, if it had, she probably wouldn't have used the ancient bonding prayer on Ialog. "I swore it had a couple of times."

"And I have been here the whole time, but you were never in danger, so I allowed the android to continue to follow her programming," she responded. "This system was designed to protect you. She gave her life for yours."

"Why did you allow my vision to come true?"

"Ialog saw everything she did. He also had her readings on a screen all the time. I allowed her to work the way he expected so he wouldn't be aware her system had been compromised by you and Storm." The robot made a strange whirring noise. "You were never in danger. This system was designed to protect. First your egg, then you. If either of you put yourself in harm's way, she was to make sure you were safe, even if it meant her destruction."

"Can she be repaired?"

"Yes. If you wish her to be."

"Please change her features so she doesn't look like me. That is very unnerving, but she has become a friend, so I'd hate to lose that part of her."

"Then she shall be revamped. I will download her memory and make the appropriate changes."

"Thank you."

The doors flew open and Vespian and Earth security poured into the room. It didn't take very long before Storm marched through the doors and headed straight to her.

"You okay?" He pulled her into his embrace. He placed one hand on her womb. He grinned when he felt a strong kick from one of the children.

"A little banged up, but we're good." She leaned into him, grateful for his comfort.

He saw the cocoon. Keeping his arm around her, he guided her as he walked over to it. "This is what the prayer did?"

"Yes. Amazing, isn't it?" She placed her hand on his heart.

"You have defeated him without me?" He said it softly, as he nuzzled her neck.

"He aimed that stupid weapon at me after you left. I had to use the bonding spell or he could have caused us both great heartache. It worked."

"What is he incased in?" He crouched down to touch the material surrounding Ialog.

"I'm not sure." She knelt down beside him. "The prayer created it, surrounded him and locked him in that." She realized by kneeling next to him her dress molded itself to her body and her pregnancy was evident. "Everyone is going to know now."

He touched her stomach tenderly, and she nodded. He touched her face. "It was going to come out sooner or later, anyway."

"I know, but I had hoped to have a feasible explanation by the time the information leaked." She leaned her face into his hand.

Kuarto came to her side and ran his scanner over her. "What happened? You have a fractured arm, dislocated shoulder, and two broken ribs."

"Nothing major." She noticed people from Earth's security watching them. Having a doctor fuss over her when they just figured out she was pregnant just made it worse. "I'll explain it all later. Just make it a little easier to breathe, and I'll make sure you know the whole story."

He shook his head as he applied the proper items to accelerate her healing process. "You go to my office first."

Heather nodded, but Storm interjected, his arms still wrapped around her. "No. She made a promise to me that she will keep. If you need to examine her, you'll have to come to our rooms."

"Fine. So what is the deal with Ialog?" asked Kuarto. "He isn't moving a whole lot."

"I used that prayer on him." Heather walked back over to where he lay.

"I still don't understand how that works." Storm walked around him.

"The words became a physical prison. I'm not sure how yet, but I'm hoping my book will explain it better."

"Is he conscious?" asked Kuarto. He looked at her.

"Very much. He's just paralyzed. It's like a stasis. His body has completely shut down, but he can hear us." She looked at Storm. "What do you plan on doing with him?"

"He deserves to die."

"But you can't kill him. The android said he won't die."

"Then we'll have to find out what the computer will tell us." Storm watched her for a moment before he turned to one of his security. "Put him in one of our most secure holds. I don't want to see him, hear his name, or even think about his presence. I will take the head of any guard that lets him escape, so make sure he doesn't."

The guard nodded before calling over three other people so they could take Ialog out of the room.

"Now, I believe we have a few things to retrieve?" Storm offered his arm to his mate. Heather smiled at him as she took his arm. He saw the slight wince when she moved her arm the wrong way. "I will allow Kuarto to heal you, but he has to come to our room."

"I am fine." She grinned at him. "Your eyes are glowing."

"Really?"

"Where are you two going?" Kuarto cut them off before they could leave.

"To get our books and my dress," said Heather. She plucked at the gown she now wore. "This thing needs to go."

"Oh, no, you don't. I'm coming with you. All we need is for you two to go off alone. We could be waiting for your return for a while."

"Doctor!" Storm tried to act like he was insulted. "You know Heather is wounded."

"Not falling for it." He gestured for them to walk in front of him. "Let's go."

They walked to where she had buried her items so Ialog wouldn't find them. She shed the dress Ialog made her wear for her Vespian style gown. She smoothed her old gown down with her hands. "Much better."

Storm held up the undergarment the ancient computer created for her to hide her pregnancy. "And what should we do with this thing?"

"I don't know. It's kind of silly for me to use now that so many know the truth."

He nodded, folded the outfit up and slipped it inside the bag that held their books.

Kuarto walked them back to the main building. He gave Heather a thorough examination while the teams secured the

BARBARA DONLON BRADLEY

area, healing as much as he could with the equipment he had.

"You know we could use his lab while we wait for the building to be secure," commented Kuarto.

"Lead the way." Storm waited for Kuarto to head to the lab before he escorted Heather.

The room had already been cleared, with guards lining the wall along the way. Nothing was going to happen to Heather ever again.

"Just get this thing off my neck."

"Sit. Let me see what I can do." He worked on her for a few minutes. Small battles broke out here and there, but Ialog's guards didn't put up much of a fight. Soon, the whole compound was secure.

After Storm supervised the securing of the equipment, he escorted Heather to a waiting vehicle. Kuarto joined them.

"What is the verdict, doctor?" asked Heather.

"Looks good, but I want to run a full set of tests on you to be sure." He looked pointedly at Storm. "In my office."

"Then you are going to have to wait because she's going straight to our bed and not moving until I say so." He had his arm around Heather and tightened it so Kuarto would know he wasn't going to budge on this.

The ship touched down in the embassy courtyard. Storm picked up his mate and walked down the gangplank. Just about everyone who worked there stood waiting for them. A shout went up when Heather was spotted for the first time.

Storm's mother stepped up to them and waited for her son to put his mate down so she could hug her. "I'm so glad you're home safe."

"Me too." Heather returned her hug. Many others greeted Heather, welcoming her home.

Once Storm had had enough, he scooped her back up and strode into the embassy. He headed straight to their rooms and dropped her onto the bed. "Stay."

"But…"

"You promised, my heart."

Heather sighed but stayed in the center of their bed. Storm walked back to the door. "You have about five minutes, doctor. Then I'm going to be with my mate whether you're here or not."

"Understood." Kuarto stepped into the room. Heather sat on the bed, waiting.

"Is five minutes enough?"

"It's going to have to be, isn't it?" Kuarto ran his scanner all over her. "I will want to check you out in about twelve hours."

"I'll do my best to make sure you can come back in, but I won't promise anything."

Kuarto smiled. "I know. He's acting like he hasn't been with you since you were kidnapped."

"Those stolen moments weren't enough and you know that. We need this time together. Make sure no one disturbs us."

He nodded and headed out the door.

Storm locked the door and turned to face her. "Now, I believe we have some catching up to do."

FOURTEEN

Heather started to work on the seams of her dress.

"Don't. I want to do that." His hand closed over hers. "I want to reveal your body slowly, enjoy you in a way I haven't been able to in a long time."

"My heart, you're acting like it has been years since we've been intimate."

"It feels like it. Those moments in the glen were wonderful and I will always cherish those memories but I have needed you in a way I can't describe." He touched her face with his fingertips. "Kuarto did give you a clean bill of health, right?"

"Yes." She lay down as he climbed on the bed with her.

"The dislocated shoulder? Broken ribs?"

"The ribs need a few more hours, but they are much better. The shoulder and the rest are completely healed."

"Good. My plans for you hinge on no interruptions. I don't want him barging in because he's worried about some reading he picked up from you."

"He did say he wanted to check me in twelve hours."

"Twelve hours." He started to work on the seals of her dress, planting kisses on the skin he revealed. "I guess we could come up for air then, but not before. I want to take my time with you. Get to know your body again. See if those favorite spots are still there."

"My heart, I'm pretty sure they haven't moved, but I'm not going to stop you from checking to be sure." She sighed as she felt his lips on her body. It had been too long since they could savor each other this way.

"Didn't think you would." He captured one of her nipples in his mouth, slowly swirling his tongue around the tip. Her sharp intake of breath made him smile. "That one is still there."

"Is that how you're going to play that?" Heather gave him a *two can play at that game* look.

"And what are you planning?"

"I have missed exploring your body as well. In fact, you always seem to go first and I don't think that is fair." Her fingers brushed against his mark.

"Since when have I ever played fair?" One of his hands slid down her stomach to slip into her folds. "When it comes to you I seem to have a one track mind."

"To possess me as many times as you can?" She arched her back as he caressed just the right spot. "My heart."

"I knew you could read minds." His lips followed his hands, suckling her core. He was greeted with a moan from her.

"Wait 'til it's my turn." Her voice came out breathy.

"I promise to take it like a man, as long as you take this like a woman." He continued to lathe her, pausing from time to time so she wouldn't climax too quickly. He knew she was close so he changed tactics, allowing her release to back off a little. Moving back up her body, he paused at her breasts, drawing the soft tissue into his mouth and causing her to arch her back once again.

She was close and nothing was going to stop it this time, he could smell it. He centered himself and filled her. His lips found her mark, increasing the intensity between them. Her body quaked just as she tightened her muscles around him. Storm set a quick pace, knowing she wouldn't take long to reach a release.

She surprised him though, changing the pace and bringing him along with her. Between her muscles milking him and the pace he forced, he found himself losing control. Her mind caressed his as he reached his climax first, her body hugging him as he found his release.

She shuddered in his arms as her orgasm grabbed her and carried her along with him.

He let out a breath. "Now that wasn't fair."

"What makes you say that?" She grinned up at him. Proud of what she did.

"You were supposed to climax first. Now we're going to have to do that all over again."

"How about that."

He laughed. "I have taught you too well."

———

Kuarto watched their readings, waiting for the right moment to interrupt them. Heather's friend Bear had been waiting to deliver a message from Earth security for several hours and couldn't understand why he had to wait. It had been almost twelve hours so he knew Heather would do her best to give him the time he asked for. Their readings settled long enough for him to take a chance.

"We should be able to interrupt them, but don't expect Storm to be happy to see us."

"He can't be that bad."

"You have no idea." Kuarto knocked on the door instead of allowing the guards at the door to open them. He could hear voices inside before the door opened. A glaring Storm greeted them.

"Can't wait?" Storm held a tray filled with finger foods, including the berries he found to help Heather.

"It has been twelve hours." Kuarto noticed he was wearing a pair of jersey pants. He bet Heather had something to do with that.

"Really? Doesn't seem like it." He did step aside so Kuarto and then Bear could enter. Behind them was the young man who had taken over the interview, Gavin. He had been freed once Storm had spoken to him the last time. Storm sighed as he allowed everyone in. He walked to the bed where Heather sat with a sheet draped over her and sat the tray down. "There are far too many people in our rooms."

"Storm." Heather held out her hand to him, which he took as he joined her on the bed, being careful not to dislodge the sheet hiding her body from their guests. He wrapped an arm around her shoulders.

"As you can see, Kuarto, Storm isn't quite ready to share yet." She gave him a quick smile. "Good to see you, Bear."

"Heather. Our government has sent me to welcome you home. They are sorry this happened and would like to know what they can do to make it up to you."

"There is nothing they can do to fix this and they know that." She tucked the sheet a little more securely so it wouldn't move as Kuarto worked on her. She sure didn't want anything peeking out when it shouldn't. "He was the reason they called me back. If they had known better this would have never happened."

"I know. And I'm sorry. I should have paid attention."

"It's done, Bear. I'm home now." She took the hand from the arm Storm had put around her shoulder for a little support.

"And she's not going anywhere." Storm tightened the hold he had on her shoulders. "Now, I would like to spend a little more time with my mate."

"She's fine. Need to get your vitamins and mineral levels back up for the children." Kuarto looked at Storm. "But I would like a chance to run deep scans to make sure there has been no damage done."

Heather nodded. She knew what he meant.

"Okay, then we'll leave you."

"Wait." Gavin spoke.

Heather looked at Storm for a moment before she turned to Gavin. "Go ahead."

"There is a rumor that you are pregnant. Is it true?"

"How about we let them set up a meeting with you in a day or two where Heather and Storm can answer your questions? Right now I know they are just happy to be back safe, but not ready to explain everything." Kuarto looked back at Heather and Storm who weren't paying any attention to anyone but each other again. They needed to get out before someone got an eyeful.

He didn't wait for anyone to agree with him he just ushered them out of the room as fast as he could. Not relaxing until everyone was safely out.

"Are they always like that?" asked Bear.

"Pretty much." What else could he say?

"Wow."

That was the way he felt when he first met them.

———

Heather took a few berries and popped them into her mouth. "I'm not sure how to explain my pregnancy."

"Your brother studies DNA, Heather. Why can't you say he has come up with an experimental drug that you are testing and until your children are born you didn't want to get anyone's hopes up?" the computer asked her.

"I wouldn't say anything that wasn't true."

"I have studied his research and he is very close to being

able to reverse sterilization in most races. You wouldn't be lying."

"We'll have to talk to him before I make any kind of announcement." She looked at Storm who had shed his pants and was starting a long leisurely trek up one of her legs. Between the kisses he planted and the touch of his tongue in the right places, she found her focus shifting.

"Later." Storm stroked her core. "Open for me, my heart."

Heather rested her head on her pillow as she spread her legs for him. His tongue dipped in as he feasted on her. She threaded her fingers in his jet black hair as wonderful sensations washed over her. How was she so lucky to find a man who worshipped her the way Storm did?

No matter what, her needs always came first.

She felt him slide two fingers inside her, causing a delicious friction. He built her up until she was close to exploding when he shifted his weight and entered her. Her orgasm was immediate.

"My heart, I'm just getting started and you want to force me to maintain control?"

"You're the one not fighting fair." Her voice came out soft and sultry.

His lips claimed her mark, sending her skyrocketing again. He pounded into her like he hadn't had been bringing her to heights of ecstasy over the last twelve hours. Her world splintered around her once again, pulling a scream out of her.

"That's my girl."

———

Another knock on the door had Storm growling. Who would be brave enough to try to interrupt him when he left explicit orders for no one to interrupt them?

"Sir?" It was Fridon. "You asked me to come when we were finished."

"Yes, I did." Heather had been sleeping, so he closed the door to their room as he went to see what Fridon had finished. Beside him stood a young man he didn't recognize. "This is the android now?"

"Yes." Excitement laced his voice. "Thank you so much for this opportunity. I have learned so much from working with him."

The door to their room opened and Heather stepped out.

"You are supposed to be resting." She must have used their mindlink to find out why he left the room.

"I know." She touched his heart for a moment before walking around the robot. "He doesn't look like me anymore. That is good."

"My other facade bothered you."

"We discussed it before. I know imitation is supposed to be flattering, but having you look like me was just a little too creepy."

"And now?"

"Much better." Heather smiled. "I am glad they were able to repair you. How about all of Ialog's protocols?"

"Gone. The main system showed me how to remove them. There is nothing dormant waiting to be awakened."

"Positive?"

"The memory of this unit has been worked through, Heather." The android touched his chest. "As per your request. Any information or recording of Ialog has been removed."

"Good." She nodded, happy to have her friend back. "I look forward to our walks again."

"As do I."

———

Heather fluffed her skirt around her, feeling nervous about the interview. "I really hate these things."

"You'll do fine," said Storm as he sat beside her. He had a protective arm around her shoulders while they waited for Gavin. "Besides, I know how to relax you if I need to. Make you boneless."

She looked up at him through her lashes, loving the promise in his voice, but she didn't get a chance to respond.

Gavin came through the door, carrying his camera. His entourage followed him, setting up lights and checking them for the camera again. He hurried to set up his camera and mike. "Thanks for seeing me. I know you just escaped a harrowing experience and have better things to do than deal with having to talk about it in front of millions of people."

He sat down once the camera and lights were set up to his satisfaction. He had an earpiece that he cupped from time to time before speaking. Heather assumed he was in touch with his news people, taking commands or suggestions as he prepared to go on the air. He gave them a silent signal that they were live.

"Heather, everyone is happy to hear you are safe at home again."

"Thank you." She looked up at Storm before resting her head against his chest, then back at Gavin and the camera over his shoulder.

"The planet also wants to apologize for allowing this to happen in the first place. We didn't know everything he said was a lie."

What could she say to that?

"I'm just glad she's with me again," said Storm. She was grateful he intervened.

"What have you done with Al?"

"He's in Vespian custody. And will be tried for his crimes." Storm didn't elaborate further.

"Then let's get to the question on everyone's mind. We

had all seen the footage of your rescue and rumors have been flying. Are you pregnant?"

"Yes." Heather rubbed her stomach. She didn't want to hide her growing womb anymore. It was time to tell the truth.

"But why did you keep it such a secret?"

"I didn't, not really. Vespian pregnancies take a little longer than a human one, and the baby is developing slower, so I wasn't really showing when we first arrived. But I wasn't sure how people would react when they found out. After all, I was sterile before I married Storm, so I just didn't see how I could announce it to the world." No one needed to know about the undergarment the computer created for her. She just hoped when they went back to look, the dresses she wore to the functions weren't as form fitting as she remembered. When she picked them out, she did so thinking about what it would hide. "We weren't sure if I could carry full term until recently."

"How is this possible, then?"

"Vespian doctors have been trying to find a cure for their sterility for a while. When I learned they had a possible cure I volunteered. I felt that as the wife of their leader it would make sense to try. If I could get pregnant, then there's hope for their planet."

"But you're not Vespian."

"No, but human and Vespian DNA are very close. There's only a few things different. There have been Vespian/human children before with little or no complications. It's frightening and exciting at the same time."

"That explains that doctor hovering around you earlier."

Heather nodded. Kuarto didn't want to be mentioned as the man with the cure. He was trying to remain hidden from those who could still want his services. "They are all very excited about this."

"So when are you due?"

"Using a standard calendar I'm to give birth in about seven months."

"But you look like you're three or four months now. Isn't that a little long?"

"A Vespian pregnancy is eighteen months, but that is based off of their eighteen-hour days and three hundred and fifty days in a year. Ours is nine months. When you convert the Vespian time to Earth's it's only a little over one month longer." Heather paused for a moment. "I'm also carrying twins."

"Side effect of the treatments you took to get pregnant?"

"Yes," interjected Storm.

"Will you share this cure with others if you find it works?"

"Yes. We know that children are as precious to you as they are to us." Storm rested his hand on her womb. "Our only concern would be a population explosion if everyone ends up with multiple births."

"I am a guinea pig. Based off my pregnancy and birth the doctors will gain a lot of information to perfect this cure, but it's not like they're going to release this to everyone in a year or so. They will continue to do research to make sure there are no side effects." Heather wanted to be sure people understood it could take time before they saw anything.

"Why did you volunteer?"

"I've known all my life I could never have children, to know the joy of being a mom, well, when I learned of this I couldn't help myself." She smiled as she shrugged.

"And the fact that you would endear yourself to the Vespian world didn't cross your mind?"

"No. My reasons for doing this were very selfish. In the past, when I was told I couldn't do something, that it would be too hard, I had to prove those people wrong. That is what happened here. In fact, the doctors fought me on this because I wasn't Vespian." She laughed as she looked up at her mate.

"They didn't see the benefit it could be to our relations until I pointed it out."

"Gavin, I hate to cut this off short, but Heather has been through a lot and I worry she'll push herself too much." Storm touched her face. She was starting to get circles under her eyes and he knew she needed rest and to eat a few more berries.

"I'm fine, Storm." She touched his face with her fingertips. *But we just started.*

"I just want to make sure you don't overdo it, my heart." He pressed a quick but heated kiss against her lips. He stood and offered her his hand. *You are showing signs of fatigue. Kuarto didn't want you to do this interview so soon after returning, but you insisted. I promised him to cut it short if you pushed yourself too hard.*

"Sorry, but I am feeling a little tired right now. Storm knew that when we sat down and promised to keep me to an easy schedule." She took his hand and stood as well. "Perhaps when I'm feeling a little better we can talk again."

"Although this is a little disappointing I'm sure the viewers will understand."

"I hope so. I'll contact you when I'm ready. Maybe we could do the next interview on Vespia," she added as they started to walk away.

"Really?" He turned in his seat to look at her. "You know how big that could be?"

"Yes, I do."

———

"Did you clear that with the council?" Storm said it softly, but she knew the tone.

"Yes." She knew he wasn't happy with her. Vespia didn't allow a lot of visitors. "I asked their permission a few hours ago. I believe it was while you were arguing with my brother, again."

"He is a pain in my side at times." Storm glowered at her. "And they said yes?"

"They agree that it would go a long way to strengthening the alliance and Gavin wouldn't see anything the council doesn't want him to see." Heather grinned up at him. "Did you see how excited he was?"

"Not nearly as excited as I am." He pulled her into his embrace where she could feel his arousal. "And I want to know when you became such a good liar."

"Liar?" She looked at him quizzically. "Oh, you mean about me getting pregnant?"

He nodded as he bent to place a soft kiss on her neck.

"A memorized speech." A soft smile played on her lips as she felt her desire for him rise.

"When did you have time to memorize anything?" Storm maneuvered her back against the wall. "I believe I have done a good job monopolizing your time."

"Oh, you did, and I loved every minute of it, but this was something I have thought about for a while." She closed her eyes while he continued to pay attention to her mark. "The moment I was kidnapped I knew my pregnancy would come out and I had several scenarios in my head. There wasn't that much to do there. That was the one that popped up first."

"Not in public, please." Kuarto stood close by.

"How did you sneak up on me?" Storm glared at him.

"I don't sneak and you were a little occupied." He gestured for them to follow him. "We need to talk about our captive and your daughter."

"Okay." Storm wrapped an arm around her waist, keeping Heather at his side. "What do you want to talk about?"

"What are we going to do with them?"

"Drop Ialog into the ocean and bring our daughter home?"

"That won't work and you know that," said Kuarto. "I'm seeing signs of the spell, for lack of a better word, dissipating. He has a little movement that he didn't have when I first saw him."

"What?" Heather felt cold. Why wasn't the prayer holding?

"Nothing to worry about." He gave her a reassuring smile. "Toki says you just need to reinforce it every couple of days until we get him back to Vespia and into that unit he came out of. The spell was never designed to be permanent."

"Is that what the council has decided to do with him?"

"That is what Toki will recommend," said Storm.

"And take the chance to allow him to accidentally be released." Heather needed to think about this. "The elders didn't know any better. That could happen again."

"What do you suggest? Shoot him into space?"

"And wait for some unsuspecting race to come across him?" Heather shook her head. "I don't think so."

"What about wiping his memory?" asked Kuarto.

"Me?" Shock filled her.

"Who else could?" Kuarto was serious. "Your mind is the most powerful. You're the one who can jump from mind to mind. You were able to enter Anseri's mind and release her memories about Ialog. You can do this."

"And do what?" The idea made her uneasy. "Give him a fake memory? That doesn't always work."

"You are just afraid to try." Now he was goading her. He knew she never stepped away from a challenge.

"Of course I am. Who in their right mind would say they weren't frightened? What if I make a mistake and not get everything? Or put something in his mind that I shouldn't?"

"Then you'll think about it."

"She will," said Storm. "Now what is wrong with our daughter?"

"Health wise nothing, but she's not happy." Kuarto looked from Storm to Heather. "She doesn't know what to do with herself."

"All she has known was studying. That was all Ialog had her do." Heather touched Storm's heart.

"And she's brilliant. Never met anyone who can retain information the way she can." Kuarto handed them a pad with all her medical records. "This should give you all the details you'll need to see what I'm talking about. We'll talk some more after you have had a chance to go through those files."

———

"He's right, you know." Heather sat on the bed with the pad on her lap.

Storm sat behind her, brushing her hair out of the way so he could kiss her mark. "Who?"

"Kuarto." Heather leaned her head back onto his chest. "Samantha hasn't really lived, and I fear she won't be able to if she stays with us."

"So what do you want to do?" He nibbled his way up and down her throat.

"Same thing we should do with Ialog. If we wipe her mind, she won't have to live with the memories she has. Give her a chance to create new ones."

He lifted his head at her words. "Are you sure?"

"Yes. I spoke to her and she wants me to do this. Give her a chance to learn and grow without knowing what happened to her."

Storm frowned. Heather could see his protectiveness coming to the surface. "But what if she gets into trouble?"

"Then she'll have to deal with it." She turned so she

could look him in the face. "We won't be able to have any contact with her."

"No."

"Storm." It really wasn't up to them. Sam was now an adult physically.

"No." He leaned in, causing Heather to lean back as well. In seconds, she found herself lying on the bed with Storm trying to distract her with heated kisses.

"My heart, we…" she had to pause when his lips found her mark once again. "… can't keep her trapped here."

"I don't want to run the risk of losing her forever." With a thought, their clothes were gone. He looked down at her and grinned. "Who did that? You or me?"

"Does it really matter?" She brushed a lock of hair from his eyes. Her legs wrapped around his hips.

"No." He slid in deep. "As long as you continue to accept me like this."

Her body shuddered as he filled her. "My body craves you in a way that still amazes me. It would probably riot if I even teased about cutting you off."

"Never tease like that." He started to move within her. A slow pace to torture them a little. "If you did, I might just have to kidnap my own mate and break down her defenses until she submits."

Heather felt a thrill run through her at the thought. "Like how?"

"Well, first I'll need to find restraints that will hold you. One's your mind can't remove." He stopped talking for a moment when her muscles tightened against him. Their mindmeld let her know the exquisite lock she had on him had him focusing only on that.

She couldn't help herself. Between the friction between them building, and the images he was putting in her head, she found herself clenching against him. Her need spiraled out of control. Heather found she wanted him to move faster so she tightened her legs around his hips, hoping to urge him on.

He gave her a wicked smile as he changed the pace. "Then I will use my mouth to taste all of my favorite spots on your luscious body." He pressed his lips against her mark once again. "Watch as desire fills your eyes, like now."

She arched against him as she felt her orgasm racing toward her. "No more talk."

"But I enjoy how it affects you. You are so close to shattering in my arms." He picked up the pace, watching her for the tale tell signs of her climax.

Heather shifted her hips, feeling him penetrating deeper. Everything tightened inside her as her release swept over her. Her muscles rippled, heat filled her. She grasped at him as her world shattered.

He was very close, picking up the pace once again he pumped into her, reaching the same overpowering climax as she did.

They lay together afterwards, clinging to each other.

"Shall I tell you all the things I want to do to your body?" he whispered it in her ear.

"You need to be anywhere anytime soon?"

"No. Why?" He propped himself up on one elbow and looked down at her.

"Because I don't think I'd let you out of this bed anytime soon."

He gave her a sultry smile. "I like the sound of that." He lowered his lips to her neck.

"But we do have to let Sam go."

"What?" He lifted his face. "No. I'm supposed to be filling your head with erotic images not help you sabotage our libidos to talk about our daughter's future."

"I doubt anything could sabotage your sex drive, my heart." To prove her point, she wrapped her hand around his hardened member. He didn't respond. Instead, he lowered his mouth to her mark and began to make her forget anything but the two of them with his lips.

"Now, where was I?" he murmured against her throat. "Oh, yes. I've found a way to restrain you so you can't use your mind to escape."

"Storm."

"Saw you do it once. Not going to take the chance you could do it again." He pressed a hot wet kiss against her collar bone before capturing a nipple in his mouth. His tongue swirled against the tip, making her squirm. Storm released it gently. "I like the idea of having you spread eagle, as you humans say. That way, I can do whatever I want."

He slid his hands up and down her body. "Then I would use my lips to caress you. I'm not sure if I should start at the top." He brushed his fingers against her mark. "Or the bottom." His hands reached down as far as they could on one of her thighs and slowly slid up the inside of her leg, over her mound, pausing long enough to dip a finger then two inside her before continuing up to cup one of her breasts then moving up to touch her lips. Her body shook as his hands worked their magic on her. "Start at the bottom, definitely."

She felt her desire grow as he whispered to her, her body on fire with need.

Storm didn't seem to be fazed at all, even though she had been massaging his hardened staff the whole time. She knew better, she could hear his voice get deeper as she aroused him. He centered himself and plunged in deep.

Her body arched up against him as her muscles clamped down hard. Her release was quick and powerful.

Storm started to move inside her. Her legs went around his hips instinctively. "There will be one problem, though."

"What is that?" Her question came out deep and throaty.

"Your legs. You wouldn't be able to wrap them around

me the way you just did." He slid his arms around her thighs and eased them off his body.

"What are you doing?" Him spreading her legs out changed the angle of her hips, and as he continued to pump into her, she felt his hardness rub against her differently. She sucked in her breath at the exquisite sensation. Next, his hands slid under her derriere, lifting it and changing the angle again. Her body clenched against him, another orgasm roaring through her.

"Oh, that will work." He lifted his head and smiled at her. "Feeling boneless yet?"

"Why isn't this affecting you the way it is affecting me?" She sounded breathless.

"My heart, I'm feeling it too, but how often do I get to experiment on you this way? I had to hold back." He captured her mouth with his, his tongue drawing hers out to dance with his. Releasing the pent up desire he had been holding back. Passion filled her again from the erotic dance.

Storm didn't hold back any more. He set a fast pace that had her body singing. Each time he filled her, her body quaked, but he felt his body shake a little too. His strokes became quicker, deeper, causing her to moan.

"My heart." He lathed her mark. Everything tightened deep inside as her world exploded once again, this time tearing a scream from her. Storm followed her with his own release, his body pounding into hers as it grabbed him and flung him with her.

"Wow."

He pressed little kisses across her face and hairline. "You are so amazing."

"Me? That was amazing. I can't even lift my head now."

"So the bonelessness has set in." He nibbled on her neck. "Now, what did you wish to speak about?"

"Now?"

"You know the Vespian way, pleasure before business. We

have had our pleasure. Now you can talk about our daughter."

Heather started to laugh. "I can't even think straight and you want me to convince you our daughter needs to go out there and start fresh?"

"Yes. I know you are capable." He lifted his head so he could look her in the face. "I don't think it is a good idea."

"She has to grow, Storm, and I'm afraid she won't be able to do that if we don't let her go."

"There has to be some sort of contact. We can't just let her go and hope for the best." He touched her face. "My father went on a mission where he couldn't contact us and we never heard from him again. I don't want that to happen with our daughter."

"We can leave her here on Earth." She was beginning to understand his fear. "Have Bear keep an eye on her."

"I don't want you doing anything until after the twins are born." He rested his hand on her stomach. "At least give her a chance to be with us for a while before she is sure."

"I agree, and that was what I told her. I will continue to keep Ialog in stasis until I give birth. Then I'll do what needs to be done." Heather paused for a moment. "You mentioned your father. I've never heard you talk about him before."

"There isn't a lot to say. I was just a boy when he left. My memories of him are from my childhood and mother never talked about him once he disappeared."

"Why not?" She found that odd.

"Not sure."

"Hmm." Heather had been in Anseri's mind and been through many memories, even if she didn't view everything she was pretty sure the information was there. "I remember your mother and father in one of those memories when I was learning about Ialog. In one of them I saw him, not his face in that particular one, but I know he was in the memories. I still have all those memories in here." She tapped her head. "Perhaps what happened to him could be here."

"You serious?"

She eased herself from under him, sat up on the bed, and sat cross-legged. "Only one way to find out." She closed her eyes as she pulled up the memories in her mind. It didn't take her too long before she found what she was looking for. Her eyes snapped open. "I have seen him."

"What are you talking about?"

"Your father, I saw him at the reserve. During some of the meals, he stood behind Ialog. I had complained about not being able to communicate with the twins because of the block. Ialog had him loosen the hold of my block so I could explain what was going on to the children." She tuned to look at him. "Where are all the people from the reserve?"

"Bear took care of them. I'm assuming they're still being held for questioning."

"I need to contact him." She slid off the bed and slipped on a shift. Pressing the keys, she reached Bear pretty quickly.

"Heather, everything okay?"

"Yes, but I have a question for you. Do you still have the people from Ialog's place?"

"Most. There were a few we let go, but they had just started working for him. Why?"

"I need to see these people. I think there is a Vespian innocent caught up with them but he might not admit it."

"So it's a male?"

"Yes."

"Good. The only people we let go were women."

"I'm on my way now." She turned off the communication and dressed. Storm was fully clothed by the time she was ready to leave. "Ready?"

"*I'm* on my way?" He stood there, proud, with his hands on his hips, questioning the odd phrase.

"It was a figure of speech. I know you'll always be there with me."

He nodded then. "Let's go."

Heather had a quick wave of nostalgia when she walked into the security center. This was where she learned she would be working with the ambassador from Vespia for the first time. Her life changed in that instant. She looked at Storm, the man who had captured her heart and knew she wouldn't want it any other way.

Bear greeted them before escorting them to main security. Each of the men they were still holding were on one of the screens. There were still three women incarcerated, but he knew Heather was only interested in the men. "I made sure they are standing where you can see their faces. Which one is the one you are interested in?"

Heather examined each man on the first set of screens. "Well, it's none of these men."

Bear moved the next set to the screens.

She thought she'd spot him immediately, but started to second guess herself when she didn't see him in this batch as well. One caught her attention, but she wasn't sure, so she froze that screen. It would stay put when Bear moved over another set of pictures.

The next set didn't have him either. Did he escape before they could grab him?

"There is one man in the medlab. He has a device on his neck that has our doctors stumped."

"Can I see him?"

"Of course." Bear led the way to the lab. Guards stood outside the room Heather and Storm were ushered into.

She breathed a sigh of relief when she saw him. Same jet black hair, same golden eyes.

His eyes widened when they walked into the room.

"He's the one. Please transfer him to Vespian custody."

"Heather."

"Bear, you know you're going to have to, anyway. He is Vespian. Just look at him."

Bear looked at Storm, who had remained quiet, to the man in question. "Okay, so they look a lot alike. There is still paperwork."

"Which I know all about. You can still turn him over to us now. Medically, you can't help him where we can. There is a doctor at the embassy who has dealt with Ialog's devices before; I'm sure he can remove that thing where your doctors can't."

"We're both going to be demoted." He went to his desk to start the process to release the man to their custody.

"I've been through it before and will make sure they know it was all my idea."

"I'll have to send four people with you."

"He's not that dangerous, is he?"

"No. He's immobile, and it takes four people to move him anywhere." Bear signaled several guards to help move him. "I'm assuming you have a transport nearby?"

Heather nodded.

It didn't take long before he was secured inside the Vespian transport and they were on their way to the embassy.

"So, you're perfection." His voice came out a little raspy, like he hadn't spoken in a long time.

"Excuse me?" Heather was afraid he was talking to her. She left her seat and crossed to his side.

"That's what Ialog called you." He looked up at her. "You're all he talked about."

That gave her a chill. "Why did you stay with him for so long?"

"I had no choice." He shifted his eyes away from her. "He found out I was following him so quickly it was embarrassing."

"How long have you been wearing the device?"

"Since he caught me about forty-three years ago."

"That's why you never went home."

"He would go to Vespia and spy on everyone, but I couldn't join him. Ialog would leave me in the ship. So close, but I couldn't go home. He would allow me a visual of my family from time to time, if I was docile." A tear slid down his temple. "He took my manhood away."

"He stole your life, which you will now get back."

"No. My mate doesn't deserve a weak mate. I couldn't care for her the way I should have. Instead, I allowed myself to be captured. I couldn't be there for my children. My son grew without a male influence."

"Now I know where you get your pride from." She looked at Storm. "Talk about stubborn."

"And you don't have a stubborn bone in your delectable body."

She glared at him. "I learned that from my mate."

"Ha!" Storm laughed. His long arms allowed him to reach for her and pull her into his lap. "You had that wonderful trait long before I met you. Bear and I have compared notes."

"Bear called me tenacious."

"And you are." Storm pressed a kiss against her mark. "I'm not complaining about your traits, just making sure you know that you're not as perfect as Ialog thinks. You might be perfect for me but you still have flaws, wonderful, beautiful flaws."

"Flatterer." She stood and went back to his father. The fact that Storm hadn't addressed the man didn't go unnoticed, but she knew if she asked him in front of the man Storm wouldn't be very happy with her. Overstepping certain boundaries was taboo, and this was one of them.

"We wish to reunite you with your family."

He didn't answer.

"Your mate is here with your children."

"It is bad enough my son and his mate had to see me this way. I don't want anyone else to see this."

"What if I could promise that we have a doctor who can remove you from your prison? No one would know."

He didn't respond, which gave Heather hope. She went back to Storm's side and used the comlink. "Kuarto, can you meet us at the landing pad? There is something you need to work on."

"You know, I get a little tired of the cloak and dagger. What do I need to work on?"

"Is your mate there?"

"No. Why?"

"Because this is very delicate, and it deals with one of Ialog's blocking devices, like the one that was on Toki. This one is much older, though."

"Fine. I'll be there." His crabby tone filled the air.

"Thank you."

"Your brother annoys me." Storm maneuvered the ship to land at the embassy.

"I think he likes you too." Heather sat down for their landing. "I truly think he says the things he does because he knows how much it annoys you. He doesn't talk that way to me normally."

"I don't know what my sister sees in him."

"That is her mate." The ship touched down and Kuarto came on board.

"So what is it that is so secretive?"

"Meet our father-in-law." Heather gestured to the bed.

"Really? Toki has never spoken of him."

"That is because Ialog stole his life from him. Can you remove the device?"

He tried to flip him onto his stomach, but found him too heavy to move. "I'm going to need a little help."

Storm came to his side, and they were able to roll the man over.

"One." He touched one key on the back of his neck with a small probe he had in his hand. "Two." He hit a second key. "Three." The device came free. He took an item out of his pocket along with his scanner. Once he checked to see what damage it had done to the back of his neck, he sprayed a coating over the raw tissue exposed. "It might be a little tender and I'll need to check it regularly, but he should be able to get his mobility back pretty quickly."

"Turn him back over." Heather knew he felt undignified lying on his stomach.

"What?"

"You can't leave him like that."

"Right." He looked at Storm and they flipped his father over. His scanner came out and he ran it over his body. He looked at the readings and smiled. "Everything is going back to normal. Do you have any movement yet?"

"A little."

"Then we wait."

Storm turned to his mate. "You are a wonderful woman to understand."

"I am mated to you, aren't I?"

———

Heather stood outside Anseri's room. She spoke to Storm's father at length to make sure this was what he wanted. Her relationship with Storm taught her so much about Vespian males. No one else could be involved.

She knocked on the door before entering. Stepping inside, she called out. "Anseri? Are you here?"

"Of course, my dear." She stepped into the room. "How may I help you..." She stopped moving when she looked past Heather to see who had walked into her room.

"Just a gift." Heather turned and left at that point. No need for her to hang around.

She walked into the rooms she shared with Storm. He stood when she walked in. "So?"

"There was no way I was going to wait to see how they reacted to each other. We'll find out soon enough."

"Would you like to see how I react to you?" He took her into his arms.

"I believe I know that, but perhaps I need to be reminded."

His lips found her mark, drawing the soft tissue into his mouth. "I think you do, my heart and I'm happy to show you every day."

———

Storm stood outside the medlab, amazed at the life his mate had brought forth. Heather and the twins were resting quietly. They were the most beautiful things he had ever seen. So tiny he feared he would crush them. Yet when he held them for the first time they amazed him with their strength.

"They are so sweet." Sam stood beside him. "What are you going to name them?"

"In Vespian society, we don't name our children right away. We wait for their personalities to blossom. They will have a naming ceremony a year from their birth." He looked at the woman who looked so much like his mate. "We could do the same for you."

"Sam suits me."

"You won't change your mind?" He put an arm around her shoulders.

"No. Mom and I have talked about this at length. I need to learn, away from the computers and downloads. The only way I can do it right is without my memories." She rested her head against her father's broad shoulders. "My memories won't be removed, just buried, releasing at a slow pace I feel I can handle."

"I wish you would stay here."

She laughed and hugged him. "I know, Dad, but I have inherited a few of your traits as well. Mom says I am as stubborn as you are. She promises to build in a few safety features, so if my life is threatened you will know and I can be protected. I don't know what they are, but I know she has my best interest at heart."

"But why Earth? Why not Vespia?"

"Because my parents won't be able to play that overprotective role they are so good at, yet I'll still have people watching over me. Mom has made her friend Bear aware of my situation. It will be his people who find me."

"I still don't like it."

"I need to start my life, Dad. It's time for my adventure to begin."

Coming Summer 2023
Unwanted Desire
The Desire Series, Book 4

———

Don't miss out on your next favorite book!

Join the Satin Romance mailing list
www.satinromance.com/mail.html

THANK YOU FOR READING

———

Did you enjoy this book?

We invite you to leave a review at your favorite book site, such as Goodreads, Amazon, Barnes & Noble, etc.

DID YOU KNOW THAT LEAVING A REVIEW…

- Helps other readers find books they may enjoy.
- Gives you a chance to let your voice be heard.
- Gives authors recognition for their hard work.
- Doesn't have to be long. A sentence or two about why you liked the book will do.

ABOUT THE AUTHOR

Writing for Barbara Donlon Bradley started innocently enough, like most she kept diaries, journals, and wrote an occasional letter but she also had a vivid imagination and wrote scenes and short stories adding characters to her favorite shows and comic books.

As time went on, she found the passion for writing to be a strong drive for her. Humor is also very strong in her life. No matter how hard she tries to write something deep and dark, it will never happen. That humor bleeds into her writing. Since she can't beat it, she has learned to use it to her advantage.

Now she lives in Tidewater Virginia with a cat who thinks he owns everything, her husband and daughter.

www.barbaradonlonbradley.com

ALSO BY BARBARA DONLON BRADLEY

Novels

Love Is…

A Portrait in Time

Love on the Run

Love's Quest Series

A Quest For Love

Magical Quest

Desire Series

Dominated by Desire

Passionate Desire

Animal Desire

Unwanted Desire (Coming Summer 2023)